LILY'S SECRET INHERITANCE

KRISTIN HARPER

D1404230

Published by Bookouture in 2022

An imprint of Storyfire Ltd.
Carmelite House
50 Victoria Embankment
London EC4Y 0DZ

www.bookouture.com

ISBN: 978-1-80314-700-0
eBook ISBN: 978-1-80314-699-7

For my sister, Dawn—
I couldn't have written this without you,
nor would I have wanted to.

PROLOGUE

Seventeen-year-old Lily Lindgren studied the way the soft, diffused sunlight cast long shadows across the clifftop and set the ocean aglow. "Did you know that photographers call this time of day 'the golden hour'?" she asked her aunt.

Dabbing a bead of chocolate-cranberry ice cream from where it had dripped down the front of her T-shirt, Dahlia replied, "I thought the golden hour was in the morning."

"It actually can be either one—the hour after sunrise or the hour before sunset." Lily pressed the button on her granddad's old 35-millimeter camera to capture the view. Then she sat down, stretched out her pale skinny legs beside Dahlia's tanned, toned calves, and propped her feet on the railing. "They call it golden because of the light."

"Mm. That makes sense." Dahlia scraped the last of the creamy residue from her bowl, licked her spoon and then set them both aside. "Do you know what I call this time of day?"

"No. What?"

"Bliss. Absolute bliss." She leaned back in her chair with a sigh of appreciation.

Lily enjoyed this part of their summer routine as much as

Dahlia did. Almost every evening after they'd eaten supper and taken care of the dishes, they'd trek through the woods and across the heathland to the one-room cottage near the edge of the cliff. The tiny structure was nothing more than a shack on stilts, but its high, south-facing deck made the perfect perch for watching the sun setting off to the west. And since the men in the family weren't as enthralled by the scenery as Lily and her aunt were, it gave them the chance to spend a little quiet time alone. Often, they brought their dessert with them.

As usual, this evening in mid-July the pair chatted casually until the sun had completely melted into the ocean and the water cooled to a bluish-gray hue. Lily angled the camera so that it looked as if they were resting their heels on the water's surface and grazing a pink cloud with their toes. Her aunt rarely allowed anyone to photograph her, but Lily figured she wouldn't mind since only her feet were in the frame. She clicked the button.

"You should make a print of that and bring it with you when you go to college next year, so you won't forget about all the girl-time we shared out here together," Dahlia suggested.

"I don't need a photo to remember this." Lily's voice unexpectedly quavered. "Besides, if I decide to get a degree, then I'll enroll in the community college in Port Newcomb. I'm not going away to school."

"Really? But you seemed so excited about the BFA program offered at that university in Brooklyn," her aunt gently reminded her.

"I was but..." A lump swelled in Lily's throat as she thought about how much she'd miss her family and their cranberry farm. Her best friend, Katie. The ocean and the trails—all of Hope Haven, really. In her entire life, she'd hadn't been off Dune Island for longer than a week and that was to visit her maternal grandparents, when they were still alive. She'd never been completely away from all her family members for more than a few days. She admitted, "I'm afraid I'll get too homesick for everyone here, especially now that you're in our family, too."

Dahlia's voice sounded tremulous as well. "Lily Amelia Lindgren, that is such a sweet thing for you to say." She cleared her throat. "If you go off to college, it will definitely be a big adjustment for all of us, but New York isn't that far away. You can come home on the weekends. Besides, I thought you wanted to stretch your wings a little. Last year you said the walls were closing in on you at school and you couldn't wait to leave so you could meet new people and experience new things."

"That was only a phase or something. I don't feel that way any more. I can't wait for senior year to start," she insisted. "It's going to be awesome."

"I hope it is, honey. But you might want to keep your options open for the future. There's still plenty of time to decide what you want to do next."

"Yeah, I guess," Lily half-heartedly agreed, even though she'd already made up her mind. She was staying right where she was, in her favorite place and with the people she loved most in the world.

PART ONE

CHAPTER ONE

NOW

TUESDAY

Of the five towns in Hope Haven, Rockfield had the least glamorous name, but it was home to one of Dune Island's most breathtaking views. Fortunately, few tourists knew about the southernmost vantage point and the locals were too busy to hike out to this cliff on a weekday morning right before the official start of tourist season. So, Lily Perkins had it all to herself, which was exactly why she'd come here. She needed a few more moments to gather her composure before meeting with her family's estate attorney.

Standing near the edge of the cliff, she shielded her eyes and surveyed the seemingly boundless sweep of glittering water. In the distance, the ocean was deep blue, but closer to the craggy coastline, a band of aquamarine swells crested and tumbled in explosions of white.

Lily inhaled the fragrant air as deeply as she could, and then she blew it out again. *It's been almost eighteen years since I've been back. That means I've been gone for almost as long as I lived here,* she realized. Yet as she took in the sights, sounds and

LILY'S
SECRET
INHERITANCE

BOOKS BY KRISTIN HARPER

Summer at Hope Haven

Aunt Ivy's Cottage

A Letter from Nana Rose

smells of the seascape, her memories seemed as clear as the waters below.

She recalled her grandfather and uncle tinkering on a piece of machinery in their workshop. Her grandmother and Mrs. Henderson kneading dough for cranberry-orange bread. Biking to the beach with her best friend, Katie Bleecker. She even had a hazy image of clamming with her parents on the tidal flats in the bay when she wasn't quite five years old.

Fortunately, she had absolutely no recollection of the day they were killed in a car accident the following winter, but other painful events came to mind. Her grandmother's death, and then her granddad's. Her uncle Martin's surgery and her aunt Dahlia's betrayal. Being the subject of gossip and ridicule in high school. Lily squeezed her eyes shut, trying to block the memories out, but they rolled in like waves, one after another and one on top of the other, impossible to stop...

"Isn't it absolutely gorgeous?" a woman's voice nearby cut into her thoughts.

Startled, Lily opened her eyes and twisted her neck to discover a young couple standing some five yards away. The man was behind the woman, caressing her shoulders as the pair peered toward the ocean.

Tourists, Lily thought. *Or else they're here to get married.* Dune Island was a popular location for weddings, especially at this time of year. She inched in their direction, intending to leave so they could have their privacy. But they were blocking the narrow path and she didn't want to step onto the surrounding beach heather, which was vital for preventing erosion of the fragile area.

While the couple began kissing and hugging as if Lily were invisible, she mused, *Did Tyler and I ever act like that in public?* Undoubtedly, they had, early in their relationship. But right now she could only picture the last year of their marriage, when their embraces had taken on more of a practical purpose, such as when Tyler needed to put his arms around Lily so he could get out of the hospital bed.

It had been over two and a half years since her husband had died of cancer. Lily no longer choked up every time at the very thought of him, the way she'd done in the months immediately following his death. But she was still gripped by a pang of... of what? Sorrow? Loneliness? No, it was more like *aloneness* she felt while witnessing the young couple carrying on as if they were the center of each other's universe.

I'm not *alone—I have my son*, she told herself, trying to shake the feeling. It didn't really help. Eight-year-old Ryan was only 300 miles away, at a cabin with his cousins and aunt and uncle in Maine, but he might as well have been 300,000 miles away as far as Lily was concerned. She hadn't spent a night apart from him since before Tyler had died. Her heart already ached from missing her boy and it had only been a matter of hours since she'd left.

If I hurry back to the car, I might have time to call him before my meeting. She coughed loudly to get the couple's attention.

"Oops," the woman uttered, wiggling out of the man's arms when she noticed Lily. But instead of moving into the clearing at the end of the path, they stayed where they were. "Sorry about all the PDA—we're on our honeymoon."

Lily congratulated them and they thanked her in unison, but they didn't budge from their spot.

"Do you know if all the public beaches are as rocky as the one down there is?" asked the woman, gesturing. "We want to find a safe, sandy place to go swimming, but we also want to, you know, have some solitude."

Pretending to be oblivious to the coy look the bride gave her groom, Lily replied, "Actually, this is the only town on the island where the beaches *are* rocky—"

"Ohh, that must be why they call it Rockfield," the woman interjected. It was a common assumption, and when she was a young girl, Lily would have eagerly informed the visitors how her hometown had really gotten its name. But today, she let the mistake slide.

"There are several sandy bayside beaches in Benjamin's Manor and Lucinda's Hamlet on that side of the island." She pointed to the right, westward. "They shouldn't be too crowded because most of the summer people haven't arrived yet. If you want to catch some waves, then you should head the other way, toward Highland Hills. The beaches there aren't officially open for the season yet, so you probably won't cross paths with anyone other than a few surfers and some seals. Be careful though—sometimes there are rip currents between the sandbars."

"Wow, thanks for the warning," the woman said. "You seem to know a lot about the island. Are you one of those lucky people who's been coming here on vacation for years?"

Lily wasn't sure whether she felt disappointed or relieved that she'd been mistaken for a visitor to the island. "Not-not exactly," she faltered. "I grew up in Hope Haven."

The woman squealed as if Lily had won the lottery. "You grew up in Hope Haven?" she repeated.

The man whistled and added, "Lucky you."

Yes and no, Lily thought. As idyllic as island living could be, she knew it had its drawbacks, too. The worst was that everyone seemed to know everything about everyone else—and whatever they didn't know, they made up.

Aloud, she acknowledged, "Mm, the scenery is magnificent." Although as she was well aware, a pretty place was like a pretty face; pleasant to look at, but it was no indication of what lay beneath the surface.

"Which town do you live in?"

"I don't live here any more. I'm just back for... for a visit." Lily didn't want to be unsociable to the friendly couple, but she wasn't about to disclose her personal business, either. "I actually have to go meet someone, so could I squeeze past you, please?"

"Oh, right, sorry." The young bride tugged her groom's hand. "C'mon, Dylan, we're blocking her way."

They moved onto the wide, sandy clearing but before Lily could pass them, the woman extended her phone and asked, "Could you snap our photo before you go? We've got a million selfies. It'd be great to have a full-length shot with the water in the background."

Even though she was in a hurry to leave, Lily could appreciate how giddy they were about being in love and honeymooning on Dune Island, so she accepted the phone. The couple started toward the edge of the cliff, but she redirected them to the opposite side of the overlook, where the light and angle were better. Posing against the backdrop of the brilliant sky and dazzling ocean, they wrapped their arms around each other's waists and gazed adoringly into each other's eyes. Lily tapped the photo button several times. Then she took half a dozen pictures of them directly facing the camera, as well as a few candid shots, before she handed back the phone.

Shielding the display screen to examine the photos, the woman exclaimed, "These are fantastic."

"Yeah, they sure are." The man glanced up to compliment Lily. "Seriously, if you can take pictures this good with a cell phone, you should be a professional photographer."

Lily fought the impulse to wince. When she was a high school senior, becoming a photographer had been her deepest ambition. But that was before her falling out with her aunt. Before her entire world had come crashing around her, shattering her dreams.

"Glad you like them," she mumbled. "Enjoy your honeymoon."

Lily tore down the path as quickly as she could, but halfway back to the car, she had to stop to catch her breath. The tightness in her chest wasn't because she was out of shape; it was because she was stressed. She was *dis*tressed. Anxious and overwhelmed.

Calm down, she told herself, drawing air in through her nostrils and then releasing it through her mouth. *If I come unglued over a completely innocent comment by a stranger, what's going to happen when I talk to people I used to know?*

Lily would have preferred not to return to her hometown at all, especially since she'd already missed her aunt Dahlia's funeral. But her family's attorney, a former classmate of Lily's named Steve, was insistent that she come to Rockfield. He wanted to discuss what she intended to do with her inheritance, which included the Lindgren family home, cranberry farm and business.

"Why do we need to meet in person? Can't we talk on the phone or schedule a video call?" she'd asked. Not that there was much to discuss about the estate anyway; Lily already knew she was going to sell it.

"There have been so many changes to the farm that you really ought to see it for yourself before you make any decisions about its future. Besides, Dahlia has been storing your grandparents' belongings for you. As you know, Selma and Lars owned several valuable antiques, as well as some possessions that might not be worth the money it would cost to ship them to you," Steve had bluntly pointed out. "You're the only one who can decide what to keep and what to discard."

A three-hundred-and-fifty-mile drive, followed by an hour-and-fifteen-minute ferry ride seemed like a long way to travel to cull through her grandmother's bric-a-brac. But there were a few items that held special sentimental value for Lily and—she was ashamed to admit it, even to herself—there were probably several she could sell.

Almost three years after her husband's death, she was still struggling to make ends meet. Tyler's extended illness, hospitalizations and treatments had prevented him from working for over two years. As a project management consultant, Lily had turned down several job opportunities so she could stay home and care for him. Between medical bills and extended periods of unemployment, they'd racked up what had felt like an insurmountable amount of debt.

Lily had been determined not to declare bankruptcy and she'd been slowly paying off her loans and maxed-out credit cards. But it was an ongoing struggle, and she could barely keep up with their mortgage, which she had already refinanced. So, even a couple extra hundred dollars she might get for her grandparents' belongings would be a big help until she was able to sell the Dune Island estate.

Fortunately, the timing of the trip to Rockfield coincided with a break in Lily's schedule. She'd just completed a software rollout for a big insurance company, and she and her son had been invited to join Tyler's sister and her family at their cabin in Maine. On one hand, Lily resented it that the meeting with Steve disrupted their vacation time together. On the other hand, she was relieved that she didn't have to take Ryan with her to Dune Island. Visiting her hometown was going to be an emotionally charged experience; Lily didn't want her own uneasiness to make her son feel upset, too.

Nor did she want the locals to scrutinize Ryan, the way they'd inevitably scrutinize her. Not that she would really blame anyone for making assumptions or gossiping about her sudden arrival in Hope Haven after all these years. *I can imagine what they must think of me, missing Dahlia's funeral, but showing up afterward to claim my grandmother's possessions*, she thought as she continued down the path.

Lily only discovered last Thursday that her aunt had died of an aneurysm three weeks ago. Steve had tried to contact her immediately, but she'd changed her number when she switched to a cheaper phone service, and he hadn't been able to reach her. She'd been so busy working overtime that she rarely bothered to collect her mail from the box. So, she hadn't read any of the attorney's written correspondence until she'd been required to sign for a certified letter from him. By then, Dahlia had already been laid to rest.

Lily may not have been close to her aunt the way she once was, but she'd still been shocked and saddened to hear of Dahlia's sudden death at only fifty-seven years old. She wished she had known about her aunt's passing before the funeral, but Lily acknowledged that she only had herself to blame. Anyone else who may have tried to contact her—including Aiden, Dahlia's son from her first marriage—would have run into the same obstacles Steve had encountered.

As soon as she'd learned about his mother's death, Lily wanted to reach out to Aiden. It wasn't that she was close to him; they weren't truly cousins, and he hadn't even been close to his own mother. But Lily had lived in the same house with Aiden for over two years when they were in high school, so it seemed appropriate to at least express her condolences.

However, they hadn't been in touch with each other ever since they'd both left the island when they were eighteen. The last Lily had heard, he was living in Vancouver, BC, but that was years ago. When she'd asked Steve for Aiden's contact info, he'd said even if he had it, he couldn't give it to her because it would be a breach of client confidentiality, since Aiden was Dahlia's son.

Just my luck, the only time someone on Dune Island decides to exercise discretion is also the only time I need to get the scoop on someone's private life, she thought wryly. *Maybe Jake will know how to get in touch with him.*

Jake Benson, an islander who was a few years older than Lily, had worked on the Lindgren family's cranberry farm during harvest season ever since he was sixteen. Lily didn't know him very well—other than having had an embarrassing childhood teenage crush on him years ago—but her grandparents, uncle Martin and aunt Dahlia had all considered him to be diligent, trustworthy and smart. After Martin died almost nine years ago, Dahlia had invited Jake to become the manager of the farm. He'd undoubtedly attended Dahlia's funeral, and Lily figured he'd probably chatted with Aiden and could tell her how to contact him.

When she reached her car, Lily slid into the driver's seat and grabbed her phone from where she'd forgotten it in the cupholder. It was already 9:38—her meeting with the attorney was scheduled for 9:30. Main Street was only a few minutes from here. She decided rather than to rush her conversation with Ryan, she'd wait until after the meeting to call him.

Talking to my sweet boy will be my reward for making it through the next hour, she told herself.

Lily pressed the ignition button and heard a clacking sound, but the engine didn't turn over. It almost seemed that the car was as hesitant to continue this journey as she was. After waiting a moment, she tried again and this time the engine started right away. She reluctantly shifted into gear, eased onto the road and headed back down the hill toward her past.

CHAPTER TWO

NOW

Lily noticed a few new shops on Main Street, but otherwise this section of town looked almost the same as when she'd lived in Hope Haven.

She passed the small Congregational meetinghouse—the town's oldest church—and the public library on the opposite side of the street. A white gazebo stood in the middle of the perfectly manicured town green. Following that were two long rows of large, opulent, nineteenth-century homes that had been converted into places for local businesses, including Steve's office. The buildings also housed boutiques, galleries, coffee shops, restaurants and bars, as well as a couple of inns.

Tourist season may not have officially begun yet, but there were so many cars parked along the brick sidewalk that Lily couldn't find an open spot. Remembering that there was a public lot behind the hardware store, she drove a couple more blocks and turned down a side street. When she reached the lot, she was astounded to see an attendant sitting at a booth next to a sign that read: PARKING—FLAT RATE $8.oo.

When did they begin charging people to park there? she wondered, annoyed. The final installment of her consultant fee wouldn't be deposited into her bank account until midnight on Friday. Having sworn off credit cards, Lily had barely managed to scrape together enough money to pay for a motel room and gas. She'd packed a lunch, along with fruit and yogurt, since she only had twenty dollars to spend on additional meals and incidentals. So, she couldn't afford to waste money on parking. She circled back to Main Street and this time she found a vacant space.

As she got out of the car, Lily caught sight of her reflection in the driver's side window. She'd left Maine shortly after midnight to catch the 7:30 ferry from Hyannis to Dune Island and now her pale grayish-green eyes were rimmed with dark circles. The wind had whipped her auburn, shoulder-length hair into tangles. She tried finger-combing her curls, but that made them appear even messier. Although Lily had changed out of her shorts and T-shirt in the women's room on the ferry, the pale blue cotton sundress she was wearing was wrinkled where she'd buckled the seatbelt across her waist.

I look like something the cat dragged in, she thought, but what did it matter? Criticism of her appearance was the least hurtful kind of remark anyone could make about her at this point. She turned and hurried down the street to Steve's office.

"Good morning. May I help you?" the receptionist chirped before Lily had fully crossed the threshold.

"Good morning. I'm Lily Lindgren—I mean Perkins." It was remarkable how quickly she'd reverted to using her family's surname instead of her married name now that she was back on the island. "I have a nine-thirty appointment with Steve Reagan, but I'm afraid I'm running a little late."

"I'll let him know you're here. Please, have a seat."

Lily sat down and leafed through a magazine and then set it aside, too fidgety to concentrate. She wiggled her foot and several grains of sand fell from her sandal and bounced across the gleaming hardwood floor.

What was that saying Dahlia used to quote all the time? she wondered. *Something about "sand between your toes getting rid of all your woes."* Lily couldn't quite remember, but it didn't apply in this instance anyway; being on Dune Island was increasing her woes, not diminishing them.

A moment later, Steve opened his door, ducking when he emerged. Because of his height, their classmates used to call him Big Fish. They also called him that because they assumed that no matter how successful he became, he'd always stay in Hope Haven, where he could be a big fish in a small pond, as the saying went. He must have grown at least six inches since he'd earned that nickname and his dark hair had gone prematurely gray.

"Lily, it's great to see you! You haven't changed a bit," he announced enthusiastically as he crossed the room.

She knew it was a cliché, as well as a lie, but she appreciated his sentiment. "Hi, Steve. I'm sorry I'm late."

"No problem." He extended his hand and when she reached to shake it, he pulled her close. She belatedly realized he'd intended to give her a peck on the cheek. Instead, his lips bumped hard against her ear.

"Er, 'scuse me." Steve's ruddy complexion turned an even deeper shade of red. Lily remembered him being socially awkward as a teenager, a trait she still found endearing in a goofy, fraternal sort of way. He ushered her into his office and offered her a seat across from a large, solid wood walnut desk.

"Very nice," she remarked as she settled into the wide, tufted-leather wingback chair.

"Yeah, my career has been good to me." A shadow crossed his face and he frowned as he unabashedly admitted, "Can't say the same about my personal life. I never did get married."

"Maybe not yet, but there's no deadline."

"Yeah, you're right." He sounded cheerful again as he took a seat behind his desk and added, "Anyway, work has been keeping me busy. And even though I don't have kids of my own, I'm a volunteer coach for the boys' varsity hockey team at 3H."

There was one regional secondary school for the entire island. It was called Hope Haven High, so the locals referred to it as 3H. When she lived here, Lily hadn't given much thought to the fact that there was an abbreviation or nickname for almost everything and everyone on the island. But now she felt as if she were re-learning a language she used to speak fluently. And Steve seemed very eager to catch up. She smiled politely.

"I remember what a good hockey player you were. I'm sure you're an excellent coach, too."

"Well, last season we were undefeated but that's more to the players' credit than mine." Steve grinned. Leaning back in his chair, he put his hands behind his head. "Our phone conversation was so brief I didn't get a chance to hear what *you've* been up to lately."

Obviously, he was inviting her to reciprocate, and Lily knew it was perfectly reasonable for him to be curious about her since they were former classmates. But she wanted to be very guarded about her personal life now that she was back on Dune Island, where gossip ran rampant. She evaded his question, answering, "You're right. It was a very short call. I was so shocked to hear about Dahlia's passing that I could barely gather my thoughts."

"Of course you were." Although he'd already expressed his condolences on the phone, Steve reiterated them again now. "I'm very sorry for your loss. Dahlia mentioned you were widowed—I was sorry to hear about that, too."

Widowed. The word still sounded strange to her ears, as if she were talking about someone else. Someone older. "Thank you." When she realized Steve was looking expectantly at her, she added, "Tyler and I were married for eight years before he passed away almost three years ago. We had one child, a son. Ryan's almost nine now—he's my pride and joy."

"I'm sure he is. Did he come with you to the island?"

"No. He's vacationing with my in-laws in Maine." Lily glanced at the grandfather clock in the corner of the room. She didn't want to be rude—Steve had always been friendly with her at school—but she wished they could just get down to the business of discussing her inheritance so she could be on her way to sort through her grandparents' belongings.

"Dahlia said that you worked in hi-tech now?"

"Not exactly. I'm a freelance project management consultant, so I work on all sorts of projects for various companies, including some hi-tech ones."

"Ahh, a project manager instead of a professional photographer." Steve was referring to the career ambition Lily had listed in their high school yearbook. "Does that mean you've hung up your camera for good or do you still enjoy photography as a hobby?"

"The only photos I take any more are of my son. You know how it is. There are hardly enough hours in the day to accomplish the essential stuff. There's not a lot of time left over for hobbies." Time constraints had nothing to do with the reason she'd given up photography, but Lily wasn't going to talk about that to Steve. Or to anyone. Tyler was the only person she'd ever told what had happened, and that was only after they'd been seeing each other for two years. "Speaking of time, I'm sorry I was late. But I'm ready to jump right into talking about the estate."

"Sure, sure, we can do that," he agreed good-naturedly, opening his laptop. "Just to confirm what I mentioned on the phone and wrote to you in an email... You understand that you're the sole beneficiary of the Lindgren estate, correct?"

"Yes, I understand." Not only had Steve sent her information about the trust, but when she was in her early twenties, Lily's uncle had told her that her grandparents had arranged for her to inherit the property, house and farming business after Martin and Dahlia passed away.

"You probably also understand that because your grandparents established a living trust instead of a will, the property doesn't have to go through probate. Which essentially means you already own it."

"Good. I'm glad there won't be a long, drawn-out probate process, because I'd like to sell it as soon as possible," Lily declared, cutting to the chase.

Steve drew his chin back in surprise. He stammered, "Oh, okay, well, that-that's certainly one possibility. But I always encourage beneficiaries to give these matters careful consideration—"

"I *have* given the matter careful consideration and I have no intention of moving back to Dune Island or being involved with the business," interrupted Lily.

"Gee, why don't you tell me how you really feel about Hope Haven?" Steve asked with a droll chuckle.

Realizing how condescending and ungrateful she must have sounded, Lily clarified, "What I meant is that my life is in Philadelphia now. It's where my husband and I settled down and bought a house. Philly is where my son goes to school. It's where his friends are. His happiness and wellbeing mean the world to me. He went through enough turmoil when his dad died—I'd never uproot him. And I certainly can't afford to keep up with the property taxes and operational costs of running the farm from out of state. To be frank, I'm already struggling to meet my personal financial obligations in Philadelphia."

If she'd been speaking to anyone else in Hope Haven, Lily would have been too embarrassed and distrustful to share that she'd been having money problems. However, she felt it was necessary for Steve to understand why she couldn't keep the estate and she trusted that as a professional, he'd keep her disclosure confidential.

"I see. In that case, selling the property and the business is definitely an option. However, as the successor trustee, my role is to administer the assets according to your family's instructions. They charged me with ensuring that you're making wise, well-informed decisions."

Lily didn't like the sound of that. "In other words, even though it's *my* inheritance, I have to convince you that what I want to do with it is best for me or else you can veto my decision?"

"I wouldn't put it quite like that. My responsibility is to *help* you make the best decision about what to do with your inheritance, Lily. Not to *stop* you from doing what you want to do."

"What does that mean in practical terms?"

Steve shifted in his chair. "Well, I'd want to be sure you understood where the business stood financially before you decided to sell it—or to keep it, for that matter. Dahlia and her business manager, Jake Benson, have made a lot of changes to the farm and business. They've also renovated the residence, so they've accrued some debt. I'd expect you to take a tour and talk to Jake, so you have a better sense of the scope of the changes. If you end up exercising the option to sell, I could connect you to a realtor. Or, if you want to list it independently, I can help you find a buyer—although Dahlia's request was that the farm and business should be offered to Jake, first."

"You think he'd want to buy it?" That would sure make the sales process a lot smoother and quicker.

"Possibly, if he can afford it. As you and I agreed on the phone, the only thing I told him was that you'd inherited the farm and you'd be visiting the house this week to sort through your grandparents' possessions. Obviously, you're free to share as much or as little about your plans for your inheritance as you wish, but I'd advise you to err on the side of discretion for now. He's worked there for years, so he might have strong opinions about what he thinks you should do—or about what *he* wants to do with the farm. It's okay to hear him out later, but you're still in the information-gathering stage, so it's best to proceed with caution."

Steve's desk phone buzzed and he paused to answer it. When he hung up, he said, "My next appointment is here, so we'll have to wrap things up, but can you meet again tomorrow? I've kept my 4:30 time slot open for you."

"I appreciate that, but I plan to leave by noon tomorrow, assuming Jake can meet with me before then."

Steve frowned. "He should be able to, but that doesn't give you and me much time to go through everything we need to discuss. That's why I suggested you stay on the island for a week."

"I thought you were referring to sorting through my grand-mother's things and I figured that would only take a day or so," Lily explained. "I'm already missing two days of vacation with my son and I don't want to miss any more time. Checking out the changes to the farm and making decisions about my grand-parents' belongings are the only two tasks I absolutely need to do in person. We can discuss everything else by phone or on a video call, right?"

"It's not optimal, but I guess it would be okay. How about if you meet me early tomorrow morning. Let's say 7:00? By then, you'll have seen the farm and spoken to Jake, so we can address any questions or concerns you might have."

Lily didn't really feel that another in-person meeting was necessary, but she was worried if she refused, Steve might not think she'd given her decision to sell the farm enough considera-tion. When, in fact, it had been at the forefront of all her thoughts ever since she'd learned that Dahlia had passed away. "Sounds great," she agreed.

Steve said he had something to give her before she left. He withdrew a small manilla envelope from a locked cabinet behind his desk and handed it to her. "There are three keys in there. One's for Dahlia's bedroom and one is for the room where your grandparents' belongings are stored. Jake turned them in to me as a matter of procedure, since you're the only person who should have access to those rooms. Dahlia gave me the third key, the brass one, a couple years ago. It's a duplicate of a key that opens a trunk she was keeping for you in her bedroom closet. She wanted me to have a spare in case you couldn't locate hers around the house. She said the trunk contains items that she considered treasures."

Lily knew he was referring to the steamer trunk that had belonged to her grandmother's grandmother, but she had no idea what treasures Dahlia might have stored in it. "She left her treasures to me, not to Aiden?"

Lily understood why she had inherited the estate itself: she was a Lindgren and Aiden wasn't. The farm had been in their family for six generations. However, she was surprised she'd inherited anything directly from her aunt.

"Yes. Dahlia specifically named you as the sole beneficiary of *all* her personal assets. That info was included in the documents I emailed you, wasn't it?"

"I'm sure it was. I got lost in some of the legalese, so I probably skimmed over it," she confessed.

"That's understandable... But I'm surprised Dahlia didn't ever tell you she'd named you her sole beneficiary. I suggested several times that she should give you a heads-up."

"She probably meant to tell me, but we both had such busy schedules that it was hard to keep in touch. Whenever we did get a chance to chat, we usually didn't discuss things like Dahlia's assets." There was more to it than that, but that was as much as Lily intended to share.

Clearly, Dahlia hadn't told Steve about their estranged relationship, either. Her aunt was very tight-lipped about their family members' private lives, even among relatives. That was part of the reason Lily hadn't known how to reach Aiden; Dahlia rarely shared any information about him except in general terms. Although her aunt's sense of secrecy might have seemed extreme to some people, Lily had always appreciated her discretion.

Slipping the small envelope into her purse, she stood to leave. "Thanks so much for all your help, Steve."

"My pleasure." He escorted her to the door. "If Jake gives you pushback about anything, let me know. But I'm sure he'll be happy to answer your questions about the business and show you the renovations he and Dahlia made. I look forward to hearing your perspective on all the changes."

"I look forward to chatting with you about that, too," Lily replied extra-enthusiastically. "See you in the morning—and this time, I promise not to be late."

As she hurried back to her car, Lily kept her head down to avoid being recognized. Not that ducking would help; her hair probably gave away her identity. When she was in middle school, she and the other students made up nicknames for everyone in their class. Hers was "cranberry-top." The name was supposed to be a play on the term "carrot-top," as well as a nod to her family's farm, and Lily had worn the title proudly. Her coppery red locks may have faded to a deeper, tarnished shade since then, but there was no disguising her unruly curls.

Maybe it's vain to worry that anyone from my past is going to care or ask me about why I'm here, she thought, but she wasn't taking any chances. Fortunately, the only people she happened to see on Main Street were teenagers who weren't even born by the time she'd left the island.

Driving toward her childhood home, Lily ruminated on her circumstances. She supposed she should have felt ecstatic. After all, once she sold the farm, not only would she be able to repay her debts, but relatively speaking, she'd be rich.

However, instead of being elated, she felt somber. Lily

hadn't expected to inherit her family's estate for another twenty-five or thirty years, because she took it for granted that was how long Dahlia would live. Even though she knew it was in her and Ryan's best interest to sell the farm, Lily always believed it would be decades before she'd have to make such a monumental decision. As necessary as it was, giving up the property and business that had been in her family for six generations was still regrettable.

Grandma and Granddad would have been devastated if they knew I was letting go of our family's cranberry farm, she thought. *But then again, they would have been devastated if they knew I'd left Dune Island for good, too.*

Lily's ringing phone suddenly sounded through the car's speakers. She saw her sister-in-law's name and pressed the button on the hands-free device. "Leanne? Is everything okay?"

"Good morning to you, too." Leanne chuckled. "Everything's great here. But it's been a couple of hours since you last called to check on your son, so I thought I'd better make sure *you're* okay."

Lily had told Leanne and Tim why she'd needed to go to Rockfield, but she'd asked them not to say anything about it to Ryan. He'd never met Dahlia, and Lily had rarely spoken about her to him. But the boy was so sensitive that Lily was concerned if he knew there was a death in the family, he'd be upset for his entire vacation. So, all she'd told him was that she had an important meeting to attend in Massachusetts.

Although it pained her to miss part of their vacation together, Ryan didn't seem to mind. She suspected he was acting more confident about her absence than he really felt, so she'd called Leanne's phone to speak to him twice before boarding the ferry, but he'd still been asleep.

"Thanks for checking. I'm fine. I was actually just about to call." Lily pulled off the road and into the "scenic viewing area," an extra-wide, sandy parking area adjacent to the marshland.

She absent-mindedly opened the window so she could smell the briny air. It was more pungent here than on Lookout Ledge, but it wasn't unbearable—not to the year-round residents, anyway. However, most tourists literally turned up their noses at the smell, much to the amusement of the locals. "Ryan must be awake by now?"

"Yes, but Tim took the boys out for a maiden voyage in the new canoe."

Ryan was a good swimmer for an eight-year-old child, but he had almost no body fat to keep him warm. Worried that if he fell in, he'd quickly become too cold to stay afloat, Lily asked, "Is he wearing a life vest?"

"Nah, none of the kids are. My husband and I believe they need to learn from a very young age to sink or swim," Leanne said drily. After a pause, she added, "Of *course* he's wearing a life vest. What kind of parents do you think we are?"

Realizing how offensive her question must have sounded, Lily answered, "I think you're the excellent kind, Leanne... and I'm the kind who worries too much. I'm sorry. If I didn't trust you and Tim as much as I do, I'd never let Ryan stay with you while I'm not there."

"Hmph." Leanne made a disgruntled sound before changing the subject. "So, how is it being back in your hometown?"

"It's all right." Lily's answer was deliberately noncommittal. Tyler was the only person she had ever confided in about the heartbreaking reason she'd left the island when she was eighteen. He had guarded her secret as if it were his own, ignoring his parents' concern and sister's nosiness about why Lily hardly ever talked about her youth. The less Tyler and Lily said about the subject, the more interested Leanne seemed to become. Lily had learned to provide just enough information to satisfy her sister-in-law's curiosity without sacrificing her own privacy.

"Have you bumped into any of your exes yet?"

"Exes, plural? I don't even have *one* ex on the island. When it came to going out with boys, I was a late bloomer."

"You must have at least gone to the prom with someone?"

"Nope, although a boy *did* ask me to go the senior dance, which wasn't as formal as the prom, but it was the next best thing. I accepted his invitation, but then I decided to go on a trip to Sweden, so I had to cancel on him." The spring of Lily's senior year in school had been so chaotic that she'd forgotten all about the senior dance until Leanne mentioned the prom. "You'll never believe what he does now."

"What?"

"He's an estate attorney—and my family used his services after their other lawyer retired. He's the attorney I met with this morning." She laughed at the irony.

"Wait a second. Your inheritance is being handled by the guy you stood up for the senior dance?"

"Yup."

"Wow, that must have been awkward."

"It would have been, if I had remembered, but it was so long ago, I'd completely forgotten about it."

"I bet *he* didn't. He must have been heartbroken."

"Nah. I doubt it. He knew it wasn't personal. We weren't dating. We weren't even close friends. He used to give me a ride to school when I was—"

Leanne cut her off. "Uh-oh, the girls are arguing about whose turn it is to use the fishing net. They're trying to catch minnows. I'd better go before they push each other over in the water—but don't worry, it's only up to their ankles. No life vests required."

"Ha, ha, very funny," Lily was about to ask her to tell Ryan she'd call him later in the afternoon, but Leanne had already disconnected.

Lily set her phone in the cupholder and gazed out the window. The bright green saltwater cord-grass and salt-hay

waved in the breeze, which was gentler here than it had been at
Lookout Ledge. In the distance, a sandhill crane stood as still as
a statue on the edge of the marsh watching the shallow water for
fish, frogs and fiddler crabs. Lily shifted her focus to the middle
of the wetland, where three boulders loomed upward from the
peat, each about twenty yards apart from each other.

This used to be one of my favorite landmarks, she recalled.

According to the travel diaries of Hope Haven's founder,
Captain Peter Alden, Dune Island was uninhabited when he
came ashore in the mid-1600s. However, his crew later discovered long, thin grooves on these three boulders, indicating that
the island's indigenous people had once used them as grinding
stones to make and sharpen hunting and fishing tools.

No one knew what had happened to the original inhabi-
tants or why they no longer dwelt on Dune Island. But in honor
of the boulders' significance, the town was later named Rockfield, which was technically a misnomer since the area was a
marsh, not a field. Lily had always appreciated the history
behind the town's name. She found it fascinating to imagine the
lives of the people who had lived on this part of the island
centuries ago.

As a child riding the bus home from school, she'd loved
cruising around the bend and seeing the boulders come into
view. Their commanding presence was a sign that she was
almost home; the cranberry farm was less than a mile down the
road, immediately following the conservation land. But today,
she felt more dread than anticipation about nearing her family's
property.

*The sooner I check out the farm and talk to Jake, the sooner I
can convince Steve it's best if I sell the estate and the business,*
she thought, motivating herself to steer back onto the main road.
*Even better, the sooner I sort through Granddad and Grandma's
belongings, the sooner I get to leave Dune Island and go back to
vacationing with my son again.*

CHAPTER THREE

NOW

Lily slowed the car as she passed the wide stand of scrub oak and pitch pine trees separating the conservation land from her family's property. At this time of the year, the cranberry vines were flowering, and she gasped to see the familiar sight: acres and acres of what looked like plush, pink carpeting.

In the spring, so many visitors to the island used to stop to take photos of the scenery that they'd worn away a patch of the Lindgrens' front lawn near the shoulder of the road. Lily's granddad was worried they'd cause a traffic accident, so he'd created a bigger turn-around area at the end of the sandy driveway. It allowed drivers to pull completely off the road, instead of idling on the shoulder. But the bare patch had been filled in now with bright green grass and the dirt driveway had been paved with asphalt. It was twice as wide as it used to be. Lily reduced her speed to a crawl so she could get a good look at the farmhouse as she approached it.

Like many homes built in this part of the country in the late nineteenth century, the Lindgrens' original house was a simple Cape style. However, over the decades and centuries, the dwelling had expanded along with their ancestral family, so now it was actually two houses attached to each other by a short interior hallway. They called the smaller abode on the right side "the cottage," and the larger one was known as "the farmhouse."

Right outside the front door, a single maple tree stretched its limbs toward the sky. Although its leaves were green now, in autumn they'd blaze brilliant red, as if they were trying to outshine the cranberry bogs to the left and in the back of the house.

Seeing the farmhouse where she'd grown up was like seeing a long-lost member of her family and Lily's reaction was visceral: her heart quickened, and hot tears stung her eyes. For a moment, she thought, *I can't do this.* She considered reversing her direction, but her intense nostalgia was replaced with surprise when she spotted a wooden sign plainly marked PARKING. The arrow indicated she should turn right, into a rectangular area that was bordered on three sides by a split-rail fence. There was probably room for twenty or more cars.

It's even bigger than the parking lot behind the hardware store, she marveled as she coasted to a stop and turned off the engine.

Peering through her window before getting out, she noticed a sign posted at the beginning of the walkway that said, "Lindgren Cranberry Kitchen & Gift Shop." Beneath the words a painted arrow pointed to the farmhouse. A second sign read, "Lindgren Cranberry Farm Information Center." Its arrow pointed to the cottage.

Last Christmas when Lily had chatted on the phone with Dahlia, her aunt had mentioned that she and Jake were considering expanding the fruit stand that the Lindgrens had hosted on their property for as long as anyone could remember. The stand was a convenient place for locals to pick up bags of fresh cranberries, as well as dried cranberries and cranberry preserves. It operated on an honor system, like all the other produce stands on Dune Island. Customers simply took what they wanted and left their money in a plastic container with a slot in the lid.

When Dahlia had asked Lily if she thought it would be okay to increase the range of products they offered, Lily had said what she always said. "You're in charge of the farm, Dahlia. If you think it's a good idea, you should definitely do it."

So although rationally she knew she didn't have any right to feel upset, Lily was completely taken back to see the changes that had been made to the driveway and house. *When Dahlia said they were considering expanding the fruit stand, I thought she meant they might add a couple extra shelves. I didn't realize they were going to turn the place into a tourist trap!*

Lily got out of the car and hurried up the walkway and through the front door of the farmhouse. She peeked into the room to the right of the foyer. The wall between what used to be her family's living room and the den had been knocked down; it was all one big open area, from the front of the house to the back. Most of the room was filled with stacks of unopened boxes and empty shelves. But in the front section there were several strategically placed displays of merchandise, including items such as cranberry candles and soaps, chocolate-covered cranberries, and cranberry note cards.

There were also several racks of deep red T-shirts emblazoned with the Lindgren Cranberry Farm logo—their family name in blue cursive above an image of a vintage cranberry scoop. Lily was familiar with the logo, which had long decorated the bags the distributor used to package their berries. But somehow, the use of her family's name on a T-shirt struck Lily as so overtly promotional that she unintentionally uttered, "Wow."

A teenage girl suddenly popped up from behind what appeared to be the checkout counter. "You scared me," she yelped, a box cutter in hand. "I almost sliced off my thumb!"

Lily was equally startled. "Sorry. I didn't know anyone was back there."

"It's okay." The girl held her hand in front of her face and wiggled her fingers, as if to make sure they were all intact and functioning. Something about her wide-set hazel eyes seemed familiar to Lily. "Unfortunately, the gift shop is closed until the Fourth of July weekend. But there's an evening jam-making class on July second if you want to register for that. Cranberry-apple. It's delicious."

A jam-making class? Lily felt like her head was spinning. She stuttered, "No-no, thanks. I already know how to make cranberry-apple jam. I grew up on this farm. My name is Lily Lindgren—it used to be, anyway."

"Oh, you're Dahlia's niece," the girl exclaimed as the realization struck. She lowered her voice to add, "I'm really sorry she died. I didn't know her too well—actually, I only met her when she interviewed me—but she seemed super nice. I was really glad she gave me the job and I'm sorry I don't get to work with her. Not that it's all about me, but, you know what I mean..."

Noticing how nervous the girl seemed, Lily tried to put her at ease. "Yes, I do know what you mean. Thank you for the sentiment. Like I said, my name's Lily. What's yours?"

"Sophie. Sophie Tuttle. I'll be wearing a name tag next week—and a Lindgren T-shirt, too, so, you know, customers can tell who's on staff." She barely paused to take a breath before asking, "What do you think of the shop? I've still got a lot to do, but doesn't it look great in here?"

"It looks... *different*," Lily answered truthfully. When she saw Sophie's disappointed expression, she explained, "This was my family's living room, so it's strange to see that it's been converted into a gift shop. But those displays are very tastefully arranged."

Sophie beamed. "Thanks. Jake said Dahlia insisted that

everything we sold had to be beautiful, edible, or useful. And it had to be handmade on the island by a local, even if it wasn't made here on the farm." She pointed to the table next to Lily. "Like, an artist in Highland Hills painted those note cards. And the T-shirts were stenciled at Big Ray's, on the boardwalk. We really should have ordered more of them. I hope we don't sell out before our grand opening on July seventh."

"Are you kidding me? There must be a hundred T-shirts on those racks! How many people will want to visit a cranberry farm during their summer vacation anyway?"

"I don't know. Lots?" Sophie said in a small voice.

Lily quickly backpedaled. "You're right, there probably will be tons of customers. I'm just having a hard time wrapping my head around the idea because when I was growing up, the only people who ever visited the farm were our friends and family members."

"Yeah, but that was a long time ago. We've had to make a lot of changes to stay in business," a man's voice said from behind her. Lily turned to see a burly, blondish-haired man wearing jeans and a Lindgren Cranberry Farm T-shirt and cap. He pulled off his work glove and extended his arm to shake her hand. "Hello, Lily. I'm Jake Benson."

Lily could feel the calluses on his palm, but his fingertips were soft and warm. "Of course. I remember you, Jake."

When she was in eighth grade and Jake was a high school senior, Lily and her best friend, Katie, both had massive crushes on him. In the fall, when Jake worked as a seasonal employee, Katie used to come to the farmhouse for supper almost every Saturday. Lily also harvested berries, but as soon as the work was done for the day, she'd rush into the house, claiming she needed to change her clothes before she ate. Then she and Katie would spy on Jake from her bedroom window as he returned various pieces of heavy equipment to the barn or chatted with Lily's uncle or granddad.

The following autumn, Jake went away to college for four years, but he always helped pick berries when he came home during his mid-term fall break—although by then, Lily and Katie had outgrown their practice of spying on him.

Lily had assumed that when she saw him again today, she'd wonder why she and Katie had ever been so crazy about him in the first place. Kind of like how she felt now when she looked at photos of the celebrity heartthrobs she'd loved as a teenager.

However, Jake struck her as being even more handsome in adulthood than he'd been in high school. Probably because back then, Lily had rarely gotten close enough to notice how bright his blue eyes were, or that they were fringed with lashes that were three shades darker than his hair and almost as thick. Or maybe it was because during the past two decades, his biceps had nearly doubled in size and he carried himself with confidence instead of ducking his head slightly, the way he'd done in high school.

Or perhaps it wasn't how he'd changed that Lily found attractive; perhaps it was how he'd stayed the same. Perhaps it was because there was something about his appearance that was still as wholesome now as it had been in their youth. In any case, she was surprised at herself for being so aware of his looks; it made her feel like a silly middle schooler again.

"I worked on the farm when Lily and I were in high school," Jake explained for Sophie's benefit. "Actually, I was in high school and she was in middle school—I think she was in the same grade as your mother."

Sophie had said her last name was Tuttle, but Lily hadn't known anyone with that name when she lived in Rockfield, so she asked, "Who is your mother?"

"Olivia. Before she got married to my dad her name was Olivia Hartley."

"You're *Olivia's* daughter?" Lily exclaimed.

Olivia Hartley had been Dahlia's son Aiden's girlfriend in

high school. It was hard to say whether she was a bad influence on him, or he was a bad influence on her, but they'd frequently skipped school and done a lot of partying together. Their relationship had been the source of many arguments between Dahlia and Aiden, so it was initially surprising to discover that Dahlia had hired Olivia's daughter to work on the farm. But Lily supposed that what happened in the past was long over and Sophie had nothing to do with it anyway.

She said, "That must be why you look so familiar—you have the same pretty eyes as your mom."

"Thanks," the teenager replied just as a young boy came into the room. Stocky and blond, with big baby blues, the child would have been the spitting image of Jake even if he hadn't also been wearing a Lindgren Cranberry Farm baseball cap and T-shirt.

Dahlia never mentioned that Jake had a son, Lily thought. Although she and her aunt only called each other a couple of times a year, it seemed like it was the kind of thing that might have come up about her business manager. All Dahlia had ever told Lily was that Jake was single.

"I washed my hands," the boy announced, holding them up as proof. "*Now* can I have something to eat? I'm starving."

"Sure. But first say hello to Ms. Lily and tell her your name," Jake instructed him. Most of the adults in that part of the country preferred for children to refer to them by the title Mr. or Ms., along with their first names.

"Hi, Ms. Lily." He waved his hand in a half-circle. "I'm Conner."

"Hi, Conner. I think my son Ryan is the same age as you—he'll be nine in September."

"Nah, I'm way older than that. I'm already nine years and two and a half months," he replied proudly, causing Lily to smile. "Is Ryan outside?"

"No, he didn't come with me. He's vacationing with his cousins in Maine."

"Ms. Dahlia was Ms. Lily's aunt," Jake interjected, addressing Conner. "She grew up here on the farm and she probably has some things she needs to talk to me about. You can start to eat your snack outside in the shade and I'll be there in a few minutes. Sophie, would you mind getting his bag from the fridge for him? Otherwise, he'll leave fingerprints all over the stainless steel."

"My hands are clean!" Conner insisted as he tramped out of the room after Sophie.

Jake explained, "My sister's ill—there's something going around the island—and her husband's traveling for work, so I had to bring Conner with me today."

Oh, so that's his nephew, *not his son,* Lily realized. Jake's sister was a couple years younger than she was and Lily remembered her as being a quiet, rather studious girl.

"That's too bad your sister's ill. Funny, though, at first I thought Conner was your son—he looks a lot like you."

"Yeah, poor kid. We're all hoping he'll outgrow it," Jake said with a forced chuckle, but his mouth quickly straightened into a tight line again. He gestured toward the hallway that connected the cottage. Lily followed him until he stopped and turned to face her. In a low voice, he said, "I'm devastated about losing Dahlia. It really was a shock."

The intensity of his tone matched the sorrow in his eyes. Although Lily was sorry he was grieving, it was comforting to know Dahlia's business manager had cared that deeply about her. She responded, "My aunt and I didn't keep in touch very often, but I know she thought highly of you—she wouldn't have asked you to manage the farm if she didn't trust and respect you so much."

"The feeling was mutual." Jake exhaled heavily. "So, I

heard you were coming to sort through your grandparents' and Dahlia's personal belongings?"

Lily nodded, even though it hadn't occurred to her until now that of course she'd be expected to make decisions about Dahlia's personal items, in addition to going through her grandparents' stuff.

"I take it Steve gave you the keys for the rooms upstairs?" Jake pointed in the direction of the cottage ceiling. "We stored your grandparents' things in the room across from Dahlia's bedroom."

"Dahlia moved back into the cottage?" When Lily left Rockfield, Dahlia and Martin had been living in the farmhouse. Her aunt had never mentioned that she'd moved back into the cottage. "I thought the sign outside said you'd turned the cottage into an information center."

"The downstairs has been converted into an *education* center, yes," Jake confirmed. "But Dahlia lived in the upstairs bedroom, and she used the bathroom at the top of the stairs. She said she didn't need any more space than that. She cooked her meals in the farmhouse, because we repurposed the cottage kitchen. Sophie probably told you about the culinary classes we're offering?"

"Not in detail, but she did offer to enroll me in one." Half-joking, Lily added, "When Steve Reagan suggested I should ask you to show me around the farm, I thought it was kind of silly considering I know this place like the back of my hand. But maybe Sophie should enroll me for a tour, after all."

Jake flipped his palms upward in a kind of irritated shrug. "Like I said, we've had to make a lot of changes in order to keep the farm in business."

He seems kind of defensive—the changes must have been mostly his idea, Lily deduced.

She diplomatically replied, "I'm looking forward to seeing and hearing more about the renovations when you have time.

Also, Steve sent me some financial information about the business earlier in the month, but he said I should review the farm's most recent records with you."

"Yeah, okay. The next couple of days will be pretty hectic, but we're closed on Sundays, so I can show you around and then we can review the financials. Does one o'clock work for you?"

Lily winced. "I actually plan to leave tomorrow, so I was hoping you'd have time to meet with me later today."

"Gee, no pressure." Jake shook his head. "There's a leak in the irrigation system I've got to troubleshoot this afternoon. Plus, I've got half a dozen other outstanding issues to address before we open the gift shop and education center to the public. Not to mention, Conner's tagging along with me. If I had known you needed to discuss financial records, I wouldn't have let him come to work with me today."

Lily regretted it that she hadn't given Jake advance notice, but until this morning, she hadn't known that Steve would essentially force her to meet with him; she'd thought she could just take a look around the farm by herself. Regardless, there was no way she was going to stay on the island until Sunday, so she proposed a compromise.

"No worries. I can poke around here on my own. If I have questions, I can ask you when you've got a spare moment or I'll ask Sophie. And if you email me copies of the financial records, we can go over them in a video call whenever it's convenient for you—or I'll review them with Steve." She paused, allowing Jake to respond, but when he remained silent, she apologized: "I'm sorry for showing up unannounced and disrupting your schedule, but Steve was really insistent that I see the changes on the farm firsthand and understand where it stands financially before I decide what I want to do with it."

"What do you mean, before you decide what you want to *do* with it?"

"You know, whether I want to sell it or—" Remembering that Steve had advised her not to discuss her plans for the estate, Lily stopped speaking, but it was too late.

Jake's eyebrows shot up so high his cap shifted backward on his head. "You'd actually consider *selling* your family's farm?"

Lily tried to do damage control. "I'm considering *all* my options. I can't rule anything in or out until I weigh all the pros and cons. That's why it's so important that I get a really good sense of what's going on with the business."

"Wow." Jake closed his eyes and pinched the bridge of his nose, but he didn't move another muscle for a very long, uncomfortable moment. Finally, he dropped his hand and blew the air out of his cheeks with a huff. "If you're making a decision of that magnitude based on what you see while you're here, then I definitely want to be the one to give you a tour and review our accounting with you. Can you meet with me tomorrow morning at 8:30, or are you catching a ferry out of here at daybreak?"

Lily could understand that it was a shock to him to learn she might not keep the farm. From Jake's perspective, it probably seemed like she was going to make a hasty decision—but he didn't know her financial situation, or her personal history with some of the people on Dune Island, including Dahlia. So, she ignored his sarcasm and said, "I'm not leaving until about noon. I have a meeting with Steve at 7:00, but I'll make sure we're done and I'm back at the farm by 8:30."

"All right. 8:30, then." Jake strode back down the hall without another word.

Not exactly the warm welcome Steve said I'd get from him, Lily thought as she entered the cottage. Rather than peeking into the downstairs "education center," she headed directly up the staircase. *Jake will be ticked off if he takes time away from work to show me the renovations and then he finds out I've already been snooping around.*

But the real reason she didn't stop to explore the education center was that she wasn't ready to encounter another part of her family's home that had been converted into a tourist attraction. *I honestly meant it when I told Dahlia that she should make any changes to the farm and the house she wanted to make. But that was partly because I never imagined I'd have to face the changes so soon.*

The upper level of the cottage had a bedroom on each side of a full bathroom. Lily used the key to open the smaller one, where Aiden used to sleep. She expected to find her grandparents' belongings, but instead she discovered a neatly made single bed. *Dahlia wasn't even living in the larger of the two rooms?* she marveled. The space was just big enough to contain a bookshelf, an armchair, and a dresser drawer, on top of which were several framed photos. Lily avoided looking at them, for fear they'd make her sentimental. It didn't matter; merely noticing the faded color of the painted walls triggered a rush of emotion.

She quickly stepped back into the hall, tugged the door shut and turned the key in the lock, as if that would help keep her memories sealed up on the other side of the wall.

CHAPTER FOUR

THEN

"Your granddad and I have made a decision," Lily's grandmother, Selma, stopped speaking to catch her breath. For the past six months, she'd been receiving treatment for stage 4 melanoma, which recently had metastasized to her lungs. Even though she was sitting next to Lily on the couch, she sounded as if she were climbing a very steep flight of stairs. "We've decided to hire a live-in home health aide. She'll bring me to my appointments and take care of the housework, including the cooking. She might even help around the farm."

Lily pouted. "Why do we need a home health aide? Uncle Martin and Granddad take you to your appointments and I'm doing the housework and the cooking."

"Yes, and you've done a wonderful job. The house is sparkling."

Lily took advantage of her grandmother's breathlessness to interject, "Then why do we need an aide living with us? Is it because Uncle Martin complained that the chicken I made last week was too dry? That only happened because I was afraid if it wasn't cooked all the way through, we'd get salmonella poisoning and your immune system is already so weak..."

She let her voice trail off, partly because she didn't want to complete the thought and partly because she was so upset, she was becoming almost as winded as Selma. Lily's grandparents had always been independent to a fault. If they were willing to allow a stranger to live with them and care for Selma, then it must have meant her grandmother was even sicker than Lily thought.

"Your cooking's coming along just fine. If your uncle complains again, tell him he's welcome to make supper for the rest of the week—although that really *could* give us food poisoning." Selma winked at her but Lily couldn't smile in return.

She didn't usually argue with her grandmother, but this time she whined, "I don't see why you want someone else to take over my responsibilities."

"Because they're *not* your responsibilities. Your main responsibilities are to go to school during the day and to do your homework after supper. Your granddad and I have appreciated your help and we'll still need you to do your regular chores in the house and around the farm. But you've taken on far too much responsibility during the past few months."

"I don't mind, really."

"*I* mind," Selma said so emphatically that she went into a coughing spasm. Lily had to get her a glass of water before she could continue. "I don't want you to be burdened with running a household or taking care of your ailing grandma. I want you to enjoy your youth, do you hear me? It goes by too fast. *Life* goes by too fast."

Unable to look at Selma for fear she'd burst into tears, Lily hung her head and picked at her thumbnail. "It's not like I'm ruining my awesome social life or anything just because I'm helping you, Grandma. Usually, all I ever do is hang out here on the farm or at the beach with Katie."

"What about taking pictures? You haven't had much time for photography lately."

"That's just a hobby," she mumbled sullenly.

"It is now, but who knows what it might turn into if you have the opportunity to develop your talent." Selma reached over and pushed Lily's curls off the side of her face, but Lily still wouldn't lift her head. "As someone who has grown up on a farm, you know that there's a season for everything, Lily. This is your season to grow and it's my season to die. Refusing to accept the help we need isn't going to keep me alive—and it might make my dying more difficult. You don't want that, do you?"

Lily was too choked up to say anything, so she shook her head, splattering tears across her lap. Her grandmother took her hand and squeezed her fingers.

"I think you'll like the aide. She's distantly related to Mrs. Henderson's husband. A second or third cousin, I think." Agnes Henderson, now widowed, was Selma's dearest friend. She lived half a mile down the beach. The two women had coffee together at the farm almost every morning, if the tide was out far enough that Mrs. Henderson could walk along the shoreline. "The aide's name is Dahlia and she's in her late thirties. It'll be good for you to have someone around to talk to about the kinds of things I'm too old-fashioned to understand."

Even though it was true that there were certain topics she felt she couldn't discuss with her grandmother, Lily objected, "You're *not* too old-fashioned."

Selma wagged a finger at her. "You know I don't tolerate lying—and that includes fibs." In that moment, her grandmother seemed so much like her healthy self that Lily's lips slipped into a small smile. "There's something else I won't tolerate... Dahlia is bringing her son with her. His name is Aiden and he's a sophomore, just like you. Mrs. Henderson confided that the girls at school think he's quite a looker and he has a bit of a wild streak. Now, I know you understand all about the birds and the bees, but—"

"Grandma!" Lily squawked, covering her ears. "I get it. You don't have to say anything else."

"Yes, I do." She feebly tugged on Lily's sleeve until Lily dropped her hands to her lap again. "Your uncle will move into the house with us, so Dahlia and Aiden can stay in the cottage. Still, we'll all be in very close quarters, so I want everyone to understand that there is to be absolutely *no* hanky-panky going on under this roof. Your granddad is going to make sure Aiden abides by this rule, too."

Lily cringed, imaging her granddad lecturing some strange boy about abstaining from any "hanky-panky" with her. "You don't have to worry about it. I promise."

"Good." Her grandmother seemed as eager to move on to a new topic as Lily was. "Dahlia will be using your uncle's bedroom, but it's so drab in there. It needs to be repainted. Maybe you can help him choose the color? He's not good at that kind of thing but you have an eye for it."

"Sure. I can help him paint, too," Lily volunteered. "It'll be fun."

It was an exaggeration to say that painting was going to be fun. But at least the task would make Lily feel as if they were preparing to welcome guests into their home, instead of preparing to say goodbye to her grandmother.

When Lars told Martin about the plan the next evening, he grumbled, "I don't see why they can't stay in the house with you. It has two bedrooms that aren't being used."

"Because Dahlia and her son need their privacy and we need ours." Selma blotted her lips with her napkin and set it down beside her plate, indicating that she was done with her meal and done with the conversation, too. "Lars, could you help me into the living room, please?"

Lily's grandmother was too unstable to walk even a short distance by herself, so someone had to escort her from room to room. But she was still strong enough to engage in her evening ritual of sipping tea in the living room with her husband.

After they left, Martin took one final bite of baked potato and then stood to leave, too. Noticing the disgruntled look on his face, Lily felt kind of sorry for him. She supposed that the cottage was as close as he'd ever come to having a place of his own, and it must have been difficult to give it up.

Now fifty-two years old, Martin was a lifelong bachelor, but he hadn't always wanted it that way. Selma had told Lily that when he was twenty-one, he'd been engaged to a local girl named Brenda. The summer before Martin and Brenda were going to get married, she and her brother died in a boating accident. Their parents were so devastated they moved off the island to one of the landlocked states in the Midwest.

Martin was grief-struck, too. For almost a year, he barely spoke more than a few sentences to anyone, including his family. Although he eventually "came around again," as Selma had put it, he was still a man of few words and he never dated anyone else.

Now the only socializing he did was to occasionally play darts with the regulars in the bar on Friday night. He was also a member of the island's environmental committee. However, most of his time was spent in the cranberry bogs or in the workshop, where he helped Lars supplement their farming income by running a small machine and equipment repair business. For relaxation, Martin liked to watch a ball game on TV alone in the cottage, or else he read the latest publications about sustainable agriculture.

Knowing he preferred to keep to himself, Lily could imagine

that it was going to be hard for him to have two more people in their household. She tried to cheer him up by suggesting, "I can bring home some paint sample cards from the hardware store tomorrow, Uncle Martin. Grandma thought you might want help choosing a color, but you should really make the decision yourself since you'll be moving back into the cottage as soon as Dahlia and Aiden leave. Hopefully they won't even be here very long."

As soon as the words were out of her mouth, Lily realized that if Dahlia and Aiden didn't stay with them for very long, it would be because Selma had passed away. Staggered by the reality, she abruptly plopped down in the chair, buried her head in her arms on the table and wept.

"Shush," Martin whispered, not unkindly. In an uncharacteristic display of affection, he placed his hand on her shoulder. "She'll hear you."

Lily nodded into her arms, knowing what he meant. If Selma heard her granddaughter crying, she'd worry, which would drain her of what little energy she still had left. Lily sat up straight again and wiped her eyes with her sleeve.

"You can go ahead and pick out the paint. Any color you want." Martin let go of her shoulder. "As long as it's not too frilly."

Lily doubted he'd meant to be funny, so she bit her tongue to keep from laughing at her gruff but lovable Uncle Martin.

By the time Dahlia and Aiden came to stay with them, Lily and Martin had painted both cottage bedrooms. Dahlia's was a soft shade of green and Aiden's was slate blue. Lily's grandfather and uncle also switched Martin's mattress with the mattress from one of the spare bedrooms in the house and they'd washed the windows, too.

Even Mrs. Henderson helped revitalize the cottage by sewing new valances for the kitchen. The material had blue and yellow stripes—not the most contemporary pattern Lily had ever seen, but at least they were livelier than the previous curtains.

"I think these used to be blue before they faded," she said as she slid the old gray fabric off the curtain rod so she could hang the new valance.

"They're not faded—they're coated in dust." Mrs. Henderson warned her, "Be careful not to shake them. We don't want to irritate your grandma's lungs. She won't be able to breathe."

Selma, who had been watching them redecorate from a nearby chair, solemnly intoned, "From dust I came, to dust I shall return..."

Lily was appalled by the reference, which she thought was maudlin, but her grandmother and Mrs. Henderson laughed so hard her grandma started wheezing. As Lily dashed to retrieve the portable oxygen tank from the farmhouse, it occurred to her that the two women cracked up over as many silly things as she and Katie did.

I bet we'll still be friends when we're their age, too, she thought.

When she returned to the cottage kitchen, she found her grandmother and Mrs. Henderson discussing a dinner menu. As ill as Selma was, she felt it was her duty as a hostess to prepare a special meal to welcome Aiden and Dahlia to the farm. She decided to serve turkey with cranberry-sausage stuffing. For dessert, she planned to make her specialty; white chocolate cranberry cheesecake.

The cheesecake was supposed to chill overnight, so the evening before Dahlia and Aiden were due, Lily helped her grandmother prepare it. Because it was an effort for Selma to stand for more than a couple of minutes, she sat in a chair and Lily brought her the ingredients. Selma insisted on measuring and mixing them herself. As she worked, she explained each step to her granddaughter, who had never prepared the dessert, which was made according to Selma's grandmother's highly guarded secret recipe.

The next morning, Selma was too weak to get out of bed, much less, to lift a 25-pound turkey. Mrs. Henderson must have anticipated the situation, because she "dropped by" for coffee two hours earlier than usual to ask if she could help with anything. Together, she and Lily prepared the turkey, stuffing, potatoes, and gravy. Selma slept until almost three o'clock and woke relatively refreshed, just in time to greet their guests.

Ever since Lily had told Katie about Aiden and Dahlia coming to live with the Lindgren family, and the embarrassing conversation she'd had with her grandmother about "hanky-panky", Katie had been speculating about Aiden's looks and personality. She'd made Lily promise to call her as soon as she'd met him.

"Just because your grandparents don't want you getting involved with him doesn't mean I can't," Katie had said. "Hot guys don't just wash up on Dune Island every day, so you have to tell me everything before the other girls find out about him."

It turned out that Aiden was as good-looking as Mrs. Henderson had indicated, and Dahlia was naturally beautiful, too. They were both tall and dark-haired, with distinctly sculpted cheekbones, and long, straight noses. They also both had big, brown, almond-shaped eyes, and olive complexions. But the similarities didn't seem to extend to their personalities. Dahlia was warm, gregarious and appreciative. She immediately pitched in to help Lily and Mrs. Henderson serve the meal. Aiden, on the other hand, didn't speak unless someone asked him a question, and then he'd mumble a one or two-word answer.

Trying to give him the benefit of the doubt, Lily figured he was nervous, not rude. However, when it came time for dessert, he announced in his first full sentence of the afternoon, "I can't eat that stuff."

Selma appeared to blanch, although she was already so pale it was difficult to tell for sure. If Lily had spoken to her like that, her grandmother would have told her to leave the room and not return until she'd learned some manners.

This afternoon, Selma merely put a hand to her cheek and apologized. "Oh, dear, I'm sorry. We should have made two desserts. I keep forgetting that so many children can't drink milk these days. What's that allergy called—lactose something?"

"I am *not* lactose intolerant," Aiden informed her. "I just can't stand the taste of cheesecake."

Lily understood why he may have been annoyed at her grandmother for essentially inquiring about the health of his intestines, and for indirectly referring to him as a child—even if he *was* acting like one. But his disdainful tone and ungrateful attitude Lily want to kick his shins beneath the table. *Doesn't he see how sick Grandma is? Can't he give her a break?*

Just when Lily thought she couldn't feel any more annoyed, Aiden added, "I can't stand cranberries, either."

Whether it was rational or not, Lily felt as if he was expressing his distaste for the entire Lindgren family. For their farm, too. From the corner of her eye, she noticed her uncle open his mouth and then close it again, as if he'd thought better of whatever he was going to say. Her granddad made a fist around his napkin, crumpling it into a wad. Although Lily couldn't bring herself to peek at her grandmother's face or to meet Mrs. Henderson's eyes, she caught Dahlia staring daggers at her son.

"I *love* cheesecake," she declared. "This one looks like a work of art—it must have taken hours to make."

"It was no trouble—Lily and I worked on it together," Selma replied with a gracious smile. "Would you do the honors, Dahlia? My hands are so shaky I'm afraid I'll make a mess of it."

"My pleasure." As Dahlia cut the pie, everyone except Aiden resumed their cordial conversation. He stared in the direction of the door and jiggled his leg under the table, as if he couldn't wait to get out of there. Right then, Lily couldn't wait for him to leave, either.

Yet in spite his obnoxious first impression, in the weeks and months to come, Lily tried to keep an open mind about him. Unfortunately, the longer she knew him, the more she realized he'd been showing his true colors since day one.

In contrast, Dahlia proved to be even kinder and more thoughtful and industrious than she'd seemed on the day she moved into the Lindgrens' home. She was a skillful, compassionate health aide and a decent cook, too. Because of the respectful way she cared for Selma, she quickly won the elder woman's trust, which in turn endeared her to Lars.

The only one who kept Dahlia at arm's length was Martin, but he kept everyone at arm's length—it didn't necessarily mean he didn't like her. Dahlia didn't seem to notice. Or if she noticed, she didn't seem to mind. She was as affable and accommodating to him as she was to the rest of the family.

Lily had to admit Selma had been right: she loved talking to Dahlia about boys and school and photography. Not to mention, she was relieved she didn't have to cook supper any longer.

Even though I like hanging out with Dahlia and I'm glad she's making all our meals, that doesn't mean she could ever replace Grandma in my heart, Lily often thought. And just because she'd grown up on a farm didn't mean she was ready to accept that there was a season for dying, either.

CHAPTER FIVE

NOW

WEDNESDAY

It was almost six o'clock in the morning and Lily knew she should get up and take a shower, but she couldn't drag herself out of the lumpy motel bed. She'd hardly gotten a full two hours of sleep overnight because the guests next door had kept their TV blaring until almost 2:00 AM. She would have requested to change rooms, but Lily knew the current motel owners from school and she didn't want to draw attention to her presence on the island by complaining about the noise.

Even after the neighboring guests had finally turned off their television, Lily continued to toss and turn, her mind racing. She'd fully anticipated that being on Dune Island again was going to spark upsetting emotions and memories, so she had braced herself for those and she'd been processing them the best she could. But she hadn't quite expected her visit to prompt so many *pleasant* recollections, especially of her aunt.

On one hand, those memories were comforting; on the other hand, they made her wistful for an earlier time in her relationship with Dahlia. Mostly, they emphasized how conflicted Lily still felt. She'd thought she'd made peace with what had happened between them a long time ago but being back in her childhood home had stirred up unresolved questions and issues. Although she no longer held any anger toward her aunt, Lily once again found herself puzzled and saddened by how Dahlia's uncharacteristic behavior that last summer she'd spent on the island had destroyed the closeness they'd once shared.

In addition to her unsettling feelings about her aunt, Lily's interaction with Jake had kept her brooding into the wee hours of the night. Although he'd been polite enough overall, Jake seemed less friendly than she'd remembered him being when they were younger. Maybe she was being hypersensitive, but when Lily reflected on his initial comment about how it had been a long time since she'd been on the island, she wondered if Jake had intended the remark as criticism. Since she hardly knew him, it was difficult to tell, but she couldn't shake the feeling that there was a negative undercurrent to his tone.

To be fair, I shouldn't have sprung it on him that I'm considering selling the farm, she thought. The first few hours of her visit to Dune Island had been so nerve-racking that Lily hadn't been weighing some of her remarks before expressing them. In hindsight, she realized her announcement may have caused Jake to worry he'd lose his job. *When I officially tell him that I am going to sell the estate, I'll make sure to give him first offer on the property. And if he can't buy it himself, I'll assure him I'll make it a condition of sale to find a buyer who will keep him on as the farm's manager,* she'd resolved, before finally dropping off to sleep.

Now it was ten minutes past six and Lily sat up and stretched. She had a kink in her spine from the rigorous bending and lifting she'd done yesterday. Although Dahlia had neatly stored Selma and Lars's possessions, there were just so *many* of them.

Lily had spent all day grouping the items into four categories: keep, sell, donate, and discard. Most of the stuff fell squarely in the "donations" section of the room.

But there were a few definite "keepers," including some family photo albums, her grandma's china, and an antique clock from Sweden. She also kept her granddad's silver watch and her uncle's baseball card collection to give to Ryan when he was older.

She'd worked for eight or nine hours, stopping only to call her son, but Lily still felt as if she'd hardly put a dent in sorting through her family's belongings. *If I'm going to finish everything I need to do today, I'm going to need caffeine and a shower, so I'd better hop to it*, she thought, finally pulling herself out of bed.

Half an hour later, as she was driving away from the motel, Lily decided that she didn't care how much a cup of gourmet coffee cost; she was going to buy one before her meeting with Steve. She figured she had plenty of time for a quick detour, since finding a parking space close to Steve's office wouldn't be a problem this early in the morning.

As she rounded a curve, she nearly collided headlong with a car that had crossed over the centerline. Sounding her horn as she swerved to avoid him, she wondered, *What's wrong with him anyway?* A moment later, she spotted the answer: a large turtle was in the middle of the opposite lane.

Aware that if she didn't assist it, the slow-moving reptile might get hit or cause an accident between two vehicles, Lily rolled to a stop on the shoulder of the straightaway. Three more vehicles zoomed by while she walked to the spot where the turtle appeared paralyzed mid-crawl. Lily carefully lifted the creature from the pavement and placed it across the road on the sandy ground. It quickly treaded down the embankment and disappeared into the tall grass.

"Oh, sure, *now* you hurry," she said aloud with a chuckle.

Returning to her car, Lily decided she'd better not stop for coffee after all. *Steve won't be happy if I'm late a second time. And if we have to extend our meeting, I'll be late for my meeting with Jake, and then I'll have two men irritated at me.*

She pressed the ignition button and the car's dashboard lights came on, but the engine didn't start. Lily waited a moment before trying again. This time, nothing happened at all. Suddenly she recalled that yesterday the engine had made a ticking sound and she realized the problem was probably her starter. She waited a few more minutes and tried again. Still nothing.

What terrible timing! Where am I going to get the money to pay for a new starter? she fretted.

First things first; she had to call Steve to tell him she wasn't going to make it to the appointment. But when she tapped on his number, the phone immediately dropped the connection. It happened again and again—she was in one of Hope Haven's ubiquitous dead zones. She'd forgotten about this minor but irritating drawback of island living.

Lily moaned as she grabbed her purse and got out of the car. The farm was three miles from there; she'd have to walk. Maybe along the way, she'd get a cell phone signal and she'd be able to call Steve. She tucked her keys under the floor mat for the tow truck driver and left the door unlocked. *If someone wants my luggage, they can take it, because I am* not *rolling it all the way back to the farm,* she thought. *Talk about drawing attention to myself!*

Briskly striding along the sandy edge of the road, Lily planned her strategy for dealing with her situation. *After I call Steve to tell him I can't meet with him, I'll call the mechanic. It shouldn't take more than three or four hours for them to install a new starter. While the car's in the garage, I'll talk to Jake. I'll arrange to have someone from the swap shop pick up the donations, since I can't bring them there myself. Even if I don't leave the island until four or five o'clock, I can still get back to Maine by midnight. So now all I have to do is figure out how I'm going to pay for the repairs.*

As much as she didn't want to, Lily accepted the fact that she'd have to borrow the money from Leanne and Tim. They could submit their credit card information to the mechanic and she'd repay them as soon as her salary was deposited into her bank account.

Lily was so lost in thought she didn't realize an SUV had come to a stop ahead of her until she practically bumped into it. On the back fender of the vehicle was a bumper sticker that read, I'M NOT ON *YOUR* VACATION.

That means the driver's a local. While Lily understood why some year-round residents were frustrated by the summer crowds or by the way the vacationers drove, she thought the bumper sticker was obnoxious. Hope Haven's economy relied primarily on tourism, so it didn't seem fair to gripe about the very people who kept their community financially stable.

When she approached the driver's side window, someone behind the wheel squealed, "Lily Lindgren! I heard you were in town."

Lily recognized the woman's voice before she even glimpsed her face: it was Claire Griffin. Her family owned a large inn in Benjamin's Manor, and she'd always looked down her nose at other business owners in the hospitality industry, especially those who operated or owned motels and hotels, instead of inns or B&Bs.

Without waiting for Lily to return her greeting, Claire told her, "When I saw the abandoned car with the Pennsylvania plates, I wondered if it was yours. Then I spotted your hair and that cinched it. You want a ride?"

When they were in middle school, Lily's classmate had dubbed herself Chatty Catty Claire, a label she'd lived up to well into high school. Hopefully, she would have mellowed a little as she grew up. Relieved, Lily accepted the offer.

"Hi, Claire. Sure, if you could drop me off at the farm, I'd appreciate it a lot." She crossed to the passenger side of the car and got in. Even though they weren't in high school any more, Lily wasn't taking any chances. She figured her best bet for avoiding questions she didn't want to answer would be to ask Claire lots of questions first. Before she'd even closed her door, Lily started babbling, "I can't believe it's been eighteen years since we've seen each other. What have you been up to? How's business at the inn? Looks like you have a car seat in the back, which must mean you have a child, right?"

"Whoa. Sounds like someone's had a lot of coffee," Claire said with a laugh. But she seemed happy to chat about herself, her family's acquisition of two more inns, and her third husband, who was a real estate agent and a transplant from Sacramento. However, Claire had very little to say about his two children from a previous marriage, except to complain that they'd be staying with her and her husband all summer. "But you know what that's like—I heard that you've got a kid, too. How old is she now? Six, seven?"

"My *son* is eight."

"Time flies. Seems like it wasn't that long ago that we heard you were pregnant. It was when your uncle died—Dahlia said that's why you couldn't travel to Rockfield for Martin's funeral. She said you had some kind of pregnancy complication." Claire glanced over at Lily's midriff. "You don't look pregnant *now* though, so that can't be your excuse for missing Dahlia's funeral. How come you weren't there?"

She should have told Claire it was none of her business, but Lily was so flabbergasted by her blatant nosiness that she answered, "I wasn't informed she'd passed away until after the funeral."

"Oh, I get it. Aiden didn't tell you, huh? Well, it's no wonder. He probably didn't want you to make him look bad."

"What do you mean?"

"You know, because he was on vacay in Australia and he couldn't make it back. If you had shown up to his mother's funeral and he didn't, that would have looked really bad for him," she explained.

Lily was appalled to hear that Aiden hadn't attended Dahlia's funeral, but she wasn't necessarily surprised. As a teenager, he'd ducked out of her grandmother Selma's funeral after the opening hymn. Dahlia later tried to excuse his absence by saying he didn't handle emotional situations well, but Lily had a hunch he just wanted to go smoke pot in the woods with Olivia.

Skipping out on Selma's funeral was disrespectful enough, but missing his mother's just because he was on vacation seemed inexcusable. *I know he was as upset by what Dahlia did when we were in high school as I was, but my understanding was that they'd come to some sort of reconciliation,* she thought. *Besides, she was his* mother. *She may not have been perfect, but there's no question that she was always very loving toward him. If I'd known that Dahlia had died, I definitely would have been at the funeral to pay my respects, despite our differences.*

"Condolences on your loss, by the way." Claire's expression of sympathy sounded like an afterthought. She hardly took a breath before barraging Lily with another verbal onslaught.

"You know, after you left for that photography cruise or whatever in Europe, we all thought you'd become famous. Instead, it was like you dropped off the face of the earth. No one heard from you and we couldn't find you on social media. Dahlia barely said a word about you. So I guess your big photography career went south before it even began, huh?"

"I-I got caught up in other passions. I traveled a lot, then I met my husband and I had my son—and I'm a project management consultant now, so never a dull moment." All those things were true, but Lily resented it that she felt the need to justify her life choices to Claire Griffin and all the other people Claire was referring to when she used the collective "we."

"We figured we'd finally get to see you once everyone in your family had passed away. That's why you're here, right, because there's no one left to take care of your family's property? You should sell it to a land developer. You could make a killing. Believe me, I know—it cost us an arm and a leg to buy the inns and they're not even on waterfront property."

"I'm not sure what I'll do about the farm. I haven't made any decisions yet, but I'd *never* sell to a land developer," Lily asserted, intending to squelch a rumor to that effect before it got started. If Jake heard anything of the sort it would only add to his worries. But Claire still managed to twist her words.

"So does that mean you're moving back here and taking over the farm yourself?" she asked. "What does your husband think of that? Is he the cranberry-farming type or is he more of a city guy? What does he do for a living anyway? You haven't said a word about him."

You haven't let me get a word in edgewise even if I'd wanted to, Lily thought. It was kind of Claire to pick her up, but there was no such thing as a free ride and it was clear Claire's payment would be information. Aloud, she stated flatly, "My husband died three years ago."

"Oh, right. Sorry, I forgot that he'd died. But that makes it easier, in a way, doesn't it?"

"*Easier?*" she repeated incredulously. Nothing about Tyler's death had made any part of Lily's life easier.

"I mean, because you don't have to consider whether he wants to move to Dune Island, or if he could find a job here, or anything like that. It's all up to you." Claire flipped her turn signal on as they neared the Lindgrens' driveway. "I can't believe you're coming full circle after all these years. It goes to show, you can take the farmgirl out of the farm, but you can't take—"

Lily cut her off. "No need to drive up to the house. You can let me out here."

"I don't mind," Claire said as she pulled into the driveway. "I've got time. I can even stay for a cup of coffee."

"No," Lily replied a little too sharply, but by this point, she didn't care. "I've got to call a tow truck and talk to the mechanic, so I'm too busy for coffee. Thanks for the ride though—and good luck with your husband's children this summer."

But better *luck to them,* Lily thought, hopping out of the SUV before they'd come to a full stop. Claire's blathering had managed to eclipse whatever good memories about Dune Island that had come to Lily's mind during the past twenty-four hours. All she could think was, *People like Claire are the reason I'd never bring my son here.*

She hurried toward the house, looking up Hank Cramer's automotive shop on her phone as she walked and feeling relieved when she saw they were still in business. Whenever her uncle and granddad had a problem with a car that they couldn't fix on their own, Hank and his sons were the only mechanics on the island they'd patronize. Even years later Lily hoped she could trust them to give her the best price and their work was guaranteed. She explained her situation and since her insurance covered her for a free tow, she arranged to have her car brought to their garage.

Next, she called Steve. It was a little past 8:00, so he was already meeting with another client. Lily left a message with his receptionist, explaining why she'd missed the meeting and requesting a return call.

She had just disconnected when Jake and his nephew pulled into the lot and got out of the truck. Jake was carrying a cup of coffee and Conner was devouring a jelly donut. Last evening all she'd had for supper was a banana and the yogurt she'd brought from Maine, because she hadn't wanted to run into anyone she knew at the market. Seeing the treat made

Lily's mouth water, but seeing Jake in his tight Lindgren Cranberry Farm T-shirt made her stomach feel topsy-turvy. She pressed her hand to her abdomen to quell the startling sensation.

"Good morning," she said in a sing-song voice, determined to get off to a better start with him today. "Looks like someone made a stop at the Donut Shanty on their way here. Are you fueling up for another long day of hard work?"

Although she'd directed her remark to Conner, his mouth was so full he could only nod. However, Jake, replied, "Yeah, my sister's still ill today, so I had to bring Conner with me again. But don't worry, Sophie will keep him occupied so we can discuss the accounting in private. She's not here yet though— you're early. I'm going to need a few minutes to get the paperwork together before we get started."

There it was again; that distinctly defensive note in Jake's tone. She couldn't blame him. "I'm not worried—I'm happy that Conner's here to give you a hand today." She smiled at Jake's nephew so he'd know he was welcome on the farm, but his eyes were closed as he tipped his head back, guzzling milk from a cardboard carton. "Take all the time you need to get the docs ready, no rush. The only reason I'm here early is that someone just dropped me off."

After Lily explained that she'd stalled a couple miles down the road, Jake seemed to lighten his tone a little. "I hope nothing's seriously wrong with the engine. You think the battery's dead?"

"The tow truck driver will check it out before they take it away, but I just had a new battery installed, so I think the problem is actually my starter."

"Well, you would know," he replied. At first, she thought he was being snide but then he elaborated, "Lars and Martin taught me an awful lot about engines and machinery. You must have learned a lot from them, too?"

"You're right, I did," she replied, moved that Jake had mentioned her granddad and uncle's mechanical aptitude.

When Lily was a teenager, they often tried to engage her in the repair business, but she'd been a resentful participant. It didn't bother her at all that engine repair was traditionally considered "men's work," whatever that meant. But she became easily frustrated when she couldn't figure out why something wasn't operating as it should—or when she made a problem worse in the process of trying to fix it.

It was only in adulthood that she appreciated how much valuable knowledge she'd gained from all those rainy Saturday afternoons she'd spent helping them change oil filters on cars, clean lawnmower carburetors, or replace air conditioner capacitators.

What I wouldn't give to hang out in the workshop with Grandad and Uncle Martin again, she thought, her eyes misty.

"Since Sophie isn't here yet, can I come on the tour with you?" Conner asked Jake.

"It's up to Lily."

"Sure," she agreed. "You can point out your favorite thing in the education center."

"Oh, that's easy. It's the cranberry puzzle. C'mon, I'll show you."

His uncle instructed him to go wash the sticky jelly from his fingers, first. After the boy was out of earshot, Jake remarked, "My sister jokes that if Conner ever gets lost and she needs to find him, instead of following his footprints, she'd follow his *foodprints*." He shook his head in amusement. "I know he's getting a little old to be reminded to wash his hands but reminding him is a lot easier than cleaning up in his wake."

"My son usually remembers to wash his hands, but he leaves a trail of toys and clothes in *his* wake. Last week I found one of his socks in our mailbox. Funny thing is, I didn't know if Ryan had left it there for some reason, or if the mail carrier had found on the walkway and put it in the box, along with our bills."

Jake laughed a deep belly laugh. Even though Lily didn't think her anecdote was that funny, she was pleased that for once she'd said something to put a grin on his face, and she smiled, too.

Then Conner came and led them into the cottage kitchen. The appliances had been replaced with bookshelves—Lily recognized some of her uncle's reference materials about sustainable farming—and a computer workstation.

"This is where people can read, or do their own research. And we have a video that plays on a loop about the farm too." Jake gestured at the space.

Before she had a chance to ask any questions, Conner hurried them into the former den, now the children's room filled with books and games. There were also several booths where little ones could engage in activities designed to teach them about cranberry plants and cranberry farming.

The wooden puzzle Conner showed her was four foot square and it consisted of hundreds of individual oversized pieces. The puzzle depicted an aerial close-up of a crate of cranberries, and there was a duplicate picture hanging on the wall as a guide.

"Sophie thinks the puzzle will be too hard for kids to put together 'cause all the cranberries look the same, but they really don't," Conner said. "See? That one's red and this one is kinda maroon and some are half-white."

"Good eye," Lily praised him. "Your uncle should give you a job at the sorting station during harvest season."

Conner puffed up his chest. "Did you know that just because some berries are half-red and half-white, it doesn't mean they aren't ripe? It's just because the white side was more shaded."

Jake started to say, "Ms. Lily grew up here, Conner, so I'm sure she—"

But Lily shook her head, signaling him not to tell his nephew that of course she knew that half-white cranberries were ripe. "Hmm, that does sound kind of familiar. Did *you* know there's a way to make the half-white ones turn completely red after they've been picked? You can either put them in the freezer or cook them. It draws the pigment out."

"Cool. I'm going to tell my teacher about that next year. Maybe she'll let us do a science experiment to prove it."

His interest in the natural world reminded Lily so much of Ryan that she momentarily wished she'd brought her son with her after all. *It's only a matter of hours until I'll be with him in Maine,* she reminded herself. *And that's a much better environment for us than Dune Island is.*

As she followed Jake into the cottage's former living room, he explained, "This area is specifically dedicated to the Lindgren farm, instead of to cranberry farming in general. If you start here and follow the timeline clockwise around the room, you'll see photos of all the Lindgren farming families—well, if photos were available when they were alive—and you can read a little bit about their lives, too."

Lily had seen these pictures of her ancestors many times and her grandparents had told her countless stories about them when she was growing up. But viewing all the photos arranged in chronological order had a profound effect on her. Probably because the arrangement emphasized the fact that she and Ryan were the only people left in the Lindgren family line. As she circled the room, moving from the oldest dates on the timeline to the most recent, Lily's chest felt tight with emotion.

She managed to maintain her composure until she spotted the final two photos. The next-to-the-last one was of her grandparents, her parents, her uncle, and herself as a little girl. The final photo was of Martin and Dahlia; Lily had taken that one. She distinctly remembered because it was one of only a handful of occasions when her aunt allowed Lily to photograph her. Seeing her closest family members again—on film instead of in person—made her ache with such deep loneliness that she could hardly contain her tears.

She choked out the words, "Excuse me, I need some air." Then she spun on her heel and fled the room.

CHAPTER SIX

NOW

It took Lily several minutes of hiding in the bathroom to steady her breathing and several more to convince herself there was no reason to feel embarrassed if Jake had noticed her weepiness. She reasoned that most people in her situation would have felt sentimental, too. Besides, she was sleep deprived. She was also hungry—and she missed her son.

It's only four or five more hours before I'm on my way, she thought, giving herself yet another silent pep talk.

When Lily emerged from the restroom, Conner wasn't anywhere in sight, but Jake was pacing the hallway with a glass of water in hand. Extending it to her, he furrowed his brows. "Everything okay?"

"Fine, thanks," she said blithely. While she was determined not to feel embarrassed, she didn't care to open up to Jake about what had brought on her tears. "What's the next stop on the tour?"

They wound their way through the gift shop in the farm-house, where Sophie and Conner were unpacking a crate of smaller versions of the wooden puzzle in the education center. Jake repeated what Sophie had already told him about Dahlia's requirements for the merchandise: everything was handmade and local.

Next, he led her to the kitchen, which was a lot bigger now because the wall that used to separate it from the dining room had been taken down. Selma's appliances from the 1990s had been replaced with the stainless steel variety. There was a large island for the instructor's use and eight smaller portable islands that could be arranged in rows, classroom style. Jake explained that Dahlia had hired a retired bakery owner to teach classes on making cranberry edibles, including desserts, stuffing, jam, and even cranberry wine.

"Now, for the upstairs." He turned toward the hallway, but Lily hesitated. She was concerned that she'd have another meltdown if she discovered her childhood bedroom had been turned into an order processing center, or something similar.

"What's up there?"

"Not a lot. Three of the rooms are completely empty. We cleaned them out because we're ordering bunk beds at the end of the summer," he explained. Lily noticed Jake kept saying "we," instead of "I," as if Dahlia were still alive. "A group of agricultural students and a professor from a university in Vermont are coming to conduct research on the bogs in the fall. As part of the arrangement, we'll provide their housing. We'll give other students, growers and scientists similar opportunities throughout the year."

His eyes shone and his enthusiasm reminded Lily of how excited Conner had been about solving the cranberry puzzle. "What a terrific idea."

"Yeah. I hope to learn as much as they do from the experience. Anyway, our business office is in the fourth room—it's the little one in the back. We can discuss the financials in there."

Relieved that her old bedroom wasn't being used, Lily followed Jake to the sparsely furnished office. Once she was seated across from him, she remarked, "Thanks for the tour.

You've made a lot of very innovative changes to the business. I'm impressed."

"But?" he prompted, as if he'd read her mind.

"But as much as I admire what you've done, when I was growing up here my family always managed to sustain the farm on cranberry sales alone. What changed?"

"Ah, well, that's where our financial situation figures in."

As Jake printed out several financial documents for Lily's reference, he explained that the farm had suffered setbacks for several years in a row. There'd been an extreme heat wave one summer. The next year, a spring frost. But the biggest obstacle the farm had faced was that the glut of berries produced by the big co-ops had repeatedly driven down the price of berries for independent farmers like the Lindgrens.

"As you know, the farm was paid off several generations ago, but real estate is at a premium in Hope Haven, which means the property taxes for the farm are sky high now, too."

Jake said that expanding the scope of the business was the only way they could meet their financial obligations and stay competitive in a market that was dominated by co-ops. As Lily reviewed the financial statements with him, she could understand why it had been necessary to enhance the business and renovate the farmhouse and cottage.

However, she was dismayed by the size of the loans they'd borrowed to make the improvements. How had Dahlia planned to repay the bank, plus cover property taxes and staff salaries? Lily suddenly felt as burdened by the farm's debt as she'd often felt about her own. All she could think was, *I sure hope Steve can find a buyer with very deep pockets.*

And she had to remember that Jake was her first choice buyer, too. "Obviously, you've given me a lot of information to bring to the table when Steve and I discuss my options—which we're still doing," she said, choosing her words carefully. "So, this question might be premature, but *if* I end up selling the farm, Dahlia wanted you to have the first option to buy it. Is that something you'd be interested in doing?"

"Of *course*, I'd be interested. I'd buy it in a heartbeat if I could. But I know what it's worth and I'd never be approved for a loan that size." Jake woefully shook his head and emphasized, "I unequivocally can*not* buy the farm or the business."

"Okay, well, that's helpful to know, so we can eliminate that option." Lily was just about to assure him that *if* she did sell the farm, she'd find a buyer who'd retain his managerial services. But her phone buzzed and she hastily stepped into the hall to answer it.

It was the mechanic, who told her she'd been right; the car needed a new starter. Unfortunately, nowhere on the island had the part in stock.

"We've located one in Providence, so they'll overnight it. We can't install it until Saturday morning, but we open at 6:00 so you should be good to go by 10:00."

"*Saturday* morning?" Lily was flabbergasted.

"Yeah, sorry about that. When we were calling around for the part, we asked if anyone else could take on the job, but the other garages are in worse shape than we are. The soonest anyone could put you on their schedule would be next Wednesday."

"*Wednesday?*" Lily echoed him again.

"Yeah." The mechanic wryly joked, "Suddenly, waiting until Saturday doesn't seem so long, does it?"

To Lily, it seemed interminable—primarily because it meant she'd miss the rest of her vacation with Ryan. It also occurred to her that even though she'd be paid by Friday night, she couldn't afford to stay at a motel again. *Like it or not, I'll have to sleep in Dahlia's room for the next couple of nights. I'll have to stretch out my grocery allowance, too.* But those were minor inconveniences compared to how crushed she felt about not being able to reunite with her son until Saturday.

"Bad news?" Jake asked when she returned to his office. After she told him, he said, "You could use Dahlia's car. It's kind of a beater, but it should make it to Maine. You could go up tonight and then bring Ryan back with you on Saturday to switch vehicles."

Lily had a knee-jerk reaction, exclaiming, "No way, I'd never bring him here!"

"Why not?" The look on Jake's face was just like Steve's expression when she'd told him she had no intention of ever moving back to Rockfield. She instantly regretted her outburst.

"Because... because my son hates road trips. Returning to Dune Island would be a major detour and you know how difficult it is to catch a ferry at this time of the year." Recognizing how feeble her excuse sounded, Lily added, "Besides, staying here will give me more time to take care of my grandparents' belongings. But I'm glad you mentioned Dahlia's car. It would be great if I could use it to haul away the stuff I want to donate to the swap shop."

Jake shrugged. "Suit yourself. The car's yours now anyway. Dahlia probably kept a key in her room, but I still have the spare, since I occasionally used her car and vice versa." He pulled a ring of keys from his pocket. As he was unfastening one of the fobs, Lily's phone buzzed again: it was Steve.

"I'll be right back." She popped into the hall again and apologized to Steve for missing their meeting.

"That's okay, it's perfectly understandable," Steve empathized. "Since you'll be staying in Rockfield tonight, do you suppose you could meet at four-thirty today after all? Or, we could meet a little later over drinks and dinner at Captain Clark's?"

Considering the inconveniences she'd caused him, Lily realized she should accommodate Steve's request. But Captain Clark's was too expensive for her budget and she dreaded the possibility of running into their former acquaintances. They'd probably assume she and Steve were dating, just as they'd assumed in high school, no matter how many times she'd denied it.

Steve must have sensed her ambivalence. "If you don't like Captain Clark's, we can go someplace else," he suggested. "Anywhere on the island—it's your choice and my treat."

Lily could almost taste the pan-seared scallops that the restaurant had been famous for when she lived here. "Captain Clark's would be wonderful. But instead of eating there, can we eat at your place?"

"Oh, sure, that's right—we shouldn't discuss your inheritance in public," Steve said. "What would you like me to order for you?"

As she was telling him her preference, Lily felt a tap on her shoulder. She turned to see Jake standing behind her, dangling a key at shoulder level.

"Here," he said loudly, dropping it into her hand. "I take it we're done with our meeting."

She covered the mic on her phone. "Yes. Thanks for—" she started to say, but Jake was already striding toward the staircase.

As she watched him leave, she couldn't help but wonder, *Is he just in a hurry to get back to work or is he angry about the prospect of the sale?*

When Lily called to inform her sister-in-law and Ryan about her delay, Leanne said it would be no problem to meet her near the Massachusetts-Connecticut border on Saturday afternoon. "He's welcome to ride all the way back to PA with us though," she suggested. "You could pick him at our place."

"Thanks, but if I'm going to miss almost our entire vacation together, I at least want to ride home with him."

"If it makes you feel any better, today's our second day of rain and we've all got cabin fever. The kids are changing into their swimsuits because I'm chasing everyone outside for a while. I told them they can either get wet swimming or get wet in the rain, but I need a little alone time, so out they go."

After Leanne gave the phone to Ryan, Lily couldn't resist the urge to remind him that if he heard thunder, he should immediately come out of the lake. "Even if you don't see lightning, you still need to go inside."

"I know. 'If thunder roars, go indoors.'" Ryan repeated the phrase he'd learned from the weather forecasters on TV.

"I'm really sorry I'm missing our vacation together," Lily lamented after telling him about her delay.

"It's okay." Ryan sounded equivocal. Or was he just distracted by his cousins?

"Are you sure everything is going all right there?"

"Yup. Everything's awesome." There was a burst of commotion in the background and then Ryan said, "Mom, I gotta go put my suit on now or I'll be the last one in the water."

"Oh, no—you can't let that happen!" Lily smiled to herself. "Have fun. I love you."

"You, too." Ryan didn't like to explicitly tell his mother he loved her in front of other children. "Bye!"

"Bye." Lily said, but she kept the phone to her ear a moment longer, reluctant to end the call.

Ryan apparently hadn't disconnected either, because she heard him yell, "Hey, great news you guys—I get to stay here alone with you until Saturday!"

Lily chuckled as she tapped the red phone icon. She supposed some parents might have felt insulted to hear their child express a sentiment like that, but she was just relieved to know for certain that Ryan wasn't lonely. *I'm lonely enough for both of us—I wouldn't want Ryan to feel this way, too*, she thought.

. . .

Lily spent the rest of the day carting items from her discard and donation piles to the car and delivering them to the recycling center and swap shop. She also posted ads online listing the things she wanted to sell—she figured whatever no one bought here in Hope Haven she'd try to sell in Philly. A few pieces of furniture were too big for her to move on her own, but Lily didn't want to bother Jake by asking him to give her a hand. Besides, she only saw him again once in passing for the rest of the day, so she left the furniture where it was.

Tired, sweaty and grime-streaked, at 5:30 she decided to call it quits so she could take a shower and change her clothes before going to Steve's house. *Oh, no—I left my suitcase in the car*, she suddenly remembered.

The repair shop was in Benjamin's Manor; there wasn't enough time to retrieve it, return to the farm and take a shower. After being late for one meeting with Steve and missing the second meeting altogether, Lily didn't want to call him now and ask if they could push dinner back an hour.

Dahlia's slacks would be way too long for me, but maybe she has a blouse that will fit, she thought, even though the prospect of wearing her aunt's clothing made her uncomfortable. In fact, Lily hadn't even re-entered Dahlia's bedroom since yesterday morning. But now she decided she should acclimate herself to the space, since she'd be staying there overnight anyway.

However, as soon as she opened her aunt's closet and saw her shirts hung neatly in a row, Lily was struck by the realization that Dahlia would never wear them again. Whether it was rational or not, she decided, *It doesn't seem fair for me to wear them, either.*

As she stepped back to shut the door, she glimpsed the steamer trunk that had belonged to her great-great-grandmother on the floor of the closet. Made of pine and bordered with slightly tarnished metal nail strips, the dome-topped trunk was missing one of its leather handles, but otherwise it was in decent shape for being so old.

Even if Dahlia hadn't stored "treasures" inside it, Lily wanted to keep the trunk. As she slid it out of the closet so she'd remember to take it with her to Philly, she noticed it didn't seem as heavy as she'd expected it to be.

Her curiosity piqued, she retrieved the brass barrel key Dahlia had left her and inserted it into the keyhole. It took some jiggling, but after a few attempts she managed to open the lock. Crouching beside the trunk, she unfastened the two latches and raised the lid tentatively, as if she was afraid something might jump out at her. However, what surprised her was that the large trunk was almost empty. It contained two cardboard boxes nested on top of what looked to be a few items of clothing.

She lifted the smaller of the two boxes from the trunk and used her fingernails to pry open the lid, which had been sealed with packing tape. There was a fist-sized ball of newspaper inside. *What kind of "treasure" could this be?* She gingerly peeled back the layers until she reached the object inside: the ring holder her uncle had crafted for Dahlia out of a long screw and a block of wood. Her wedding ring was on it.

Lily gasped and tottered backward onto her bottom, as if she'd literally been bowled over from all the memories the ring evoked.

CHAPTER SEVEN

THEN

AUGUST, PRIOR TO LILY'S JUNIOR YEAR OF HIGH SCHOOL

Shortly after Dahlia and Aiden arrived, Lily's grandmother's health took an unexpected turn for the better. Her appetite improved, her energy increased and her breathing was easier. She even had a little color in her cheeks. Lily attributed this phenomenon to Dahlia, whose presence in their lives made them all a little more radiant—including Martin.

Granted, the changes he underwent were slow and subtle, but the fact that they occurred at all was astonishing to Lily. She noticed he'd started shaving every day instead of twice a week and changing his shirt before supper. Instead of gobbling down his meal and loping off to the cottage, he'd linger over dessert, talking with Dahlia. Even more amazing was the way his eyes sparkled and how frequently he smiled—until then, Lily had never realized what nice straight teeth he had.

It seemed that Dahlia had grown infatuated with Martin, too, but Lily couldn't be sure because Dahlia was so warm to everyone. It was also difficult to know because Lily had never seen any physical affection between the two of them. At school, if people were dating they would be *all* over each other. Not that she wanted to see Dahlia and Martin make out or anything —she shuddered at the thought—and it could have been because they were always around Lily's grandparents, but it also might have meant they weren't interested in each other. Lily dropped a few hints to Dahlia, trying to find out, but Dahlia was extremely discreet when it came to expressing her opinions or feelings about other people.

However, a few months after Dahlia and Aiden had moved in, Lily inadvertently brought Martin and Dahlia together for an evening. She had bad cramps and ended up turning down Dahlia's invitation to go get ice cream. Aiden wasn't home, and Selma and Lars had already drank their tea and gone upstairs to bed. So Dahlia asked Martin if he'd give her a ride to the boardwalk.

"Sure, I'll get my keys," Martin said.

"Great. I've got to change this shirt and I'll meet you here in the living room."

Lily went upstairs to go to bed but then she came back down again to get the hot-water bottle her grandma kept beneath the bathroom sink along with the first-aid kit. She filled the bottle and was tightening the stopper when she heard Dahlia and Martin's voices in the living room.

"How do I look in this dress?" she asked.

"Fine."

Coming from Martin, that was a compliment, but Dahlia sounded disappointed. "Fine? That's all you can say?"

"You look nice." Martin's second compliment was as bland as his first. Hearing it, Lily squeezed her eyes shut and shook her head. She wished she could help him choose the right words, just like she'd helped him choose an appealing color of paint for Dahlia's bedroom.

"Gee, thanks a lot," Dahlia retorted.

"What do you want me to say? You have a mirror. You've heard people's comments about you. You already know how you look."

"I wanted to know how *you* think I look. But I guess now I do. You think I look *fine* and *nice*."

Even as teenage girl who'd never had a real relationship with a boy, Lily understood what Dahlia was really asking was how Martin felt about *her*, not what he thought of her dress or her appearance.

Martin must have caught on because he elaborated in a husky voice, "I think you look beautiful, Dahlia. You'd look beautiful in a burlap sack. You're way too beautiful to be seen in town with an old toad like me."

Lily giggled and then quickly pressed her palm against her mouth, holding her breath until Dahlia answered.

"Thank you." It was obvious from her voice that she was beaming. "You know, we can stay in if you want to, but you're not an old toad, Martin. Toads don't have strong hands and starry eyes like you do."

There was a rustling sound and then all was quiet. Lily gingerly crept out of the bathroom and up the stairs, hoping desperately that her grandparents wouldn't wake up and catch Dahlia and Martin kissing.

"You can come in. I'm awake," Selma rasped. It was mid-August and Dahlia and Aiden had been living with the Lindgrens for almost six months.

Lily hesitantly approached her grandmother, who was semi-reclining in the hospital bed that Dahlia had arranged to have delivered to the house. Selma couldn't sleep on a regular mattress any more; lying flat made it too difficult for her to breathe, even though she received oxygen around the clock now.

Because she could no longer climb up and down the farm-house stairs, Lars and Martin had cleared the table and chairs from the formal dining room and set up the adjustable bed in its place. Then, they'd brought in Lars's recliner from the living room so he could sleep beside his wife.

"Don't be stubborn, Lars. You need a good night's rest," Selma had protested.

"You're right, I do," he'd replied. "And I won't get one unless I'm sleeping next to you."

The hospital bed may have been a necessity, but Lily couldn't get used to seeing it beneath the chandelier, where the table should have been. Nor could she get used to how fragile her formerly robust, broad-shouldered grandmother appeared lying in it, dressed in a flannel nightgown during the late-summer heatwave.

Selma patted the mattress, indicating Lily should sit beside her. "I need to talk to you."

Lily hoped her grandmother didn't want to discuss dying again. She didn't think she could bear it. Perching on the edge of the bed, she kept her voice light. "What's up, Grandma?"

"Martin and Dahlia, that's what." She coughed twice. Short, sickly coughs. "I don't have enough air to dance around the topic, so I'll say it outright. They've grown rather, ah, *fond* of each other."

Relieved, Lily giggled. "Yeah, I noticed."

"Well, I shouldn't be telling you this yet, but..." Selma stopped to catch her breath and Lily could hardly endure the suspense until she continued, "Martin is going to ask Dahlia to marry him."

"He *is*?" Lily yelped. "*Sweet!*"

"Shush. Someone might hear you."

She knew that was unlikely, because Dahlia had gone to the grocery store, and Lars and Martin were in their workshop out back. Who knew where Aiden was, but he wasn't home.

Regardless, Lily lowered her voice to a conspiratorial whisper. "When's he going to propose?"

"As soon as he gets a ring, which is what I need to talk to you about."

"Does he want me to find out Dahlia's ring size for him?"

"He might, if he purchases a new one, but I've been considering giving him my mother's ring to give Dahlia."

"The emerald and diamond one from Sweden? Oh, Grandma, that's a great idea! She'll love it."

Selma held up a finger, signaling she had more to say but she needed a minute before she had enough breath to continue. "The trouble is, I was saving the ring for you."

Lily didn't hesitate. "That's okay. I love your mother's ring but Uncle Martin's your son and he should have first dibs, not me. I'm just your granddaughter."

"Don't you dare call yourself *just* my granddaughter, Lily Amelia Lindgren." Selma's voice was surprisingly strong—it was almost fiery—and there was a spark in her eyes as she added, "You've been as much of a child to me as Martin has been."

"I know, Grandma. I only meant that Uncle Martin's older than I am, so he should be first in line to inherit your mother's ring. Especially since I already have my mom's."

Selma closed her eyes, apparently considering Lily's suggestion. She kept them closed so long that Lily wondered if she'd fallen asleep. Suddenly, she opened them again. "I suppose what you're saying does make sense. I'll give Martin my mother's ring now and you'll receive mine after I die."

Lily pretended her grandmother hadn't mentioned dying. She hopped off the bed and gave her an exuberant embrace, momentarily forgetting how frail Selma was. "This is so exciting! Once you give him the ring, do you think he'll propose right away?"

"I hope so. I'd like to know they're engaged before—"

Lily deliberately butted in so her grandmother couldn't

refer to her impending death again. "I can't wait until he shows Dahlia the ring. She's gonna *love* it."

"If not, Martin can buy her a different one. The important thing is that she loves *him* as much as he loves her—and I'm convinced she does."

It turned out that both Selma and Lily had been right; Dahlia was thrilled that Martin had proposed and she was wild about the ring, too.

"I can't believe I get to wear a family heirloom like this," she'd gushed to Selma and Lily the day after she'd accepted Martin's proposal. "But I'm really worried the stone will come out of its setting or the ring will slide off my finger when I'm gardening or helping in the bogs."

So, Martin constructed a ring holder out of a five-inch screw and a block of wood. He attached it to the wall next to the key rack near the door. If Dahlia went outside to work, she'd slide her ring onto the screw. When she was done working outside for the day, she'd put the ring back on her finger. She was so meticulous about this habit that Martin joked it was like watching her punch out for the day on a time clock.

"Don't let him fool you," Selma warned her, "On a farm, there's no such thing as "punching out" at the end of the day. Your work will never be done, no matter what the clock says. Are you sure that's how you want to spend the rest of your life?"

"Yes, because it means I'll get to spend the rest of my life with Martin."

They set their wedding date for two weeks after Martin proposed. Dahlia said they intended to have a very simple, fifteen-minute ceremony near the cliff in front of the dune shack.

When Selma heard their plans, she objected, "Two weeks hardly gives your family and friends any time to make travel arrangements. And the restaurants and inns are always booked at this time of year, so where will you have your reception?"

Although Dahlia rarely spoke about her family, from the little she did say, Lily concluded that she had one brother, her parents were divorced, and they'd both died a few years ago. It didn't seem that her family was close, nor did she ever mention any good friends, which was surprising, since Dahlia was such a caring person.

Sometimes Lily got the sense that she'd come to the island to get away from people she used to know. She figured when Dahlia and her husband got divorced, their friends probably all took his side and stopped talking to her. Lily didn't have any specific reason to suspect this, except that's what usually happened in the movies; the nicer spouse was left without any friends because the meaner spouse spread so many nasty rumors about them.

"The six of us and Mrs. Henderson are the only people we want to attend the ceremony," Dahlia said. "Afterward, we're going to have a lobster and chowder dinner at the house. Captain Clark's restaurant will deliver it. We want everything to be very low-key."

"I know what you're trying to do," Selma scolded her, shaking a finger. "But you shouldn't rush to get married because you're afraid I'll die before the wedding. And you shouldn't skimp on your reception because you're worried I'm too delicate for a big to-do."

"We're not rushing or skimping because of you, Selma," Dahlia claimed, although Lily sensed her grandmother's suspicion was right. "I've already been married once, so a big wedding isn't important to me—our marriage vows are. I want to take those vows as soon as possible so Martin doesn't have time to change his mind about becoming my husband."

"Ha!" Lily involuntarily sputtered. "As *if*."

The other two laughed at her reaction and Selma conceded that perhaps it was for the best that they kept the occasion informal. "Knowing my son, he'd break out in hives if he had to speak in front of a big crowd. But there must be something I can do to help with your wedding?"

"Actually, there is." Lily appreciated it that Dahlia spoke right up—it showed how genuine her request was. "I'd absolutely love it if you'd make a white chocolate cranberry cheesecake for our wedding dessert. Maybe Lily could help you?"

"Sure! And I can paint the trim and door of the dune shack with the paint left over from when Uncle Martin and I did the bedrooms. I'll take the wedding photos, too." Remembering Dahlia's aversion to being photographed, Lily qualified, "Unless you don't want your picture taken."

"Thanks, Lily. I'd love it if you'd snap a few photos," she gamely agreed. "Just nothing too formal. Nothing posed, okay?"

"Got it."

"What kind of bouquet would you like to carry?" Selma asked.

"I don't want one. The rosa rugosa and wildflowers blooming near the cliff are all the flowers I need. Seriously, I want this to be a very, very low-key event."

Despite Dahlia's wish to keep the ceremony as casual as possible, Lily suggested that she should wait inside the dune shack until everyone had arrived at the edge of the cliff. "Then you can come down the deck stairs and Uncle Martin can take your arm and the two of you can walk over to the minister together."

Surprisingly, Dahlia gave in, but she said she wanted Aiden to escort her down the stairs and walk her to the cliffside, where Martin would be waiting for her.

Even more surprisingly, Aiden agreed to do it. He'd been going through a pleasant phase that summer, which Selma attributed to what she called his blossoming relationship with Olivia. Lily was skeptical of that theory; frankly, she suspected Aiden was high. But she didn't want anything to dampen the festive atmosphere in their household, so she kept the suspicion to herself.

When the day of the wedding arrived, the weather was sunny and warm, without being humid, and the waves provided gentle background music as they lapped the stony shore. Emerging from the dune shack in a long, champagne-colored sundress, Dahlia clearly took Martin's breath away. Yet despite his nervousness, he didn't bungle a single word of his vows. And although Aiden wasn't exactly smiling, he wasn't scowling, either.

The only glitch that occurred was when the wheelchair Dahlia had borrowed for Selma's use got stuck in the sand before the wedding. Halfway between the woods and the dune shack, Lars couldn't push it any farther and they had to abandon it. He and Martin locked their arms together and carried Selma between them the rest of the way to the cliff.

After the ceremony, as the two men lifted her to bring her back to the house, Selma protested, "Dahlia's the one who should be carried over the threshold—I'm not the bride."

"Yes, you are. You're *my* bride of fifty-four years," Lars said and sweetly kissed her cheek.

As far as Lily was concerned, the afternoon couldn't have been any more romantic.

CHAPTER EIGHT

NOW

Did Dahlia stop wearing her wedding ring after Uncle Martin died? Or was she working outside so often lately that she figured she might as well lock it away for safekeeping permanently now? Lily wondered. For the past thirty minutes, she'd been lying flat on the bedroom floor, alternately weeping and smiling at the ceiling as she reminisced about the past.

She especially missed her grandma and granddad, but some of her memories filled her with joy, too. *I never would have remembered some of those details if I hadn't come back here,* she thought. Regardless of why Dahlia had put the ring in the trunk —and regardless of what had come between them—Lily was touched that her aunt had taken special care to make sure Lily knew she still considered the ring a treasure.

Enough thinking about the past. She warned herself, *If I don't get up, I'm going to be late in the future.*

As was placing the cardboard box back into the trunk, Lily recognized the article of clothing on the top of the stack. It was the yellow bathing suit she'd bought during her senior year in high school—it still had the tags on it. *These are all my clothes,* she realized as she rifled through the two piles of blouses, jeans and shorts. *Dahlia must have saved everything I left behind in my dresser drawer.*

Lily hardly considered the clothing to be a "treasure," but since she needed a clean shirt, it was a serendipitous discovery. Although she knew she couldn't button her high school blouses any longer, she figured her Hope Haven High class T-shirt might fit.

She sniffed it and then gave it a shake, holding it up in front of her. It was wrinkled, but it smelled fine. However, when she put it on, it felt ridiculously tight, so she crouched down and pulled the fabric over her bended knees to stretch it out. When she stood up straight again, the shirt bounced back into its original shape, but it wasn't quite as clingy.

There wasn't enough time for her to shower, so she washed her face and tamed her curls as well as she could, then applied a coat of mascara and lipstick. "Good enough," she declared to the bathroom mirror.

Pulling out of the parking lot a minute later, Lily spotted Jake cutting across the front lawn. She waved, but he must not have seen her, because he kept ambling toward the farmhouse. He wasn't wearing his Lindgren baseball cap and a breeze tousled his sun-kissed hair.

As he lifted a brawny arm to push a lock from his eyes, a strange thought popped into Lily's mind. *I wish I were eating dinner with Jake this evening... Maybe I should invite him to join us?* Just as suddenly, she dismissed the idea. Considering that he was probably on edge about all that was happening with the farm, Lily realized dining with him socially might be awkward.

Besides, it wasn't her place to extend an invitation, since Steve was the host, not Lily. *I doubt he'd mind, but then we'd have to share our meals with Jake and I'm way too hungry for that*, she thought, giggling as she coasted down the driveway.

Steve's home was in Highland Hills, which was surprising for two reasons. First, very few locals lived in the remotest town on the island, where most of the houses weren't winterized. Secondly, Lily always assumed Steve would reside in their hometown of Rockfield.

When she expressed her surprise about his location, he replied, "I'd bought a house in Rockfield when I returned from law school and I lived in it for about five years. To be honest, I relocated in Highland Hills because I had to get away from my parents—they were driving me nuts."

Lily grinned at the notion that moving one town over was the same as getting away from his parents, until she realized Steve was serious. "You chose well. This house is gorgeous."

Actually, it was the view that was gorgeous, not his home. The style of the boxy abode was the polar opposite of Steve's office; it was sleek and modern, and made almost entirely of glass and steel. The design didn't especially appeal to Lily, but she loved that the house was located atop of a grassy, rolling sand dune, and it offered an unimpeded view of the waves breaking against the sandbars in the foreground.

"Could we eat on the deck, please?" she requested.

"Sure, but will you be warm enough? It's breezy out there."

"I don't mind. I've missed having the ocean in my back yard. I want to take it in as often as I can while I'm here."

As ravenous as Lily felt, she forced herself to eat slowly, relishing every bite of the tender scallops basted with garlic basil butter. While they dined, Lily told Steve what she'd learned about the farm. "I have to admit, at first I was skeptical about the renovations and about expanding the business beyond farming. I figured the last thing this island needs is another souvenir shop."

Steve chuckled. "Not a fan of imported shells and saltwater taffy, huh?"

"Nope. You probably won't ever catch me in a Lindgren Cranberry Farm T-shirt, either," Lily said. "But aside from that, the gift shop is really quite charming. All the products sold there are locally grown or crafted. They're very high-quality goods. And you should see how informative and engaging the education center is. Plus, there are cooking classes! People are going to love it. During tourist season, I bet there will be a line out the door and down the driveway."

"That's great to hear, but I didn't expect this reaction from you. You're so enthusiastic, you almost sound like you're pitching the farm to *me*."

Lily hadn't realized quite how impressed she'd been with the changes Jake and Dahlia had made until she'd described them to Steve. "Like I said, at first, I was skeptical. But it was easy to see that every enhancement Dahlia and Jake made is very purposeful and innovative—yet they still managed to retain the farm's most important traditions. I really admire what they've accomplished."

"Does that mean you're leaning toward keeping the estate after all?"

"Sadly, no. I'm still leaning toward selling it." She paused and corrected herself. "I'm not just *leaning* toward selling it. It's what I intend to do, once I can convince you I'm making an informed decision."

Lily set down her fork. It was time to level with him. She still didn't want to disclose her complicated history or conflicted feelings about her aunt Dahlia and Hope Haven. But after confirming he wouldn't repeat anything she said, Lily opened up to him about her dire financial situation.

She ended by saying, "The bottom line is, the money from

the sale of the estate would be a lifesaver. I'd be able to repay all my debt, as well as contribute to a fund for Ryan's education, and a retirement fund for me. We'd finally have some financial security again."

"I can see why that would be appealing. But let me play devil's advocate for a moment... If you sold your house and relocated to the farm, you could use that money to pay off a good chunk of the farm's loans."

"No, I couldn't. I took out a steep second mortgage. Meanwhile, the property values in my area nosedived. If I sold my house now, the amount I'd get wouldn't cover what I owe. So then I'd have still have to repay my mortgage, *plus* the farm's loans." She concluded by saying, "Frankly, I've been so worried about money for so many years that the last thing I want to do is take on any more debt. It's not good for my health to feel so pressured all the time and it's not good for my son to have such a stressed-out mother."

After discussing her debt and reviewing the farm's accounts in more detail, Steve finally agreed that selling the estate was in her and Ryan's best interest. "As I mentioned, I can help you find a realtor, but Dahlia requested that it should be offered to Jake Benson, first."

"I already asked him a hypothetical question about that," she admitted sheepishly. "He said he absolutely couldn't afford to buy it."

"I expected as much." Steve took a sip of Chardonnay. After confirming that she'd prefer to sell the estate independently instead of through a realtor, he offered, "I can help you list the property. I've also got a pretty extensive network of colleagues and clients who have the kind of capital it would take to purchase the farm, so if you'd like, I could put feelers out to them."

"Thanks, I'd really appreciate that. There's one thing I have to emphasize, though. Jake has worked on the farm since he was a teenager. My family thought very highly of him and he's poured so much effort and energy into positioning the farm to succeed in the future. So it's very important that we find a buyer who'd guarantee to keep him on as the farm's manager, assuming he wants to continue in that role."

"Sure, you can make that a condition of the sale. I was actually going to suggest that we include him in the sales process, too. He could show potential buyers around the farm, make sure they're a good fit, that kind of thing. Since he's the expert on the business, his perspective will be invaluable."

Lily was relieved. Jake would surely be happy to be involved in the process once he knew his job was protected, and she would have the benefit of his expertise. But with running the cranberry farm itself plus the new business venture of the gift shop and education center, all without Dahlia as his partner, would he have the time? "I'd love that. But I'm hesitant to ask him to take on that responsibility because he's already got so much on his hands as it is."

"Let me talk to him about it then," Steve suggested. "I'm confident he'll want to participate, especially once I assure him we'll work around his schedule."

Pleased that they'd come to an agreement about her plan to sell the estate, Lily lingered on the deck with Steve, chatting for another hour. By then, the sun had set behind them and the breeze had picked up, causing Lily to shiver. Steve offered her a sweater, but she said she probably should return to the farm for the evening.

"Thanks so much for dinner—it was delicious. I'm sorry I couldn't make it to your office this morning, but I think this worked out even better."

"Yeah, when you didn't show up today, it was like a flash-back to high school," Steve said with a laugh, but Lily didn't get the joke.

"What do you mean?"

"You know, it was like when you canceled on me for the senior dance."

Leanne was right, he does *remember,* Lily realized. "I'm sorry I changed our plans to go to the dance together, but I had to catch a flight to Sweden right after final exams."

"Yeah, I was only kidding. I didn't take it personally—even though some of our classmates said you only left the island so you wouldn't have to go to the dance with me."

Even though he was laughing it off now, Lily got the feeling that as a teenager, Steve had been deeply hurt by their peers' teasing. She felt compelled to say, "That's absurd. I didn't leave the island to get out of going to the dance with you, Steve... To be honest, I left the island because I was grief-struck after my granddad passed away. I needed to be somewhere else for a while. To be some*one* else for a while."

"I think I know what you mean. After all, I moved clear across Hope Haven when I needed to be somewhere else for a while." Steve gave a self-effacing chortle and she smiled, too. "I wish you were here under different circumstances, Lily, but I'm glad you came back."

Although she couldn't honestly agree that she was glad she came back, she could earnestly reply, "Seeing you again has been a highlight of my trip, Steve."

Driving back to the farm, Lily reflected on their conversation about the senior dance. *I'm not the only teenager who was affected by rumors and teasing when I lived in Hope Haven,* she thought. It made her feel even more confident that she'd done the right thing by telling Steve she wanted to sell the farm. *I*

wouldn't ever want Ryan to be the object of that kind of kind of
small-town gossip.

As she coasted up the driveway, Lily was struck by how empty the dark house and cottage appeared. She pulled into the parking area, but instead of getting out of the car, she sat inside it for nearly fifteen minutes.

"You're being silly," she scolded herself.

It didn't matter; she still didn't want to stay alone in her childhood home, especially not in Dahlia's room. She shifted into reverse and drove next door to the conservation land parking lot.

Lily opened the windows a crack and reclined her seat. Vaguely aware that this wasn't the first time she'd refused to go into the farmhouse after the death of a family member, she closed her eyes and tried to sleep.

CHAPTER NINE

THEN

AUTUMN, LILY'S JUNIOR YEAR OF HIGH SCHOOL

Because Martin and Dahlia had been so secretive about their relationship, no one outside their family except their old friend Mrs. Henderson knew they'd gotten married until after the wedding. So, a week later, on her first day of classes as a high school junior, Lily was inundated with questions and opinions about the couple.

"My dad wants to know how a mangy old dog like your uncle ever landed a babe like Dahlia Ford," a boy in Lily's homeroom class remarked before she'd even sat down.

Another student claimed he'd heard that Lily's grandmother promised to leave Dahlia a parcel of waterfront property if Dahlia married her son. Others speculated that Dahlia was pregnant with someone else's baby who didn't want children, so Martin agreed to provide for the child financially if Dahlia became his wife.

The rumors were so ludicrous they might have been laughable if they weren't based on the two hurtful beliefs: Martin could never "get" a woman like Dahlia, and Dahlia was somehow using Martin or the Lindgren family. Lily knew nothing could be further from the truth and she dismissed the substance of the gossip out of hand. But it was still upsetting to hear her classmates make disparaging comments about her uncle and new aunt.

In response to their comments, she'd say things like, "That just shows how much you know about true love." Or, "It's too bad your life is so boring you have to make up ridiculous stories about other people's relationships." Sometimes, she'd suggest that the gossipers were jealous. Other times, she'd just mutter, "Oh, shut it," beneath her breath. Nothing she said ever seemed to make a difference; certain classmates kept fabricating wild stories and making mean cracks about Dahlia and Martin for weeks.

Although Lily and Aiden never discussed their peers' remarks with each other—or anything much at all, for that matter—she assumed he'd heard the comments and was as upset by them as she was. Lily wouldn't have dreamed of telling anyone else in their family what some of the kids at school were saying because she didn't want to hurt anyone's feelings. So she was appalled one evening when Aiden repeated the gossip, like a second-hand insult, to his mother.

It was late September and Dahlia and Lily were clearing the supper dishes. Aiden came into the kitchen and began badgering his mom to give him money to go to a concert in Boston with Olivia.

"No way," Dahlia refused. "You don't have your license yet and Oliva's only had hers for three months."

"So?" Aiden had a way of sounding condescending with just a single syllable.

"*So* it's illegal for her to drive with an underage passenger in the car, unless there's an adult in the car, too. I don't want either of you to get hurt or in trouble," Dahlia explained, even though the answer should have been obvious. "Furthermore, it's a school night and I don't have an extra two hundred dollars to shell out for a ticket."

"Why don't you dig for it in your husband's pockets then?" sneered Aiden.

Dahlia froze mid-stride. "Ex*cuse* me?"

"Everyone at school says you just married Martin because you're a gold digger."

Lily was mortified, but Dahlia snorted with laughter. She laughed so hard she had to set the stack of plates she was holding down on the table again so she could clutch her sides.

"Tell your classmates there are easier ways to dig for gold than becoming a cranberry farmer's wife." She wiped the corner of her eye with a dish towel. "And warn Olivia that she needs to brush up on Massachusetts driving laws before she loses her license."

Dahlia may have been amused by the hearsay that she was just interested in Martin for his money, but Lily still wished her peers would lose interest in the topic of her aunt and uncle's marriage.

Unfortunately, she got what she wished for about a week later. Apparently, Aiden had done something to upset Olivia and she'd threatened to break up with him. So, as a grand gesture of contrition, he'd spray painted the words I'M SORRY OLIVIA in huge red letters on the grinding stones in the conservation land. One word per rock.

Most of the people in Rockfield were understandably angry about his blatant disregard for their town's legacy. Defacing a historic landmark was a misdemeanor that could have been punishable by fine and imprisonment. But because Aiden was a minor, he was only required to pay for the cost of cleaning the rocks. Even then, he never contributed a dime toward the expense; Martin and Dahlia paid the fee on his behalf since he didn't have any money of his own.

For the rest of the month, Aiden's graffiti was the most talked-about topic among their classmates. Some of the boys were impressed by his nerve and a few of the girls thought it was romantic. But the majority decided that Aiden was either senseless or shameless. Or both.

Lily felt utterly humiliated. By spray painting the majestic grinding stones, Aiden had also left a smudge on her family's good standing in the community. Lily's granddad and uncle received as much flak from their peers as Lily had received from hers. She'd even overheard Martin telling Dahlia that someone had called for his resignation from the town's environmental committee.

Hearing the embarrassment in her uncle's voice made Lily so angry at Aiden for disgracing her family that she could hardly glance in his direction.

But when her anger simmered down, she felt kind of sorry for him. As a newcomer to the island, he probably hadn't under-stood the significance of the landmark. Or he hadn't known that the residents prided themselves on keeping their parks and beaches in pristine condition. Lily supposed it must have been difficult for him to adjust to life in a small town and she felt bad that Aiden had made such a public spectacle of himself.

However, her empathy was wasted because he couldn't have cared less that people were gossiping about him. Nor did he show any remorse for what he'd done or for how it had affected his family and the community. The only thing he seemed to care about was that Olivia had accepted his apology.

. . .

By the time the chatter about Aiden's stunt finally died down, harvest season was nearly over. Heavy rain was forecast for the final week of berry picking, so the Lindgrens and their staff were racing to gather the last of the fruit. Unfortunately, one of the farm hands, a recent high-school grad, called in sick, so the crew was short-staffed. Dahlia couldn't lend a hand in the bogs because Selma was so weak that she didn't want to leave her alone in the house.

Of course, Aiden was of no help; he claimed he needed to meet with his calculus tutor after school all week, but Lily knew that he and Olivia were partying with some off-island kids in Hyannis. She pleaded with her granddad and uncle to allow her to take the worker's place during the day as well as what she did in the afternoons after school, but they wouldn't let her cut any classes.

So, when the bus dropped her off that afternoon, she hurried up the long driveway to change her clothes before she joined the others picking berries. As she walked, she scanned the bogs for her granddad's trademark red-and-black plaid flannel shirt, but she didn't see it. Lily came to a standstill. Shading her eyes, she squinted toward the barn and the workshop. Then she surveyed the bogs again. She saw several crew members, but her granddad wasn't out there, and she couldn't spot her uncle, either.

Deep down, Lily knew there was only one reason Martin and Lars wouldn't be working in the bog during the final week of harvesting. She numbly marched up the driveway, but instead of going inside the house, she dropped her bookbag near the split-rail fence that bordered the front lawn. Gaining momentum, she jogged past the cranberry bogs. When someone called her name, she broke into a hard run, tore through the stretch of woods, across the heathland and up the rickety deck stairs. Her breathing ragged and her vision fuzzy, she leaned against the shack wall and sobbed until her legs gave out and she collapsed in a heap.

Sometime later, when she felt a hand on her shoulder, Lily knew whose it was without looking up. "I wanted to stay home, but Granddad and Uncle Martin wouldn't let me. They made me go to school," she bawled, her words barely intelligible. "If I had been home, I could have..."

She was blubbering too hard to complete the thought, but Dahlia understood. She sat down and enveloped Lily in her arms. "There was nothing you could have done, sweetheart. It was your grandma's time to... It was her time to go."

"But I didn't get to say goodbye," Lily howled. "She left without even saying goodbye."

"I know it hurts, I know," Dahlia murmured, rocking back and forth for a long time before she spoke again. "Your grandma passed away in her sleep, Lily. You were at school, your granddad and uncle were in the bog, and I was fixing a snack for the crew. I think Selma felt content that everyone was right where they should be. I think she understood she had somewhere she needed to be, too, and she was ready to leave because she knew we'd look after each other."

Lily nodded, sniffling, but she didn't say anything. A few minutes passed before Dahlia asked if she wanted to go to the farmhouse. "Your granddad and uncle are worried about you."

She panicked at the thought. "I can't. Not yet. I can't."

"Okay. We won't go back until you're ready."

The two of them sat there, leaning against the rough wooden wall of the shack without speaking for an hour or more, while the tide gradually pulled away from the cliff and the sun dropped closer to the horizon.

Everything is leaving, Lily thought, as more tears rolled down her cheeks.

Even after the sun set, the temperature fell, and Martin came to out to get them, Lily couldn't bear to return to the house. She buried her head in her arms against her knees, while Dahlia took her husband by the hand and led him to the stairs.

"How are you and Lars doing, love?" Lily heard her ask in a hushed tone.

"I'm okay, but I've never seen Dad like this. Mrs. Henderson dropped by—she's with him now, but I'd better get back there soon."

"Yes, you're right. You should go be with him. Lily and I might stay out here for a while, so don't worry about us if it gets late. She can't face going into the house without Selma there."

Hearing Dahlia express exactly how Lily was feeling almost made her burst into tears again. But her eyelids were nearly swollen shut and she suddenly felt too exhausted to cry. When her aunt sat down again, Lily yawned and rested her head against Dahlia's shoulder.

She had almost drifted to sleep when Martin returned with a heavy wool blanket, which he unfolded and spread over Lily and Dahlia's outstretched legs. Before leaving, he squatted down to kiss his wife. Then he turned to his niece and cupped her cheek.

"Lily." That was all he uttered, but it was enough. Lily understood he meant to express that he was sorry she was hurting and that he was hurting, too.

Nuzzling her cheek against his big bearish paw of a hand, she whispered, "I know, Uncle Martin. I feel the same way."

Lily woke at sunrise, her neck stiff and her bottom sore from sitting on the hard deck all night. For a moment, she couldn't make sense of what she was doing at the shack. When she remembered, she nudged her aunt.

"Dahlia. Hey, Dahlia, I want to go inside to see Granddad now."

"Good, because my bladder's about to burst," Dahlia mumbled in a groggy voice, which made her niece giggle. It only lasted a moment, but it gave Lily a ray of hope that maybe she wouldn't feel like crying forever.

PART TWO

CHAPTER TEN

NOW

THURSDAY

Lily woke to the sound of a mourning dove's soft, sorrowful call. *Coo-oo, coo, coo, coo. Coo-oo, coo, coo, coo.* Reclining in the driver's seat, she rubbed her neck and gazed out the window at the bright blue sky; it was going to be a gorgeous day.

Maybe this afternoon I'll take a walk to see if Mrs. Henderson is here for the summer yet, she thought. Her grandmother's dearest friend had moved to Florida shortly after Lily left Dune Island. But Dahlia had said that every summer the elderly widow returned to her Rockfield home with her daughter's family.

Lily's overnight recollections about her grandmother were so vivid and poignant that she anticipated visiting Mrs. Henderson would feel a little bit like chatting with Selma herself. Besides, a visit to the elderly woman was long overdue; Lily was ashamed that she'd never kept in touch with their family friend, who'd been such a kind presence in her life during her youth.

I should bring her a bag of chocolate-covered cranberries, she thought, recalling how Mrs. Henderson had delivered treats and meals to the Lindgren house for over a year after Selma died.

Lily put her seat in an upright position and got out of the car to stretch. The combination of lifting heavy boxes and sleeping in the vehicle had wreaked havoc on her upper back and shoulder muscles.

Coffee is the cure for what ails me, she decided, and drove to a nearby convenience store. The cup she purchased there was a surprisingly tasty alternative to expensive gourmet coffee and she bought a fruit cup to go with it. Then she brought her purchases to Lookout Ledge.

The warmth of the sun and the sight of the shimmering water heightened her enjoyment of the simple breakfast. To her delight, just as she'd finished eating, Ryan called to tell her about the snake the children had found under the woodstove in the cabin. His youthful exuberance made her feel exuberant, too. Before disconnecting, he even whispered, "Love you, Mom. Bye."

Half an hour later as she was heading up the walkway to the farmhouse, Jake was coming down it, with a toolbox in hand.

"Good morning, Jake. Looks like it's going to be a beautiful day, doesn't it?"

"Hey, Lily." He gave her an obvious once-over and appeared to wrinkle his nose.

Realizing she hadn't showered yet and she was still wearing her 3H class T-shirt, Lily took a step back and crossed her arms over her chest. "Did something in the house need to be repaired?"

"Something in the house *always* needs to be repaired," he groused, but didn't elaborate.

"That's how my granddad felt, too," she empathized. "My grandma and I used to get frustrated about it, but he seemed to love keeping busy with DIY."

"Hmpf." Jake made an ambiguous noise and shifted his toolbox to his other hand.

Obviously, he was eager to continue down the walkway, so Lily quickly said, "So, listen, I spoke to Steve last night and I can tell you about our conversation when you have a few minutes to spare."

"I don't know when that will be," Jake barked. "I've got a to-do list a mile long—and my sister is still as sick as a dog, so Conner's going to be shadowing me all day again."

Although she didn't appreciate Jake's tone, Lily recognized how stressed he was, so she treaded lightly. "Sounds like you're really busy. Is there something I can do to help?"

He shook his head. "It would take twice as long to explain what needs to be done as it would take to do it myself."

"Okay, but if you change your mind, just holler."

"Right."

Shaking off residual feelings of guilt about Jake, for the rest of the morning Lily finished loading the remaining items she wanted to get rid of into the car. She also went into Dahlia's room to collect her clothes to donate to the thrift shop. But she couldn't do it. Her aunt wouldn't have minded if someone acquired her old clothes, but it bothered Lily to imagine anyone except Dahlia wearing them.

Other than her wardrobe, books and a few framed photos, Dahlia had very few personal possessions, which made Lily feel sad, initially, the same way she'd felt when she'd realized her aunt was living in a single, small room. But as she gathered her aunt's sparse belongings, Lily recalled one of the only responsibilities Dahlia had ever grumbled about doing was dusting Selma's knickknacks. Her aunt had confided she found the accumulation of material possessions to be burdensome and she said if the shack overlooking the ocean had running water, she'd be perfectly content to live in it. So, Lily imagined that downsizing the cottage and house must have felt liberating to Dahlia.

It's probably part of the reason why she was so particular about only selling useful or beautiful crafts in the gift store, too, she realized.

As she boxed up the books in Dahlia's bookshelf, she spied a copy of *Cape Cod*, by Henry David Thoreau. Lily plunked down on the bed and read through a few pages. She had given this book to Dahlia the first Christmas she'd lived with the Lindgren family. Her aunt had been tickled to receive it and judging from its dog-eared pages, she'd read it several times. *I'm keeping this*, Lily thought and set it aside.

Finally, she turned her attention to the framed photos on top of the dresser. They included a picture of Dahlia and Martin on their wedding day, a school photo of Aiden when he was about nine or ten; and, for some reason, a photo of what looked like Martin as a newborn.

Picking it up, Lily realized it wasn't her uncle—it was Ryan. There was definitely a family resemblance to Martin. Her eyes smarted when she remembered that she'd sent the photo to Dahlia shortly after Martin passed away. Moved that her aunt had kept it on display all these years, Lily put it atop of the book by Thoreau. Then she added her aunt and uncle's wedding photo to her "keep" pile, too.

"What should I do with this?" she mumbled as she picked up the photo of Aiden as a boy. She supposed she could send it to him, but she still didn't know where he lived. "Besides, if he didn't care enough to show up to his mother's funeral, I doubt he'll place any sentimental value on an old photo."

"Who are you talking to?" Conner asked from the hallway, startling her. Lily was going to tell him it wasn't polite to spy on people—she would have told her son the same thing—but the boy looked like he'd been crying.

"I was talking to myself. I do that sometimes when I'm

trying to decide something. What are you doing inside? It's such a beautiful day, I thought you'd be helping your uncle clean the sprinkler heads."

"Nah. He told me I had to go entertain myself for a while."

Sounds like Jake's still stressed out, Lily thought. She didn't know whether she felt sorrier for him or for Conner.

"Well, it's not very entertaining, but I'd love your help bringing these boxes of books down to the car so I can take them to the swap shop. They aren't too heavy."

"Can I go with you?"

"Sure, if your uncle says it's okay. I also need to swing by the garage to pick up my luggage, so we'll be driving around for a while. Are you okay with that?" Lily asked, since she knew how much Ryan hated being in the car for more than five minutes.

"Definitely. I'd ride for two hours to go to the swap shop—they have all kinds of cool stuff there," Conner said, a smile returning to his lips. "And the best part is, it's all *free!*"

At the swap shop, Conner picked up a slightly distressed bodyboard, which, as he pointed out, was "perfectly good, just a little faded." He also acquired a soccer ball and promptly challenged Lily to a match when they got back to the farmhouse. So, they set up four empty boxes as makeshift goal posts on the front lawn and after twenty minutes of playing, the score was tied.

"I've got some things I need to do now," Lily announced, resting her foot on the ball. "So whoever scores the next goal wins."

Quick as a flash, Conner stole the ball from her and dribbled it across the lawn. He was within three yards of her goal posts when she stole it back from him. Since his goal was wide open, she swung her leg back and kicked the ball as hard as she could, hoping to score an easy goal. But the ball bounced off the trunk of the maple tree, hit the house and then rolled past the flower bed and into Conner's goal.

"No way!" he shouted.

Lily was doing a victory dance when she noticed Jake had just stepped out of the farmhouse, with a bucket in his hand. "Did you see me score that goal?"

"Yeah. You could have broken the window."

Lily thought he was joking until she noticed his scowl. His foul mood was becoming tiresome. *I know he's stressed out, but I thought he'd be happy that I took Conner off his hands for a couple of hours*, she thought.

"Conner, come and get this bucket and take it to the workshop for me. I'll be there in a couple of minutes, I need to talk to Lily," Jake told his nephew.

As the boy trudged off, Lily called, "Good game, Conner!" Then she asked Jake, "What's up?"

"I've got a few minutes to hear what you and Steve discussed last night."

"You want to discuss that *here* on the front lawn?"

Jake shrugged. "Sophie's inside, so she can't hear us and I don't want to leave Conner on his own in the workshop for very long."

"All right. Well, since you're in a hurry, I guess I'll dive right in... I've definitely decided to sell the estate—"

Jake interrupted her, muttering, "Big surprise."

"Excuse me?"

"It was clear from the moment you got here that you were going to sell the farm." Jake removed his cap and pushed a damp lock of hair out of his eyes to glare at her. "I kept hoping that maybe, just maybe after you saw all the improvements Dahlia and I made, you'd reconsider. And I have to admit, you were so flattering about the changes that for thirty seconds, it almost *seemed* like you might reconsider. But clearly, that was all part of your act."

Lily's cheeks burned with embarrassment and she could barely look Jake in the eye. Even though she didn't appreciate his tone, she couldn't deny that he was right about her desire to sell the estate. "It's true that I knew from the start I couldn't keep the farm," she admitted. "But as I told you, Steve insisted I take a tour and talk to you about the business, first. He also advised me not to disclose what my intentions were until my decision was final. I'm sorry if you feel deceived, but—"

Jake cut her off. "Deceived? I don't feel deceived. I felt *ticked off* that you wasted my time. You may not have noticed, but while you've been bopping around here like a teenage kid and flirting with your high-school boyfriend, I've been working my tail off to prepare for the opening of *your* family's gift shop and education center. So, yeah, I resent it that I had to spend two hours of my *own* time the other evening putting together a financial report. And I resent it that I had to cut into my work schedule to give you a tour and to discuss something with you that you had absolutely no interest in hearing about!"

Jake had made so many wrong assumptions that Lily hardly knew which one to address first. She tried not to let her annoyance show as she began, "Listen, just because it's not possible for me to keep the farm doesn't mean I wasn't interested in taking a tour and learning about the expanded business operations and finances. And by the way, I wasn't flattering you or putting on an act—I'm genuinely impressed by the changes you've made to the farm and your vision for the future."

"Pah." Jake made a derisive noise, but Lily ignored it and kept speaking.

"Furthermore, Steve is *not* my old boyfriend and I haven't been *bopping around*. What I have been doing is meeting with my attorney, plus happily entertaining your nephew for several hours, because as you've repeatedly expressed, you have a million other things to do." She let out a big puff of air before adding, "I was *trying* to be helpful."

"You're about ten years too late for that," he muttered.

Lily couldn't believe she'd heard him right. "What did you just say?"

Instead of repeating himself, Jake answered, "Here's an idea. How about if you or Steve email me whatever it is you need me to know about the future of the farm. That way, I can read it at *my* convenience. Meanwhile, unless or until I hear from one of you, I'll assume it's business as usual—which means I've got work to do."

Then, he shoved his cap back onto his head and stalked away before Lily could utter a word.

CHAPTER ELEVEN

NOW

Once her shock wore off, Lily was fuming. If her phone hadn't buzzed just then, she would have charged after Jake and told him just how immature, unreasonable and hotheaded he was being. But she recognized the Philadelphia area code on the display screen, so she answered the call—and she was glad she did because it was a recruiter from a large media and technology company.

He requested to set up a video interview with her the following Tuesday for a project expected to last at least a year and a half. Usually, Lily had to find a new consultancy position every six months. It would be a relief to have job security—especially if the farm didn't sell right away.

By the time the call ended, she felt calmer, but she still felt it would be best if she didn't come anywhere within shouting distance of Jake for a while. Maybe even for the rest of her time in Hope Haven.

If the tide's low enough, I'll take a walk along the shoreline to visit Mrs. Henderson, she thought.

The ocean lay about a half a mile behind the Lindgrens'

farmhouse. To reach their cliffside property, Lily had to cut past the bogs, across the back yard, through a thick stand of stubby trees they referred to as "the woods," and over a wide stretch of heathland.

There once was a tottery wooden staircase leading down the fifty-foot cliff to the water's edge. Dahlia had mentioned on one of their rare phone calls that the staircase had been washed away in a Nor'easter, so Lily wasn't expecting to see it now. However, as she peeked over the ledge, she was alarmed by how much of the upper face of the cliff had been eroded. The land used to slope gradually toward the ocean. But now there was a steep, twenty-foot drop-off separating the clifftop from the natural rocks and boulders at the bottom.

Lily glanced to her right: erosion had also eaten away the upper portion of the cliff bordering the conservation land. However, the base of the neighboring precipice was reinforced with a rock revetment, which supported a heavy-duty steel staircase, designed for the public's use. Lily had intended to cut through the conservation land, and then go down those stairs. From there, she'd stroll along the shoreline to Mrs. Henderson's house.

However, the waves were breaking high on shore and Lily couldn't tell if the quickly changing tide was going out or coming in. She didn't want to walk halfway to Mrs. Henderson's house and then suddenly find herself trapped among the rocks without access to a staircase. She ambled over to her family's cliffside shack instead.

Lily's great-granddad had built the little structure in the 1950s for his wife. Elevated on stilts, the wooden hut provided shelter from the sun and rain, as well as an excellent location for gazing at the seascape. Although the perch had been repaired and reinforced countless times, it had become rather ramshackle by the time Lily left the island. So, she was glad it didn't appear any worse for the wear since she'd last seen it and she scrambled up its staircase to the deck.

"Oh!" She half-laughed, half-moaned at her first glimpse of the glorious seascape from the familiar viewpoint. Throwing her arms wide, as if to embrace it, she tilted her face toward the sun, closed her eyes and breathed in until she thought her lungs would burst.

When she cried, it wasn't necessarily from joy. It wasn't from sadness, either. It was more like her salty tears were her body's way of expressing the depth of her connection to the ocean. Her connection to this view. It was a part of her and now she realized it always had been, even after she'd left it.

Lily must have stood there for fifteen minutes, watching the swells wrinkle the vast, green-blue sweep of water. *I could stay here all day and all night and it would never get old*, she thought.

Out of the blue, it occurred to her that she really *could* stay there all night—she could sleep in the shack on a lounge chair. *It can't be any more uncomfortable than sleeping in the car. And I'd rather sleep out here than in Dahlia's room anyway.*

First, she'd have to remove the boards from the shack door and windows. Considering how much Dahlia loved sitting on the deck, Lily thought it was unusual that she hadn't removed them yet. But then she figured her aunt must have been too busy preparing for the grand opening of the farm's shop and education center to come to the shack that spring.

I can remove the boards in no time, she thought, hopping down the stairs. *And I can put them up just as quickly before I leave.*

When she got back to the yard, Lily spied Jake's truck in the parking area. *Uh-oh, I hope he's not still in the workshop with Conner*, she fretted, since she wasn't ready to speak to him right now. Fortunately, he wasn't there, but she collected the tools and supplies she needed as quickly as possible, in case he returned. She thought she was home free, but when she stepped outside, she nearly collided with him.

"Hey, what are you doing with that stuff?" he asked. Even though it wasn't really his business, Lily told him anyway.

"I'm borrowing them to take the boards off the shack door and window. Don't worry, I'll return them and I'll board the shack up again before I leave. I just need to get some air flowing through it, otherwise I'll be too hot to sleep tonight."

"You're going to *sleep* out there? You can't do that!"

"Yes, I can. Because as you made a point of reminding me, this is *my* family's farm," Lily retorted. Immature or not, she took smug satisfaction in hurrying away and leaving *him* speechless.

As a teenager, Lily had developed a routine for taking down the boards, stacking them, putting up the screens and cleaning the interior of the shack. She could get the entire job done in under an hour. It may have taken her a little longer than that this evening, but not much.

As she wiped off the lounge chair that she'd pulled down from the open storage loft, she told herself, *A couple of pillows and a summer quilt and I'll be perfectly comfortable out here.*

She returned to the farmhouse and was happy to see Jake's truck was gone. More tired than hungry, Lily skipped dinner in favor of taking a shower and brushing her teeth. While she was at the cottage, she also called Ryan because she wasn't sure that she could get a cell phone signal out by the cliff. She was going to tell him about going to the swap shop with Conner but she felt oddly disloyal because she'd been spending her son's vacation time with Jake's nephew. More accurately, what she felt was a bit resentful that Jake didn't appreciate it.

After describing how he'd spent his day, Ryan abruptly said, "I've got to go, Mom. We're getting ready to roast marshmallows now." There was some garbled background conversation and then he added, "Aunt Leanne says don't worry, she won't let me burn my fingers or eat too many marshmallows and get a stomachache."

Lily chuckled to show she wasn't offended by her sister-in-law's teasing, even though it was getting kind of old. "Have fun, sweetheart," she said.

"Okay. Bye." Lily thought he'd hung up but then Ryan whispered, "I miss you. But it's almost Saturday."

Hearing him say that was almost enough to make Lily jump in Dahlia's car and zoom straight to the ferry dock. The only thing that stopped her was knowing that if she went to Maine now, she'd have to bring Ryan with her to Dune Island to switch vehicles on Saturday. So, she went into Dahlia's room and collected a spare pillow and fresh linens from the top shelf of her closet.

When she spied the steamer trunk pushed against the wall where she'd left it, she remembered that she still hadn't opened the second cardboard box that Dahlia had included among her "treasures." Lily set the bedding down and unlocked the trunk. This box was slightly larger and heavier than the box that contained Dahlia's ring and ring holder, and its contents were wrapped in a blue vinyl pouch and cushioned in packing material.

Is it Grandma's antique butter dish? Or something Granddad carved? she wondered, unzipping the little bag.

A moment later, Lily recognized that it was the digital camera Dahlia had given her for her eighteenth birthday. Her aunt had included a small, inscribed card with the gift. Lily had saved the card, tying it to the camera strap with a short piece of twine. Seeing her aunt's elegant cursive sparked bittersweet memories and Lily promptly stowed the camera in the trunk again.

She left the cottage in a daze, hardly aware that she'd

walked across the back yard, through the woods, and up the stairs of the shack. She stood on the deck a long time, reminiscing about all the dreams she used to have and all the other evenings like this one, when she and her aunt used to watch the sun imbue the water with lavender and the sky with brilliant bands of orange and pink.

CHAPTER TWELVE

THEN

*LATE SUMMER, BEFORE LILY'S SENIOR YEAR OF HIGH
SCHOOL*

The uppermost curve of the orange sun had barely dipped
below the flat purple line of the horizon when Dahlia slapped
her hands against her thighs and jumped up from her deck
chair.

"Aw, don't get up already," Lily protested. The "blue hour"
—the hour following sunset—was Lily's second-favorite time of
day and she didn't want to return to the farmhouse quite yet.

"I'm not leaving. I need to get something from inside."
Dahlia darted into the shack and out again, the screen door
banging behind her. She was holding a square box wrapped
simply in brown paper and encircled with a length of twine. A
tight bow looped around a sprig of wild roses and a small
rectangular card dangled from the knot. She extended the gift to
Lily, who tipped her head to the side, puzzled.

"What's this for? My birthday isn't until spring."

"It's your graduation present."

"But I haven't even started my senior year yet." Tomorrow was the first day of classes, which was another reason Lily wanted to linger on the deck. Once school began, she'd have to do homework in the evenings.

"When you see what it is you'll understand why I have to give it to you now." Dahlia pushed the box into her hands. "Go on. Open it."

Lily tugged at the end of the string and the bow came undone. She carefully tucked the roses behind her ear before reading the card aloud. *"It's not what you look at that matters, it's what you see—*Henry David Thoreau." On the other side of the card, her aunt had written, "Happy Graduation, Lily! With much love, from D."

"Just rip it," she impatiently urged her niece as she struggled to unwrap the gift without tearing the paper. So Lily hastily tore it open. The photo on the side of the box indicated it contained the exact digital single-lens reflex camera that she'd been saving to buy.

"Is this for real?" she marveled.

"Of course it's for real, silly." Dahlia grinned, but Lily bit her lip and shook her head.

"How can you and Uncle Martin afford to give me something this expensive?" Money was always tight on the farm and last year they'd suffered an especially big setback when two major Boston markets decided not to sell Lindgren cranberries in their stores any longer.

"It's not from your uncle, it's just from me. And don't worry about how I can afford it—I have my ways." Dahlia looked very pleased with herself. "I know how adept you've become at using your granddad's old 35-millimeter camera. But now that you have this, you can enroll in the digital photography class at the community center."

Lily's face broke into a grin but almost immediately her

features fell when she recalled that the first session of the workshop started in September and ran through early December. She had been helping her family harvest cranberries after school and on weekends during the fall for as long as she could remember. Lily was proud of her skills and stamina, and she couldn't imagine not spending Saturdays in the bogs. The work was tedious and demanding, but it was also one of the most satisfying experiences she'd ever had.

Not to mention, her family needed her help now more than ever. In the year following her grandmother's death, Lily's granddad had slowed down considerably. Martin was already trying to compensate for Lars's fatigue—he couldn't be expected to compensate for Lily's absence, too. Nor could they afford to hire more workers than the handful they already employed.

"Thanks, but the first half of the course lasts until December and I don't want to miss harvest," she said.

"You won't miss it. You can still help after school during the week and as soon as you get home from the class on Saturdays."

"But it wouldn't be fair to stick you and Uncle Martin with the extra work while I'm gone."

"Aiden will help pick up the slack."

Not going to happen, Lily thought.

Aiden put more effort into avoiding working on the farm than he spent doing any actual work, much to Martin's consternation. Lily's uncle had strong expectations about everyone pulling their own weight on the farm. It was their family's livelihood, after all. But Aiden acted as if the work was beneath him. Only last week Lily had overheard him muttering to himself, "Just because my mother married an island hick doesn't make me a farmer's son. *My* father owns a talent agency."

Lily knew that Aiden's attitude and refusal to participate on the farm—or in any household chores, for that matter—was creating tension between Dahlia and Martin. So she was careful not to say anything about Aiden that might add to Dahlia's stress.

She traced a finger over the lettering on the top of the box. "I love the camera and maybe I can sign up for the second session of the class in the spring. But I don't need to enroll in the first session. Because even if you and Aiden and Granddad don't mind covering for me, Uncle Martin will never allow—"

"I've already spoken to him, and he agreed you should take the class."

"He did? How did you ever convince him to let me do that?"

"As I said, I have my ways." Dahlia's lips twitched with a saucy smirk. "Consider it a done deal."

Lily jumped up and threw an arm around her aunt's back, hugging the box to her chest with her other arm. "Thank you, Aunt Dahlia. Thank you so much."

Because Lily had been calling Dahlia by her first name long before Dahlia married Lily's uncle, she rarely addressed her with the title, 'aunt'—except on occasions like this, when she was so happy she couldn't contain herself.

"Kyle says that using Granddad's camera put me at an advantage, not a disadvantage. He says that when people use a digital camera all the time, they can get lazy and let the cameras do almost all the work for them," Lily told Katie and Dahlia.

It was the second Saturday in October of their senior year. Because it had rained all morning, Lily and her aunt weren't harvesting this afternoon because picking the berries while they were wet made them susceptible to becoming moldy faster. Since the Lindgrens' produce was sold to the fresh fruit market, instead of to a processing company, they had to be especially careful to maintain its quality.

Although the sun was beginning to peek through the clouds,

the air was still damp and Katie complained that it was too cold to sit outside. But Aiden and Martin had been bickering and Dahlia said she needed to hang out in a "testosterone-free" zone for a while. Since she had agreed to pluck Katie's eyebrows for her—Katie was too squeamish to do it herself—the two girls had no choice but to accompany Dahlia to the beach shack.

Short and heavy-set, Lily's best friend had never really given much attention to her appearance until now. She hadn't cared about hair styles or fashion trends, but she was determined to make herself over during her senior year. She'd proudly announced that she'd lost twelve pounds during the summer and next week she was going to get her frizzy brown hair professionally straightened. Lily would secretly miss her curls, but she didn't say anything. Katie couldn't afford to get her eyebrows done, too, which was why Lily's aunt had volunteered to do them for her.

"Ouch!" she exclaimed as Dahlia plucked a tiny hair from the corner of her brow.

"That didn't hurt," scoffed Dahlia. "You're lucky I'm not waxing."

Katie fidgeted in the wooden chair. "Maybe I should just keep my unibrow."

"You don't have a unibrow. Your brows are very nicely shaped, they just need a little cleaning up."

"Speaking of cleaning up, Kyle says that sometimes he prefers the grainy appearance of film compared to the sharp, clean quality of digital photos," Lily interjected. "Kyle says grittiness gives an image character."

"Oh, is that what Kyle says?" Dahlia teased.

Lily lowered her camera and turned to face her aunt. "What do you mean by that?"

Katie answered on Dahlia's behalf. "She means you're always saying, 'Kyle says this, Kyle thinks that.'"

"Nuh-uh." Lily made a negative sound.

"Yuh-huh," Katie countered, pulling away from Dahlia's tweezers to rub her brow. "You are in love with Kyle Wright."

"I'm so *not*."

"Good, because he's way too old," Katie muttered. "He must be at least thirty or thirty-five. Even if he didn't get arrested, he'd be fired just for going out with you."

"First of all, he's not a schoolteacher—he's not even anyone's employee—so he wouldn't get fired," Lily argued.

Every year, the island's cultural center sponsored a fellowship for an up-and-coming artist, writer or photographer. In addition to receiving free housing in a magnificent seaside setting, the fellows were paid small stipends. In return they offered free workshops to the residents, as well as a public display of their own work in the fall and again in the spring.

This year's fellow was Kyle Wright, a photographer from New York who wore a leather jacket and torn jeans, and whose dark thick hair flopped forward, nearly obscuring his soulful green eyes. He was an engaging, encouraging instructor and his passion about photography was infectious. Everyone in his workshop was crazy about him, including Lily—but not in the way Katie had suggested.

"And second, I'd never want to go out with him anyway," she said.

"You'd better not." Dahlia shot her a serious look. "It's okay to think he's all that, but Katie's right—he's way too old for you to be in love with him."

"Dahlia! I'm *not* in love with him." At least, Lily didn't think she was. Granted, she was enraptured by what he was teaching her about photography, and it was exhilarating to know he thought she was talented. But that wasn't really the same thing as being in love, was it? "I think Kyle's super creative and smart, but I could never *like* him, like him. I mean, have you seen his feet?"

"His feet?" Dahlia echoed.

"Yeah. He wore sandals to class in September and his toes are really long and he's got these big tufts of hair on his toe knuckles. It's disgusting." She shuddered, which for some reason, cracked Dahlia up. Her hair cascaded over her shoulders as she threw back her head.

Lily didn't know what she'd said that was so funny, but she was happy that she could make her aunt laugh, especially because Dahlia always seemed anxious when Martin and Aiden weren't getting along.

She continued, "Even if I wanted to go out with Kyle—which I *don't*—but even I was old enough to go out with him, it would be a waste of time because he has a girlfriend in New York. Her name is Natasha and she came to visit him last weekend. I saw them in Gibsons' market and Kyle introduced me to her."

In fact, Kyle had introduced Lily as, "Dune Island's budding Anna Atkins." His girlfriend seemed to understand the reference, but Lily hadn't known what he'd meant. As soon as she got home, she'd looked up Anna Atkins online and learned she was a famous botanist, as well as a photographer. *He must have called me that because of all the close-ups I've taken of the cranberry vines and wild roses*, she'd thought. She treasured the compliment too much to share it, not even with her aunt and best friend.

"What about you, Katie? Is there anyone at school you like?" Dahlia asked.

"I *wish*," she answered honestly. Lily loved it that she and her friend could openly confide in Dahlia, who seemed more like a big sister than an aunt. They never had to worry that she'd lecture them or repeat anything they'd told her.

"How about that tall boy, the one who gave you girls a ride home from the boardwalk when you got caught in that thunderstorm last month? He seems nice."

"You mean Steve Reagan? He's got a thing for Lily."

"Does not," she contradicted.

"Then why did he ask you on the very first day of school to go to the senior dance with him next *June*?"

"He likes to plan ahead, that's all. Besides, it's not even definite. He asked if I'd go with him if neither of us has anyone else to go with, so I said okay, we could go as friends. If Steve likes anyone, it's *you*." Lily nudged Katie's shoulder.

"Hey, don't do that. You're going to make me poke her in the eye," Dahlia warned.

At the same time, Katie protested, "Steve doesn't even notice me."

"Aha—so is *that* why you're doing this makeover? You want to get his attention?" Lily was only teasing to get back at her friend for suggesting she was in love with Kyle.

"No, I'm just sick of being the frumpy one in my family." Katie's cousin, Lexi, had been voted homecoming queen at their junior prom.

"Frumpy—are you kidding me? Look how glam you are!" Dahlia handed Katie a small hand mirror. "Isn't she, Lily?"

Dahlia had shaped her friend's eyebrows into a dramatic arch. Lily's heart welled with pride over her aunt's ability to bring other people's beauty to light. "Yeah, she is. Can I take your photo, Katie?"

"Make sure you don't get me in it!" Dahlia cautioned, so Lily waited until her aunt had moved out of the frame.

"You look so pretty. You could be a model," Katie remarked to Dahlia. "Why don't you want your photo taken?"

Lily had posed the same question to her aunt at least a dozen times, but she never got a straight answer, so she'd given up asking.

"Thanks, but no thanks," Dahlia said.

Lily snapped the photo and then showed the display screen to Katie, who made a crack about how her eyebrows made her look surprised. But Lily could tell by the way she studied the picture that she was pleased with the effect.

"If you don't like Steve, what about Will Jackman? You said he was hanging out at the shop a lot this summer." Katie's uncle owned Bleecker's, an iconic ice cream shop on the boardwalk in Lucinda's Hamlet, so Katie worked there on the weekends and during the summer tourist season.

"He was only interested in me because I gave him extra scoops of ice cream for free. Besides, we've known each other since we were in diapers—literally. My mom has a photo of us running through a tidal pool together." Katie rolled her eyes.

Dahlia clarified, "So you wouldn't go out with a guy just because you grew up with him?"

"Sort of. I mean, because we grew up together, I feel like I already know everything there is to know about him. Bo-ring."

"Yeah, I feel that way about the boys at school, too." Lily gave an exaggerated, wistful sigh. "I wish some really amazing guy would move here so I'd know what it feels like to fall madly in love with someone."

Dahlia had been watching the girls and listening intently while they were speaking, but now she gazed toward the rumpled ocean. Navy-blue in the October light, its waves softly folded themselves against the rocky shore.

After a moment, she said, "Infatuation can be thrilling, for as long as it lasts. But trust me, girls, there's something even better than falling head-over-heels in love. And that's being with a man who steadies you. A man who makes you feel as if you have solid ground beneath your feet. If you find a man like that, hold on tight and don't let go."

Lily suspected Dahlia was comparing her ex-husband—whom she'd almost never mentioned—to Martin. This intimate glimpse into her feelings about him warmed Lily's heart.

Studying her aunt's profile, she thought, *If I could take her*

photo right now, I'd title it, "Dahlia Dreaming." Then I'd give it
to Uncle Martin, so he'd know how much she loves him.

But her aunt would never agree to have her picture taken
and Lily figured her uncle didn't need a photo to know how
Dahlia felt about him anyway. So instead, she pointed her lens
toward a juniper tree, carefully positioning it off-center in the
left third of the frame, just like Kyle said she should do.

CHAPTER THIRTEEN

NOW

FRIDAY

Lily woke to the scratchy pitapat of a squirrel or chipmunk scurrying across the roof. She checked the time on her phone: 7:38. Usually she'd be wide awake and out of bed by now, but she was tired because memories of her aunt had kept her from falling asleep until two or three o'clock.

It wasn't necessarily that the occasions and conversations she'd recalled were troubling; rather, most of the recollections that had come to mind last night had been about positive, happy times. But once again, even Lily's fondest memories of Dahlia had been tarnished by her awareness of what had happened to destroy their relationship. It had made her feel conflicted, as if her memories were playing tug-of-war with her emotions, so she'd been too agitated to sleep.

Since I can't seem to control how I feel when I think about the past, I should try harder not to think about it so often, she resolved. It wouldn't be an easy task, since almost everything she saw or did on Dune Island triggered a memory. *But when something springs to mind, I don't have to dwell on it.*

She eased out of the lounger, groaning because her back and shoulders were even sorer than they'd been yesterday morning. She stepped out onto the deck to stretch, but a dense curtain of fog prevented her from enjoying the view. After she'd warmed up her muscles, she hurried toward the farmhouse to get Dahlia's car keys so she could go buy coffee.

As she emerged from the other side of the woods, she noticed the heavy fog had already lifted from the bogs. Now, only a delicate mist veiled the pink blush of flowering cranberry vines. *How I've missed this sight*, she thought before continuing toward the farmhouse.

Her intention was to dart into the cottage to grab her purse, but her plans were waylaid when Steve called to her from the parking area. She did a doubletake when she realized Jake was standing with him.

I hope Steve didn't get an earful from him about how I've been wasting his time, she fretted. She had completely forgotten to tell her attorney friend that Jake had requested they only communicate about the farm by email from now on.

After both men had greeted her, Steve announced, "I stopped by to chat with Jake and he kindly agreed to help us find the right buyer for the farm."

"Really?" Lily didn't mean to sound as surprised as she felt. Had Jake realized that it was in his best interest to be involved in the sales process? "That's great. Thank you, Jake."

"No problem," he said with a sheepish half-smile.

Steve proceeded told them he'd gotten the ball rolling with the listing and he would set up a phone meeting with them both to discuss it soon. He also said he'd connected with a wealthy off-island colleague who was interested in touring the farm. "He's coming to Hope Haven for vacation over the Fourth of July weekend. I realize that's when the farm is hosting its grand opening and the place will be overrun with customers, so you might be too busy to give him a tour. But if you can swing it, it might be an opportune time to show off the business."

"I'll do what I can to make it happen," Jake confirmed.

While Lily appreciated his willingness to help, she was surprised he was being so accommodating. Why the sudden change of heart since yesterday? *Oh well, I have a hard enough time trying to make sense of my own up-and-down emotions. I don't need to try to figure out Jake's moods, too.*

After Steve left, she started toward the cottage to get her purse, but Jake asked, "Could you hold on a sec? There's something—" Before he could finish his sentence, Lily's phone buzzed and she glanced at the screen. So he waved her off, saying, "Go ahead, take your call. I can talk to you later."

Why don't you just email me so I can read whatever it is you want to say at my *convenience?* She smiled facetiously to herself.

But her smile quickly faded when the caller said she was reaching out on behalf of the Cramer family. She told Lily that two of the mechanic's grandchildren had been injured in an off-island accident and they were expected to be hospitalized until Monday.

"Oh, I'm so sorry to hear that. What can I do to help?"

It wasn't an empty offer. Gossiping aside, most of the locals supported each other with acts of kindness during times of illness or mourning, regardless of whether they were close friends or not. Lily hadn't realized how much she'd appreciated this island custom until Tyler got cancer when they were living in Pennsylvania. She kept wishing one of her coworkers would drop off a casserole or mow their lawn, the way one of her Hope Haven acquaintances would have done.

"Thanks for asking, but the Cramers aren't even on the island right now—the whole family is staying in Boston near the hospital. That's why I'm calling. I have to let you know that unfortunately, the shop is closed. It looks like your car was scheduled for a starter installation. Unfortunately, they're not going to be able to take care of it until they return. We'll tentatively aim for Wednesday morning. Sorry for the inconvenience, but they want to be there for their family."

"Of course, I understand," Lily automatically replied, because what else could she say? "No problem."

But all the way to the convenience store, she felt like crying as she considered her two most practical options. *I can either ask Leanne and Tim to keep Ryan with them until Wednesday, or I can meet them tomorrow and bring Ryan back here with me.*

It wasn't a difficult decision to make. Even though the thought of bringing Ryan to her hometown filled her with anxiety, she absolutely couldn't bear to be separated from him for five more days. She immediately began planning ways to protect her son from having a negative experience while he was in Rockfield.

First of all, I've got to get a better grip on my own emotions, otherwise my uneasiness about being here will rub off on him, she reminded herself. *Secondly, we'll have to do our best to stay away from people like Claire Griffin, because who knows what kind of baloney she might say in front of him.*

Even though she'd personally been trying to avoid her former acquaintances since she'd arrived on the island, Lily had mixed feelings about her and Ryan keeping to themselves on the farm. She didn't want him to feel too isolated.

But she rationalized, *There's plenty to do on the farm and he'll love exploring the conservation land and the beach. Besides, it's only for a couple of days, so it's not as if we're going to develop some kind of anti-social lifestyle.*

It would be easy enough to limit their trips into town or to other public places, but how would they avoid Jake? *He may have been acting friendlier this morning, but that could change if he gets stressed out again,* she thought. *I don't want Jake to feel like we're in his way, but I don't want my son to feel like he's unwelcome on the farm, either...*

As she was ruminating, Lily pulled up to a stop sign, where a trim, middle-aged pedestrian had just stepped into the crosswalk in front of her. Although she could only see his profile, something about the way he carried himself seemed very familiar. *That's not* Kyle Wright, *is it?* she questioned, a funny feeling in her gut. She leaned over the steering wheel to try to get a better look at the man as he reached the opposite sidewalk. Was it really her former photography instructor?

The driver behind her honked his horn and Lily jerked back against her seat. Her foot slipped off the brake and hit the gas pedal, causing the car to lurch forward. She quickly lifted her foot and the car's momentum slowed. *So much for getting a better grip on my emotions*, she thought, chuckling at herself. *I'm so preoccupied with the past I'm practically jumping out of my skin when I think I see someone I used to know!*

After she'd finished her coffee and had called Leanne to tell her she'd had another change of plans, Lily wandered down the beach to Mrs. Henderson's house. Her grandmother's friend wasn't home, but the windows were open, which meant she must have moved in for the season. Lily was hopeful she'd eventually get a chance to chat with her.

She spent the rest of the morning and the early afternoon assisting Sophie. Regardless of Jake's claim that Lily's help wasn't needed, the teenager had gratefully accepted her offer to organize a system for tracking and storing extra merchandise in the basement.

By 3:00, Lily felt so famished she thought, *I don't care if I end up bumping into my entire high school class—I need to go to the market and get something for supper.*

As she headed toward her car, she noticed a silver sedan idling in the farthest corner of the parking area. *That must be Olivia*, she thought, and waved to Sophie's mother, who didn't wave back. Lily may have been mistaken, but it appeared that Olivia had deliberately turned her face in the opposite direction.

Did I just get the brush-off or didn't she recognize me? Lily considered crossing the lot to strike up a conversation with her, but she wasn't confident that Olivia would be receptive. *Given how hard I've tried to avoid certain acquaintances, I don't want to put her on the spot if she isn't interested in having a conversation with me*, she decided.

A few minutes later, as she neared the boardwalk in Lucinda's Hamlet, which was known as Lucy's Ham to the locals, Lily had a sudden desire for a cone from Bleecker's Ice Cream Shop. And maybe it was because of all the reminiscing she'd done the previous night, but she also had a strong urge to touch base with Katie.

It must have been two or three years since Dahlia had mentioned anyone in the Bleecker family in their infrequent phone calls. She'd said that Katie's uncle had retired and her cousin Lexi had assumed responsibility for the business. Lily figured if she didn't see Katie at the ice cream shop, Lexi or a staff member would be able to tell her if she still lived in Hope Haven and how to contact her.

However, before Lily even reached the shop, she spotted Katie setting up a flavor menu board on the sidewalk.

"Katie Bleecker—you look fantastic," she exclaimed. It honestly seemed as if her childhood friend hadn't aged more than five years. She hugged her warmly, but Katie barely lifted her arms to reciprocate.

"Hi, Lily." Taking a step back, she wiped her hands on her apron. "I heard you were on the island."

"Yeah, news travels fast in Hope Haven." It was a trite thing to say and she didn't mean anything by it, but Katie visibly bristled.

"Don't worry. It's not as if we're all sitting around talking about you—especially not right before the start of tourist season." She motioned to the line of people trickling out the shop's open door. "We're short-staffed today, so I've got to go help ring up sales."

Lily quickly apologized. "Right, sorry. I won't keep you. I just wanted to say hi. Maybe we'll get to catch up with each other another time."

"Maybe, but it's a busy time of year." Before squeezing past the customers, Katie stopped to add, "I was very sorry to hear about Dahlia."

Even though her final sentiment sounded sincere, Lily felt so slighted by her friend's general aloofness that she completely forgot to purchase an ice cream cone. All the way home, she mulled over their interaction.

It's not as if I expected Katie to drop everything to talk to me, but I didn't expect her to be so frosty, either, she thought. *Is she truly just stressed because the shop is short-staffed? Or is it that she's just not as warm and affectionate as she used to be when we were young?*

A less likely possibility was that Katie was angry at Lily. But why? The girls had exchanged postcards and occasional texts the summer after Lily left the island. As far as she could remember, they hadn't had any conflicts during that time; they just sort of drifted apart.

In fact, it was Katie who'd dropped out of touch first. After half a dozen notes went unanswered, Lily had assumed her friend was too busy with her college courses to correspond with her and she stopped communicating, too. But until now, Lily never would have questioned whether Katie treasured their youthful friendship as much as Lily did.

After getting the cold shoulder from two people in a row,

Lily had lost her appetite. Instead of going to the market, she headed straight back to the farm. It wasn't quite 4:00 when she got there, but Jake's truck was gone.

His to-do list couldn't have been that *long if he's already left for the evening,* she thought. *Maybe he cut out early because he's got a date.*

It wasn't as if Lily necessarily cared what he was doing. It was that without anyone else on the property at all, seeing the deserted house made her feel as lonely this afternoon as it had made her feel the other evening. Or maybe it was being snubbed by Olivia and Katie that was making her feel so solitary.

Rather than going inside the cottage or farmhouse, she trekked out to the cliffside shack and settled into her lounger on the deck. Within fifteen minutes, she had been bitten half a dozen times by the tiny but notoriously aggressive insects called "no-see-ums" that were especially prevalent when the weather was as humid and overcast as it was today.

Lily carried the chair into the shack and unfolded it into a reclining position. *A nap will make the time go by faster until I get to see my son,* she told herself. *And as long as I'm asleep, I won't be able to think about Katie or Olivia or anything else about with my past...*

CHAPTER FOURTEEN

THEN

SPRING, LILY'S SENIOR YEAR OF HIGH SCHOOL

Spring had always made Lily feel buoyant and hopeful. She loved it when the first crocuses and daffodils poked through the ground because it meant it wouldn't be long before she could exchange her sweaters and shoes for T-shirts and sandals. Also, her birthday was in early April and after that, there were only about eight weeks left of classes.

This year, she was especially looking forward to the end of the academic year because the seniors took their exams a week earlier than the rest of the student body. Then, during the final week of school, the graduating students were excused from classes and homework. Instead, they participated in seniors-only events, including the senior dance, a beach party, movie night at the drive-in theater, and graduation ceremony rehearsals.

The week of celebration culminated with Hope Haven High's traditional "senior leap" off Herring Run Bridge into the tidal river beneath it. Ordinarily, jumping from the bridge was strictly prohibited and violators who were caught received a hefty fine. But on the final day of school, the graduating students were allowed to take a symbolic "leap into the future" with their classmates during high tide.

Lily anticipated this event more than any other during senior week. She'd even bought a new swimsuit for the occasion. It was a simple yellow maillot, similar to the style she normally wore, except this one had skinny straps and high-cut legs. Trying it on, she'd felt... not exposed, really, but more aware of her body than she usually felt.

When she'd stepped out of the dressing room, Dahlia had gasped and put her hand over her mouth.

"It's too revealing, isn't it?" Lily tried to tug the fabric farther down on her thighs, which weren't quite as skinny as they used to be.

"No. It's perfect."

"Then why are you looking at me like that?"

"I just realized how grown-up you're becoming." Dahlia's eyes shone. "You're a strong, lovely young woman, Lily, inside and out—and that's definitely the suit you should get."

Lily couldn't wait to wear it, but what really kept her on pins and needles was waiting to hear the outcome of the photography contest she had entered that winter. Kyle was the one who'd told the workshop about it. As a member of a professional photography association, he was allowed to enter one workshop participant's collection in a national competition. The winning photos would be featured in a prominent publication, both online and in print, and the winner would be awarded a $5,000 prize.

Kyle had chosen to submit Lily's photos of the cranberry bog and they'd advanced to the final round of judging. With each passing hour, she drew nearer to hearing the results of the competition, which were supposed to be announced sometime after April 15. According to the guidelines, the winner would receive a phone call; everyone else would be notified by email.

"I'm trying not to get my hopes up," she confided to Katie as they were eating lunch in the school cafeteria. "But this means so much to me."

"Even if you don't win, it's already a huge compliment that Kyle chose your photos," her friend reminded her. "Unless he chose them because *he's* had a thing for *you* this whole year. Which is still kind of a compliment, I guess."

Lily frowned at the possibility. "No it isn't."

"I was only kidding," Katie said, rolling her eyes.

"Sorry. It's just that sometimes I get the feeling that Kyle's being extra complimentary because that's what kind of guy he is, not because my photos are anything special." She sighed and admitted, "That's one of the reasons I really, really, really want to win this contest."

"You do? Really?" Katie echoed and they both cracked up. "You probably *will* win, Lily. Just don't forget about me when you're famous."

"I don't want to win so I can be famous. I want to win because it will mean that someone besides Kyle thinks my photos are good."

"*I* think your photos are great."

"Thanks, Katie." Lily smiled at her friend and took a drink of milk before quietly confiding, "I also want to win because of my granddad. He's been so different since my grandma died. It's like he doesn't care about growing cranberries any more. If I won the contest, maybe it would make him remember, you know, how hard he's worked on the farm and all the things he loves about it and that it's still part of who we are, even if Grandma isn't here."

Lily's eyes smarted and for one mortifying second, she thought she might cry right there in the middle of the cafeteria and she ducked her chin to her chest. But then Katie nudged her foot under the table.

"Hey. You know what?" she asked, pausing until Lily looked up again. "I really, really, really want you to win the contest, too."

When Lily returned home that afternoon and found her aunt resting her forehead against her arm in the corner of the laundry room, she thought Dahlia was crying. *It's no wonder, considering all that's been going on around here.*

Not only had Lily's granddad been struggling ever since Selma died, but her uncle was also going through a rough patch that spring. Martin had had spinal surgery in February and it hadn't been successful. In fact, after the operation the numbness and weakness in his legs had worsened and his back was in constant agony. No matter whether he sat or stood or lay flat in bed, he couldn't get comfortable. But he seldom took medication because he was concerned about becoming addicted.

In addition to helping him manage his pain and practice physical therapy exercises, Dahlia was doing to her best to keep Martin's spirits up. She made all his favorite meals. She massaged his scalp and shoulders. And, when the pain was so severe he could hardly see straight, she tried to distract him by reading aloud from his agricultural magazines.

She'd also gone out of her way to shield her husband—and her father-in-law—from any additional stressors. Which meant that when Aiden asked for money or wanted to borrow the car, she gave in without any argument. Dahlia also assumed responsibility for answering the business cell phone and handling the email correspondence and accounting. Lily got the feeling that the farm was having money problems and her aunt didn't want the men to find out about it. Her efforts to minimize their stress may have paid off for Lars and Martin, but they seemed to be taking a toll on Dahlia.

Yet when Lily reached forward to tap her shoulder and ask if she could do something to help, she realized her aunt wasn't crying—she was speaking on the phone.

"My husband absolutely can't find out about this," Dahlia was pleading. "He's still recovering from spinal surgery and if he hears what's been going on, I'm concerned he'll suffer a major health setback. I'll let him know eventually, but now is not the time."

The caller must have agreed because a moment later Dahlia said thank you and disconnected. When she turned around, she flinched to see her niece standing right behind her.

"I was coming to give you a hand folding clothes," Lily explained.

"Oh." Dahlia bit her lower lip. "So you heard what I was talking about?"

"Yeah, part of it. It sounded like bad news. Did another market decide not to sell our berries?"

Dahlia looked momentarily confused but then her expression brightened. "No. It was a call about a... about an outstanding debt. I'll take care of it though, so promise me you won't mention it to Martin or your granddad."

"I won't," she assured her aunt. "You seem kind of tense. Is there something else I can do to help? You want me to make supper?"

Dahlia smiled wanly. "No, thanks. I'm roasting a chicken, easy peasy. You probably have homework, so don't worry about folding the clothes, either. I'll take care of them."

But instead of going to her room to study, Lily traipsed outside to the workshop to borrow her granddad's screw gun and a broom. Every winter, Lily and Lars boarded up the doors and windows of the shack. Every spring, Lily took them down again. It was one of her favorite annual traditions. Even though the weather was still chilly during the nighttime hours, Lily figured it wasn't going to snow this late in the season, so she might as well remove the boards today.

As she made her way through the woods and across the heathland, she thought about her future. *Kyle says most photographers need to work in other fields for a long time before they can support themselves taking photos. So it's important to find a satisfying way to earn a living in the meantime,* she recalled. But other than being a photographer or working on the farm, she couldn't imagine any other job she'd like.

Maybe I should enroll in business admin classes at Port Newcomb's community college this fall. Although she wasn't especially interested in the subject matter, the way Lily saw it, the information she learned would be useful if she ran her own photography business, like she hoped to do one day.

Her daydreams kept her mind occupied as she removed the boards from the door and the windows and put in the screens. She swept the sand and spider webs from the shack's interior. Then she brought the boards inside and stacked them in a neat pile in the corner of the room, where they'd be out of the way for the summer. Lily was going to retrieve the deck chairs from the storage loft, but she'd stirred up so much dust that she began coughing and had to step outside.

Standing on the deck, she surveyed the small, whitecapped waves that rose in peaks across the green expanse of water. The tide was out and the feathery breeze that caressed her skin was unseasonably warm. She considered picking her way down the steep, ramshackle stairs to the base of the cliff, where she could ditch her shoes and go beachcombing.

But then she remembered she'd promised her aunt she'd wait until they were together before she dipped her bare feet in the water for the first time of the season. Besides, she needed to get back to the house to set the table.

Tomorrow, I'm going to convince Dahlia to come out here

with me, she decided as she hiked through the woods. Considering all the time her aunt had spent catering to the men in the family, Lily figured she'd appreciate escaping to their "testosterone-free zone" for a little while. *We can bring dessert with us*, she planned. *It'll be like a celebration of spring.*

And maybe, just maybe—she barely dared to hope—by this time tomorrow evening, they'd have something else to celebrate, too.

The following day, Lily was late returning home from school because there was a substitute bus driver who had reversed the route, which meant she was the next-to-the-last student to be dropped off.

Aiden's so lucky, she griped to herself as she trudged up the driveway. He didn't have a class scheduled during seventh period, so he was allowed to go home forty-five minutes earlier than she did. Not that he ever actually went home; he usually went who-knew-where with Olivia.

Lily was also miffed because it seemed unfair that he got away with doing absolutely *nothing* to help around the house or on the farm. He was clearly taking advantage of his mother's concern about Martin's stress levels. Whenever Dahlia asked Aiden to do something, he'd raise his voice and complain and she'd immediately change her mind and complete the task herself.

Maybe I'm *the one who needs some time in a testosterone-free zone*, Lily thought, but she knew that Aiden's behavior wasn't what was really bugging her. She was frustrated because another day was almost over and the photography association hadn't announced the competition winner. It was maddening.

She went into the kitchen to tell Dahlia about her idea of bringing dessert to the shack that evening. A basket of fresh cranberry muffins was on the counter, but there was no sign of her aunt and no sign she'd been baking, either.

Mrs. Henderson probably dropped these off, Lily thought. Agnes checked in on them at least once a week since Selma died. Usually, she brought muffins or a casserole. No matter how many times they invited her to stay and eat with them, she never did. Lily figured it was because she felt strange being in Selma's house without her friend there, too.

Lily peeked into the cottage and didn't find Dahlia there, either, but Martin was snoring in the recliner. *He probably took one of the sedatives the doctor prescribed*, Lily surmised, since her uncle virtually never slept during the day. Knowing that he must have been in excruciating pain to finally take medication, Lily tiptoed back down the hall to grab her camera from the farmhouse. Photographing the seascape always put her in a better mood, so she figured she'd head out to the shack.

On her way, she popped in to greet her granddad, who'd been spending more time in his workshop than in the bogs lately. "Hi, Granddad. Whatcha doing?"

"Repairing this air conditioner for the Warrens before the summer heat sets in." He glanced up at her. "Any news about your contest yet?"

Touched that her granddad had remembered, Lily put on her best face. "Nope, not yet, but I'm sure I'll hear soon," she replied. "Do you know where Dahlia is?"

"She was burning brush behind the house a while ago but I don't know where she is now. If you see her, tell her it's almost time to go—my cardiology appointment is at four forty-five."

Last week when he'd tried to renew his license, Lars had failed the vision portion of the test, so he couldn't legally drive until he got stronger lenses. Dahlia was as concerned about his safety on the road as she was about Aiden's and Lily's, and she insisted on driving Lars everywhere until his new glasses arrived.

"She must be at the shack since she isn't anywhere else and both cars are home. I'll go get her," Lily agreed.

Sure enough, as soon as she came around the corner of the shack, she spotted her aunt standing on the edge of the deck. Hugging her midriff with one arm and pressing her opposite hand to her cheek, Dahlia was obviously lost in thought.

Lily knew she shouldn't do it, but her aunt's contemplative profile against the backdrop of the distant ocean was so photogenic she couldn't resist. She lifted her camera to her eye, imagining the "rule of thirds" grid, the way Kyle had taught her to do. When she'd captured the angle she wanted, she pushed the shutter button.

Before she could take a second photo, her aunt twisted her head in Lily's direction. She lowered her camera just in time and called, "Hi, Dahlia. Did you notice I took the boards off the windows? I thought we'd eat our dessert out here tonight—I noticed Mrs. Henderson brought us muffins."

"Mm, we'll see. It depends on how Martin's doing." Her voice was somber and her brow furrowed. Had she seen Lily taking the photo of her?

"He's sleeping right now," she reported, hopping up the stairs. "Granddad wanted me to tell you it's almost time to take him to his cardiology appointment."

Dahlia smacked her forehead. "I completely forgot about that. Could you take him? I just got out here and I really need a break."

Lily was surprised; it wasn't like Dahlia to forget a medical appointment. Something major must have been troubling her. "Sure, I'll take him... But, um, are you all right?"

"I *will* be if I can just get a little peace and quiet," she snapped.

It was understandable that her aunt needed a little solitude, but Lily felt stung by her tone. "Don't worry, I'm going."

As she scurried down the stairs, Dahlia called after her, "Lily, wait!"

She paused but didn't turn around. "What?"

"When you're in town, can you pick up a couple gallons of milk?"

Lily nodded and strode away without answering aloud so she wouldn't disturb her aunt's peace and quiet.

"What did the doctor say?" Lily asked her granddad when he got into the car. She had waited in the parking lot while he'd gone into his cardiologist's office.

"Not a lot. Most doctors won't say much of anything until they run a bunch of expensive tests. It used to be that doctors knew just by looking at a person what was wrong. They didn't hesitate to give you their opinions. I suppose nowadays they're all so afraid of being sued that they won't say *boo* without an X-ray or an MRI to back them up."

Lily had heard this kind of grievance from her granddad many times before. "Does the doctor want to run one of those expensive tests on you?"

"Nah—he wants to run *three* of them." Lars grunted. "First one's called a stress test. Good name for it, huh?"

"Yeah." Although she was glad to hear a glimmer of humor in his voice again, Lily was alarmed that the doctor wanted her granddad to undergo testing.

Lars must have noticed her expression, because he said, "Don't worry. My old ticker may not be as fast as it used to be, but it's still strong enough to keep the cranberry juice pumping through my veins."

This was an old joke between them. When Lily was a little girl, her granddad told her the difference between regular people and cranberry farmers was that the farmers had cranberry juice instead of blood running through their veins. At that age, Lily had taken his remark literally. So, a little while later when she scraped her knee and it bled red blood rather than pink cranberry juice, she was devastated, because she wanted to have cranberry juice in her veins, like her granddad did.

"I'll bet that's what the doctor will say after the tests, too." Lily stole a sideways glance at Lars and smiled. She figured she wouldn't ask about the other tests—Dahlia would wheedle that information out of him this evening.

A few minutes later, she stopped at Gibsons' market and dashed inside to buy the milk they needed. She was coming down the dairy aisle with a gallon jug in each hand when one of the stockers, Claire Griffin, who also happened to be Lily's classmate, stepped into her path.

"What are you doing here?" Claire's tone was accusatory, almost as if she'd caught Lily shoplifting.

Even though the answer seemed apparent, Lily held up the two jugs and replied, "We ran out."

"Seriously? You're here buying milk while your family's farm is burning down?"

Lily tried to fathom what in the world Claire possibly could have meant. Then it dawned on her that someone had probably smelled smoke from the burn pile while they were hiking in the conservation land and they'd called 9-1-1 to report a fire. As with so many other stories on Dune Island, the account of what had happened was undoubtedly altered and exaggerated the more times it was told. Lily giggled when she realized Claire's rumor *about* a wildfire was going to spread *like* a wildfire unless she put it out.

"Dahlia was burning brush today, no big deal," she said. "We have a license."

"Do you have a license to burn the meadow in the conservation land, too?"

Lily shook her head, confused. "What are you talking about?

Before she could answer, Mr. Gibson, the store owner, strode toward them and ordered Claire to go clean up a spill in the condiment aisle.

"What was she talking about?" Lily repeated, looking up at Mr. Gibson. "Did the conservation land really catch on fire?"

"Yes. But I believe the blaze was contained quickly and—"

Lily interrupted him, her voice rising to a squeak, "Was anyone hurt?"

"No. No one was hurt. No one at all. No," he repeated, as if he understood how much Lily needed to hear that word. She pushed the containers of milk into Mr. Gibson's arms and fled the store.

In the parking lot, Dan Jordan, one of Martin's pals from the bar where he played darts, was leaning over her granddad's side of the car, talking to Lars through the open window. When Dan saw Lily approach, he stood up straight and tapped the roof.

"You take care," he told Lars, then he nodded at Lily and ambled away.

It was clear from her granddad's expression that Dan had told him about the fire. In a way, Lily was relieved because she didn't know how she would have broken it to him. Lars must have been able to tell from the look on her face that she'd heard the news, too, because when she got into the car and she reached to change gears, he put his hand over hers.

She paused while he said, "The most important thing to remember in all of this—the thing to be thankful for—is that no one was hurt. Anything else that has come to harm will be restored, in time."

Lily wasn't sure whether he was talking about the farm and conservation land or their family's reputation in the community —or both—but she nodded her agreement.

He continued. "Dahlia has been carrying too much on her shoulders lately. It's possible she had other things on her mind and she didn't extinguish the burn pile properly. Maybe a breeze caught some embers and lofted them. I don't know what happened yet. But there are three things I do know for certain." He counted on his fingers as he listed them. "One, whatever happened, it was unintentional. Two, Dahlia is going to feel devastated about it. And three, she won't ever make this mistake again. So we're going to support her, no matter what, right?"

"Right," agreed Lily, nodding so vigorously her head hurt.

CHAPTER FIFTEEN

THEN

To everyone's relief, the fire damage was relatively minimal. The flames had scorched two acres of the Lindgrens' property and not even a full acre of the conservation land was burned. Dahlia provided a sworn statement to the police, confirming that the fire was unintentional: she hadn't realized the burn pile wasn't completely extinguished before she'd trekked out to the shack.

As a matter of procedure, the police also questioned the rest of the family. Lily felt guilty when the officer asked if it seemed like her aunt had been distracted when she'd seen her at the shack, but she answered honestly. In the end, Dahlia received a fine and she was also ordered to pay restitution to the fire department for their services. But she wasn't penalized with the threat of jail time because the fire wasn't the result of a willful and malicious act of arson.

Regardless, she felt inconsolably guilty. She wouldn't stop catastrophizing about what *could* have happened and she kept apologizing to her family. In turn, they claimed the fire was more *their* fault than hers.

"I should have been helping you instead of puttering around in the workshop," Lars told her.

"If I hadn't taken a pain pill, I wouldn't have fallen asleep," Martin lamented. "Then I might have smelled the fire sooner."

Lily chimed in, "I *did* smell it and I didn't say anything. I thought the scent was just lingering in the air because Granddad said you'd been burning leaves earlier in the day."

Aiden was the only one who didn't try to comfort Dahlia. When Lily went into the cottage that evening to tell Dahlia she was going back to the store to buy milk for breakfast, she heard him mouthing off to his mother.

"Where were you, anyway?" Dahlia was questioning him. "You better not have been drinking with Olivia."

"Get off my case already."

"You're eighteen now, Aiden, which means that legally, you're an adult." Dahlia's tone had a sternness to it that Lily hadn't heard until now. She pivoted on her heel and started down the hall, but she could still hear her aunt's voice loud and clear. "It's time for you to grow up. You need to start being more responsible and making better choices."

"The best choice I'll ever make is that I'm getting as far away from you as I can the second I finish school," he jeered. "And since I *am* a legal adult, no one can stop me!"

Who would want *to stop you?* Lily thought, furious that he was speaking to his mother like that, especially after all she'd been through this afternoon. As a tiny act of revenge, she decided she wasn't going to the store for milk after all. *Aiden's the only one who eats cereal for breakfast anyway, so if he wants milk, he can go get it himself!*

When the school bus rumbled to a stop in front of the farm the next morning, virtually all the students had moved to the right side of the vehicle and were peering out the windows. They were obviously trying to catch a glimpse of where the fire had blackened the grass and made a torch of two or three pitch pines. Lily braced herself for her classmates' remarks and climbed aboard.

As expected, most of their twaddle was about how careless or inept they thought Dahlia was. One kid claimed his father said he always knew that someone as beautiful as Dahlia couldn't have had a brain in her head. Someone else commented that she was lucky she didn't get jail time. Another student claimed the fire had killed two eagle hatchlings in the conservation land, even though the only eagles ever seen on the island nested miles away, in the wildlife sanctuary.

"First, Aiden graffitied the grinding stones, now Dahlia trashed the conservation land. It must be a case of like mother, like son," a girl named Gretchen Turner opined. "Or maybe it's because they're newcomers."

"It's not just newcomers who have no respect for Dune Island's ecosystem. Lily has lived here her entire life and when I told her about the fire, she *laughed*," Claire Griffin announced.

Although she felt no need to defend herself, Lily was compelled to stand up for her aunt. But once again, it didn't seem to have any effect on her acquaintances' jabbering. By the time her last class was let out, she couldn't stand to hear another word on the topic. Rather than taking the school bus home, she decided to walk two miles to the nearest public bus stop.

She'd barely gone three blocks before it began to pour. So when Steve Reagan pulled alongside of her in his vintage convertible sports car and offered her a ride, she accepted. The only thing he said about the fire was that he hoped Dahlia was doing all right. Other than Katie, none of Lily's peers had expressed concern for her aunt.

Lily was so grateful she touched his forearm and told him, "Thanks a lot for giving me a ride, Steve. I couldn't deal with taking the bus today."

He slowly bobbed his head up and down, as if he understood. "I can pick you up and take you home from school whenever you want," he said. "I go right past the farm anyway."

From then on, Lily got a ride from him. Almost immediately, her classmates began spreading rumors that the two of them were going out. It was annoying, but at least they weren't chitchatting about Dahlia as often. By the end of the week, Lily was hopeful that they'd lost interest in the topic of the fire altogether.

However, on Friday she discovered her optimism was premature. She had just sat down in the cafeteria to have lunch with Katie, when Sean Miller, the president of the student environmental club, approached their table.

"Did you tell her yet, Katie?" he asked. Katie gestured to her mouth, indicating she was chewing and couldn't respond.

Lily didn't want Sean hovering over them while they ate, so she asked, "Tell me what?"

"Katie was supposed to give you a heads-up, as a courtesy." He paused to shoot Katie an annoyed look. "The student environmental club has decided to circulate a petition to boycott Lindgren cranberries because of your family's disregard for the environment."

"Wh-what?" Lily spluttered. The Lindgrens had long been admired for their commitment to sustainable agriculture practices. Other growers on the island frequently sought out Lily's granddad and uncle for advice about enhancing the environmental quality of their property. And every spring, the family would organize, fund and lead a volunteer clean-up event in the wildlife sanctuary. The notion that the community would penalize them for an accidental fire was outrageous and Lily jeered, "Good luck with that. Nobody in Hope Haven is going to sign your stupid little petition."

"For your information, three businesses are already seriously considering signing it, Lily—and Bleecker's ice cream shop is one of them."

"Yeah, okay." Lily's voice dripped with sarcasm, a trick she'd picked up from Aiden.

"Tell her, Katie," Sean demanded.

Lily looked at Katie, who wouldn't look back at her. "For real? Your uncle's actually signing a petition to boycott our farm?"

Katie lifted one shoulder and let it drop, still avoiding Lily's eyes. "I don't know. Maybe."

Lily was too stupefied to respond, but Sean repeated, "Like I said, the environmental club thought you should have a heads-up before the petition picks up any more support. I hope you know it's nothing personal."

After he walked away, Lily practically hissed at her friend, "Yes, it is. It's *very* personal. I'm your best friend and Dahlia has always been so nice to you. Your family has known my uncle and granddad for decades. How could you let your uncle do this to us?"

"He hasn't signed it yet. The only reason he's even considering it is probably because Sean's going out with my cousin Lexi." Katie's eyes were watering. "Besides, it's not as if we buy that many cranberries from your farm anyway, so even if he does sign it, it won't make a big difference."

The Lindgrens' farm was the sole cranberry supplier for all the markets on Dune Island. They also sold dried berries to local bakeries and to Bleecker's ice cream shop for use in their homemade products. Granted, the quantity of dried fruit the Lindgrens sold was negligible compared to the volume of fresh berries they sold to several large off-island markets in Massachusetts. But the islanders took pride in reciprocating support for each other's businesses. Most tourists seemed to favor foods prepared with local produce, so ultimately the cranberries increased sales for the Bleeckers, as well as for the Lindgrens.

"It's not about the quantity. It's about the *relationship* and it *will* make a big difference," Lily retorted pointedly.

"You're right. I shouldn't have said that," Katie acknowledged. "I feel terrible about all of this. That's why I didn't tell you sooner. I tried super hard to convince my uncle not to sign it, but you know what Lexi is like. She always gets her way. I don't know what else I can do to change my uncle's mind."

Katie's face was blotchy and a tear dripped from the corner of her eye. As disappointed and humiliated as Lily felt because of the petition, she recognized that it wasn't her friend's fault. She gave her a wry smile and joked, "You could threaten to boycott the ice cream shop."

Katie made a sound as if she wanted to laugh but it came out like a gurgle. "I'm really sorry, Lily," she cried, the tears flowing freely now.

"It's okay. I know it's not your fault." Lily pushed a napkin across the table. "You'd better stop crying or else someone's going to start a rumor that I slapped you or something."

Katie sniffled. "Yeah, they'll say we had a catfight over Steve Reagan."

Lily chuckled, glad that things were back to normal between her and her best friend again.

On one hand, knowing that the photography association wouldn't announce the competition winner during the weekend was exasperating to Lily. On the other hand, it gave her a welcome break from obsessively checking her email or staring at her phone, willing it to ring. The weekend also provided her with a reprieve from hearing more gossip about Dahlia, the fire, and the boycott of the farm.

Lily decided to spend Saturday afternoon taking photos of waves breaking against the rocks. She wasn't very skilled at action shots and she was looking forward to developing her technique.

Maybe Dahlia will go wading with me, now that she doesn't have to help Uncle Martin so much. All week, Lily's uncle had been pushing himself to resume his usual activities, in spite of his pain. Today he was helping Lars repair an outboard motor in the workshop, which would keep them occupied for hours.

By the time Lily had completed her own chores, a drizzly fog had rolled in. Even though the weather wasn't conducive to the kinds of photos she wanted to take, she figured it was still warm enough for beachcombing and she went next door to ask Dahlia to join her.

Lily hadn't realized that Aiden was home until she was halfway down the hall to the cottage and she heard him yelling, "You have no idea how humiliating this is for me. You're a total embarrassment!"

Lily abruptly spun around. It literally made her sick to hear Aiden yelling at his mother like that. She understood how difficult it was for him to cope with all the gossip from their peers, but it wasn't as if Dahlia had *intended* to embarrass him.

After getting her camera from her room, she scribbled a note saying she was going to the community center. Kyle had set up a high-quality printer for workshop participants to use and she decided to print out the photos she'd taken before the fire.

Maybe I'll get to see Kyle, too, she thought. His fellowship had ended, and he was leaving the island the following Tuesday or Wednesday. Lily secretly hoped that she'd hear the competition results before he left. Whether she won or lost, she wanted to talk to him about it in person. So, she'd been putting off saying goodbye, but she realized today might be her last chance.

However, the room reserved for the photography workshop participants was empty. When Lily printed out her photos, she was surprised to see one of Dahlia standing on the deck of the shack. Until then, she'd forgotten she'd furtively taken it right before she'd brought her granddad to his doctor's appointment.

At the time, Lily had thought her aunt's expression was contemplative, but as she studied it now, she recognized that her aunt looked harried. She looked absolutely exhausted. *No wonder she needed time alone.* In retrospect, Lily realized she shouldn't have felt so put out when Dahlia had snapped at her. *I definitely shouldn't have taken her photo without her permission, either.*

She was so lost in thought she didn't notice that someone had come into the room until they were right in front of her. It was Kyle and Natasha, his girlfriend from New York. Lily quickly slid Dahlia's photo into the folder with her other prints. After greeting her, Kyle told Lily he'd come to collect the last of his things; he was leaving on Sunday afternoon.

"Oh, that's too bad. I was kind of hoping you'd be here when the competition results are announced," Lily openly admitted.

"Yeah, Kyle's great at giving moral support." Natasha interjected, wrapping her arms around his waist. "That's one of the reasons I can't wait to have him back in New York with me."

"Lily doesn't need moral support—she's going to win," Kyle told Natasha.

"Well, even if I don't, I wanted to say thanks for everything you taught me. And for, you know, believing in my ability and helping me improve and all that stuff..." Lily suddenly felt very awkward trying to express herself, especially in front of Natasha.

But Kyle pushed his hair out of his eyes and grinned. "I had a great time being your teacher. You remind me of myself when I was your age, except you have a lot more potential than I did. A lot more natural talent, too. You're going to go far, Lily."

In contrast to all the negative remarks she'd heard that week at school, Kyle's praise was so overwhelmingly uplifting that it made Lily's cheeks burn. "Thank you," she squeaked. She quickly gathered her things and wished the pair a good trip to New York.

She was barely out the door when she heard Natasha giggle and ask, "Did you see her blush? I think someone has a little schoolgirl crush on you. It's a good thing she doesn't look anything like her aunt, or I'd be worried you'd fall for her."

"Knock it off, Natasha," Kyle growled. "That's totally inappropriate."

Lily was initially surprised that Natasha even knew who her aunt was, until she remembered that Natasha had met Dahlia at Kyle's gallery exhibit last fall. Lily recalled how excited she'd been to introduce her aunt to Kyle. They'd hardly had a chance to shake hands before Natasha had dragged him away to say hello to her friends who'd just arrived from New York. She'd been so dismissive of Lily and her aunt that it had almost seemed as if they were invisible.

Obviously, Dahlia had made more of an impression on Natasha than she'd let on. Lily speculated, *maybe Natasha is jealous because Kyle made a remark about how attractive he thought Dahlia was or something.* It wouldn't have been the first time a man had commented on her aunt's appearance. Not that it mattered to Dahlia; when it came to compliments about her looks, the only man whose opinion she cared about was Martin's.

When Lily got home she found Dahlia sitting at the table in the farmhouse kitchen. Her eyes were red-rimmed and she was blowing her nose into a tattered tissue. Lily hadn't ever seen her aunt crying like this before and she could only guess that Dahlia had somehow found out about the proposed boycott. Lily rushed to her side.

"What's wrong?"

"He's gone and he's not coming back," she wailed.

For a moment, Lily thought Dahlia was referring to Kyle, which didn't make any sense. Her next thought was that Dahlia was referring to Lars or Martin; she'd meant that one of them had died and she couldn't bring herself to say the words.

"Who isn't coming back?" When Dahlia didn't answer, Lily panicked and asked the question louder, "*Who* isn't coming back?"

"Aiden."

Relieved, Lily sank into a chair. "He's threatened to leave before, but he never did, so maybe he's just saying that again because he's angry or something."

"No, this time he meant it. He's really gone." Dahlia cried harder, her shoulders shaking. "I accepted a long time ago that he'd leave once he turned eighteen, but we had an agreement. He promised he'd finish school first. Now he's going to miss his final exams and he won't graduate. I don't get it. He was doing so much better here than in Jersey. But now he's going to throw away two years of hard work just to spite me."

Lily was taken aback to hear Dahlia openly admit how frustrated she'd been with her son. Usually, she didn't say a single word to anyone about Aiden's behavior, no matter how obnoxious it was. What was even more astonishing was that Dahlia indicated her son was doing *better* in Hope Haven. *If this is the new and improved Aiden, I'd hate to meet the New Jersey Aiden,* she silently mused as she patted her aunt's hand.

"I'm sorry you're so upset, Dahlia. But I really don't think Aiden left for good. I mean, he probably doesn't have much money, right? I bet he'll be back as soon as he runs out of cash."

Dahlia didn't look convinced. She pushed her chair away from the table and rose to her feet. "I need to be alone for a while. Can you make supper tonight? There's steak in the fridge."

"Sure. Do you want me to bring a plate to your room when it's ready?"

"No, thanks. I'm going out."

Maybe it was because Dahlia rarely left the farm in the evening by herself, but for the next several hours, Lily had the dreadful feeling that her aunt had fled the island for good, too, just like Aiden. Even after she heard Dahlia's car rolling up the driveway a little past nine o'clock, Lily couldn't shake the sense of foreboding.

Why do I feel like this? Dahlia might be upset, but she's going to be okay, she tried to reassure herself. *Eventually, the gossip about the fire will die down and the petition for the boycott won't get enough signatures. People will move on to talking something else—they always do. The worst of this is behind us now.*

But after tossing and turning for hours in her bed, Lily knew the only thing that would calm her was to concentrate on something entirely different. She thought of what Kyle had said to her this afternoon. "You have a lot of potential... A lot of talent... You're going to go far," she repeated, over and over again.

CHAPTER SIXTEEN

NOW

FRIDAY

Despite her resolution not to dwell on the past, Lily had spent the last two hours mentally reliving the fire and its aftermath. It wasn't as if she'd *intended* to think about it. It was more like she'd been drifting in and out of memories, while simultaneously drifting in and out of sleep.

Now, she woke to the sound of her stomach growling. She was so groggy that for a moment, she couldn't figure out if the fire had ever happened or if it had only been a dream. A nightmare. However, within seconds, the haziness of sleep evaporated, and Lily knew that the fire—and everything else that occurred during her senior year of high school—had been undeniably real.

Yes, it happened, but it happened eighteen years ago, she reminded herself. *It's in the past and that's where I have to leave it.*

She refocused her thoughts on practical matters in the present. Until her salary was deposited, she only had enough cash to buy supper for herself tonight. But first thing in the morning, she'd go get groceries for her and Ryan. *I'll come back and put everything in the farmhouse kitchen before I catch the ferry to meet Leanne and Tim and pick up Ryan,* she schemed, her project management skills kicking in. *I'd also better make a motel reservation, before there aren't any lodging vacancies on the island. Dahlia's room isn't big enough for both Ryan and me, and I still don't feel comfortable staying in it anyway.*

Planning for her son's arrival gave Lily a burst of energy. She flew out the door, intending take a drive to the market, but when she reached the staircase, she stopped short and her posture stiffened. Jake was standing at the bottom, balancing a pizza box on his palm at shoulder level and gripping a large brown paper bag in his other hand.

"Pizza delivery. Salad and drinks, too," he announced, a smile crinkling the skin around his eyes. Instead of his usual Lindgren T-shirt, he was wearing a short-sleeve button-down chambray shirt. "Can I come up?"

As hungry as she was, Lily hesitated. She appreciated that Jake had been through a lot of upheaval at work lately and she was grateful that he'd agreed to help Steve find a buyer for the farm. But that wasn't quite the same as apologizing to her for what he'd said and how he'd behaved toward her yesterday. She didn't feel like she could let his attitude slide, but she didn't especially want to confront him about it, either.

"Please, Lily?" he urged, his brows knit as he peered up at her from the bottom step. "I've been waiting since this morning to apologize and to explain why I've been behaving like such a jerk."

That was all she needed to hear—for now. Lily stepped aside and beckoned him. "C'mon. I'm starving."

Because it was drizzling out, they decided to eat inside the shack. Jake pulled a couple of short deck chairs down from the loft and they sat opposite each other. The lounger served as a low picnic table and when Jake leaned forward to arrange their food and drinks on top of it, Lily noticed his sandy-blond locks were damp. *Is that from the rain or did he go home and take a shower?*

It occurred to her that his first choice for a dinner date might have canceled on him, but even if Lily was the runner-up, she was too hungry to take offense. He seemed as ravenous as she was and they ate with gusto, making small talk in between bites.

When they'd both finished their meals, Jake scratched his chin and cleared his throat, obviously gearing up to transition into a more serious conversation. "Like I, um, like I said earlier, I want to apologize for my attitude in general and especially for the things I said to you yesterday. I've been majorly stressed but usually I handle it better than that. It was completely unfair for me to take out my frustrations on you."

Lily met his eyes and nodded. "I understand. Tourist season is a terribly busy time of year and the farm's grand opening is right around the corner. You've been under a lot of pressure, especially since you don't have Dahlia here to help you."

"That's true, but stress wasn't my only issue. I guess I sort of panicked when you confirmed you're selling the estate and the business. I was worried that I'd be out of a job or that a new owner might not share the same vision for the farm that Dahlia and I had. Then all our hard work would be for nothing." Jake's face fell and he looked down at his knees, as if he were visualizing the scenario he'd just described.

"I was going to tell you that we'd only sell the estate to someone who'd retain your managerial services," Lily said. "But you stormed off before I could."

"I know. Steve told me this morning that you'd made it a condition of the sale." Jake looked utterly chagrined. "I felt like a complete idiot—and I deserved to feel that way, after all those things I said to you. I'm sorry."

"I accept your apology. But there's something I'd like you to understand." She leaned forward for emphasis. "Like I said before, just because I'm selling the farm doesn't mean I don't appreciate all the work you've done to keep it in business. I was being sincere when I said I was impressed by the changes you've made. I truly care about the farm's future, which is why it's so important to me that we find a buyer who will employ you as the manager, for as long as you're willing to stay."

"Thanks for saying that." Jake hemmed a little. "Er, this isn't really any of my business, so if you don't want to explain, that's fine. But I'm curious about why you've decided to sell the estate?"

Lily figured he deserved an answer; after all, any decision that affected the farm affected Jake, too. So she told him the same things she'd told Steve; primarily that the money from the sale would help her repay the formidable amount of debt she and her husband had amassed when Tyler was ill. Also, that she didn't think it would be good to uproot her son from their home and friends in Philadelphia.

"Oh, I see."

Lily had the sense that he didn't believe her, so she pressed, "Is there something else you want to ask?"

"Well, the other day when I suggested that you bring Ryan here for a couple days, you had a pretty intense reaction. I know you said he hates road trips, but it almost seemed as if... as if you hate it here."

Maybe it was because the room had grown dim and raindrops were gently pattering the rooftop, creating a sense of intimacy. Or maybe it was that Lily was tired of trying to process her emotions and her thoughts on her own. But for whatever reason, she found herself opening up to Jake in a way she wouldn't normally do.

"I don't *hate* it here. Actually there are a lot of things I love about Dune Island and especially about the farm. Things I've missed and things I hadn't even realized I missed about this place until I came back again. Of course, I miss my family most of all. Even though it's been years since my grandma and granddad died—my uncle Martin, too—being here makes me so lonely for them that sometimes I can hardly stand it." Feeling close to tears, Lily swallowed. "That's why seeing the photos in the education center reduced me to a sniveling wreck."

"Ug. I'm such a dolt." Jake clutched the top of his head. "I knew you were upset when you shot out of the room, but I assumed it was because you disapproved of the timeline. I was worried you felt like I was exploiting your ancestors—which wasn't my intention in creating the display. I wanted to honor your family, not exploit them. I certainly didn't mean to make you cry."

"I appreciate that and I'm not blaming you—I was only giving you an example of how sentimental I've been since I came back to Hope Haven," she explained. "I have so many memories associated with this place... Not all of them are of my family and unfortunately, not all of them are pleasant, which is one of the reasons I didn't want Ryan to come here. Dune Island isn't always the most positive environment. Some of the people here are very gossipy and their remarks can be extremely upsetting—especially to a child."

"You mean, like the hurtful comments people made after the conservation land caught fire?" Jake gently questioned her and Lily nodded. There was no need to ask him how he'd known about those rumors; he'd undoubtedly heard them, too. His voice was even quieter when he asked, "Is that why you left the island?"

Lily blinked, momentarily speechless. He was getting too close to the truth for her comfort, and she answered his question with a question. "Who told you that—Dahlia?"

"No. She'd never discuss something like that with me and neither would Martin. I was making an assumption based on the timing of when you left Dune Island, that's all," he explained.

Realizing Jake didn't know about her secret heartache or what really happened, Lily relaxed a little. "It's complicated, but you're right. The damaging comments people made after the fire played a role in my decision to leave Dune Island." She took the opportunity to change the subject. "But I'm here now and despite my qualms, my son will actually be joining me tomorrow."

After filling him in on the Cramer grandchildren's accident and her car situation, Lily requested that Jake not mention in front of Ryan that she had inherited the farm. "If he found out that I still technically own the estate, he'd want to live here. Then I'd have to tell him we can't afford it, which would break his heart."

"He'd want to live in Hope Haven even though he's so happy living in Philadelphia?" Jake teased.

"Ryan would want to live in a tree house or in a zoo or on a rowboat, if he could," Lily said with a laugh before turning serious. "But what he wants and what he needs are sometimes two different things. And since he's a child and I'm his mother, I'm responsible for deciding what's best for him."

"No argument there," Jake acknowledged, grinning.

He bent his arms, interlocking his fingers behind his head. Even though the room was almost dark now, Lily could still make out the pale undersides of his biceps. She had to admit her curiosity was stoked about whether he was seeing anyone or not.

She hinted, "So, what kinds of things do you like to do when you're not working?"

"When I'm not working? Let's see if I can remember... Oh yeah, I like to sleep. And eat. Occasionally, I like to take a shower."

"Oh, c'mon. You're not *that* overworked, are you?"

"Nah. I'm just that boring. Dahlia was the same way. She used to joke that we were like two berries in a bog, instead of two peas in a pod."

Lily's shoulders slumped with disappointment. Without giving it a second thought, she blurted out, "Were you two in a relationship?"

There was a rustle as Jake lowered his arms and sat up straight. "No way, not like that."

His objection was so authentic that Lily intuitively believed him—and she instantly regretted her question. "Sorry, that was intrusive," she apologized. "Your personal relationship with Dahlia was none of my business."

"It's fine," Jake said. Yet he made a point of clarifying, "But we didn't have a *personal* relationship. We worked together, and I considered her a friend in the same way I considered Martin to be a friend. The reason Dahlia called us two berries in a bog was because we were alike in the sense that the farm was our main interest. The work is so demanding and so satisfying that we didn't have a lot of time or desire for other pursuits. I had a world of respect for Dahlia and I enjoyed working with her, but we never even really socialized together."

"Well, I'm glad you and *I* socialized together this evening." Lily switched on her flashlight so she could see to gather their used paper plates and napkins. "Thank you for dinner—it hit the spot."

"I enjoyed it, too. I'm glad we got the chance to talk and it was nice not to have to eat by myself for once," Jake said, unwittingly satisfying Lily's curiosity about whether he was seeing anyone. "If there's anything you need while your son is here, let me know."

After he left, Lily sat on the deck, reflecting on their conversation. Although the misty rain had let up, the sky was pitch-black and she could barely see the deck railing five feet in front of her. As relieved as Lily was that she and Jake had cleared the air between them, she regretted asking him if he'd been in a relationship with Dahlia.

"Why in the world would I ask him something like that?" she muttered to herself. But the reason was painfully obvious, no matter how hard she tried not to remember.

CHAPTER SEVENTEEN

THEN

SPRING, LILY'S SENIOR YEAR OF HIGH SCHOOL

"Come on, Dahlia. Dipping your toes in the ocean will make you feel better," Lily wheedled her aunt after lunch on the Sunday following the day Aiden left the farm. Dahlia had stayed in her room all morning because she had a headache. Considering how puffy her eyes were, Lily assumed she'd gotten the headache from crying.

"Yeah, Dahlia, go enjoy the water with Lily," Martin urged. "I'll take care of the dishes."

"I can give him a hand," Lars chimed in.

"Wow, you two really must be fed up with my moping around here if you're willing to do the dishes just to get rid of me," she retorted, poking fun at them as well as at herself. "If it means that much to you, I guess I'll go."

A few minutes later as they were walking through the woods, Lily tried to get her aunt's mind off Aiden by telling her she'd seen Kyle the previous day at the community center. "I'm glad I got to say goodbye to him, because he's leaving the island today."

"Oh, yeah? Did he, uh, say anything other than goodbye?"

Uh-oh. She must be able to tell from my face that he compli-mented my photography, Lily thought. But it seemed vain to repeat his remarks, so she kept her answer vague. "He said he liked having me in the workshop. His girlfriend was with him, though, so it wasn't like we talked a lot about photography or anything."

Dahlia smiled as they approached the clearing and caught their first glimpse of the ocean through the stubby scrub oak trees. The water was so blue that the sky literally paled in comparison, and the air was perfumed with the scent of lily of the valley and rosa rugosa. "I feel better already," she said. "Hey, you didn't bring your camera."

Lily shrugged. "Kyle says sometimes you need to set your camera aside and just be present in the moment."

"I'm going to miss hearing what Kyle says," Dahlia gently teased.

"Yeah. Me, too."

As they neared the shack, Dahlia suggested they lounge in the sun for a while because she was too cold to go beach-combing in bare feet at the moment. Lily took the stairs by twos ahead of her so she could pull the deck chairs down from the storage loft. But she came to an abrupt halt when she noticed a small square of cardboard taped to the door of the shack.

"Look, someone left a note."

"What does it say?"

Lily took it down and read the words aloud before her mind could comprehend their meaning. Addressed to Dahlia, it said, "You're lucky I didn't tell your husband that you and Kyle were hooking up in your cozy little love shack while the farm was burning. Next time, you'd better think twice before you play with fire!"

Confounded, Lily reread the message silently and then said,

"I don't get it. Why would anyone write something like this? Kyle's never even been here."

Dahlia snatched the note from her hands. "Let me see that." Her cheeks darkened from bright pink to deep red as she examined the note and then flipped it over. The back was blank. She ripped the cardboard into little bits before Lily could stop her.

"Hey! I could have studied the handwriting to figure out who wrote it."

"It doesn't matter who wrote it—it's rubbish and it's going straight into the trash."

Ordinarily, Lily might have agreed that ignoring the inane rumor was the best way to deal with it. But this note went way beyond the kind of ridiculous baloney kids spread at school. Someone had planned ahead—they'd even brought adhesive tape to post the note—to deliberately malign Dahlia.

"Somebody trespassed on our property on purpose to harass you," she exclaimed. "We should report this to the police."

"Considering the fire, I don't think I'm really in the position to complain about trespassers."

"But what they wrote is a lie and that makes it libel or slander or something. It's illegal. Seriously, we could sue them."

"Yes, it's definitely a lie that..." Dahlia squeezed her eyes shut and shook her head, as if it pained her to say the words. "It's definitely a lie that there's anything going on between Kyle and me, but I did see him walking on the beach the day of the fire. I waved to him and he came up to say hello."

"Wh-what?" Lily couldn't believe her ears. "How come you never told me that?"

"My mind was a mess after I spoke to the police and the fire department." Dahlia rolled her eyes as if mocking herself. "I guess I forgot to mention it later because it wasn't important."

Lily felt queasy. Despite her aunt's nonchalant response, something about her story wasn't adding up. "I can see why you'd wave to each other, but why would Kyle come all the way up the stairs to the shack to talk to you? You hardly know him."

"True, but I went to his exhibit last autumn with you and I've crossed paths with him in town from time to time. He knows I'm your aunt. He was just being friendly."

Again, it struck Lily as odd that Dahlia had never said anything about occasionally bumping into Kyle in town. Had she been hiding that information or was it really so inconsequential that she didn't think it was worth mentioning?

"What did you talk about when he came up here?"

"I don't know. The weather, maybe. The view? I can hardly remember—except that he made a comment about how talented you are. I felt very proud to be the aunt of his star student."

Dahlia's proud smile made Lily feel guilty for doubting her and for acting so territorial about her instructor. Yet she couldn't keep from asking, one more time, "So that's all you did? You just talked?"

"Yes, I promise. We just talked. In fact, he never even stepped foot inside the shack." She puckered her face into a knot, as if she'd just bitten into a lemon. "Whoever wrote the note must have been down on the beach. They probably saw us on the deck and made up the story as a prank. I don't know why anyone would do something like that, but their mind is in the gutter and they have a twisted sense of humor."

Her concerns finally allayed, Lily sighed. "It was probably one of the kids on the student environmental committee." She reluctantly told her aunt, "They were... they were kind of upset with you about the conservation land burning. But that doesn't give them the right to put a note like this on our door and I still think we should report them. Or we should at least ask Uncle Martin to post a no-trespassing sign. Some of those kids might not care about respecting people's personal lives, but they do care about respecting property boundaries. They probably wouldn't come up here again if they saw a sign."

Dahlia chuckled, even though Lily was being serious. "I'd prefer we didn't mention this to anyone, especially not your uncle or granddad. Martin's already worried about me as it is. He's just getting on his feet again and I'm concerned this will stress him out, and that'll have a negative effect on his recovery."

Her words had a familiar ring to them, but it took a moment for Lily to remember when she'd heard them before. It was the day she'd found her aunt in the laundry room, talking on the phone. *My husband absolutely can't find out about this... he'll suffer a major health setback,* she'd said. Lily had assumed Dahlia was talking to someone about the cranberry business, but what if she was wrong? What if she'd been warning Kyle that Martin couldn't find out Dahlia was having an affair with him?

Pushing the ugly thought from her mind, Lily agreed, "I won't say anything about it to anyone, I promise. But, um... these kinds of things have a way of getting around, especially at school."

"Oh, dear. I'm really sorry about that." Dahlia sounded so contrite that Lily felt bad for her, especially because Aiden had just blamed her for embarrassing him.

"That's okay. I'm used to their gossip. I can handle it," Lily assured her. Besides, maybe the kids would be more interested in talking about Aiden running away than about Dahlia and Kyle's supposed affair.

Dahlia wiped sweat from her forehead. "You know what? It's actually hotter than I thought it was going to be out here. Instead of lounging around, let's take a walk by the water. We'll cool our feet and forget about this nonsense."

"Sounds good to me," Lily agreed.

However, for the rest of the day, the note was all Lily could think about. *Who would have been upset enough about the fire to hike down the beach or through the conservation land to post a note like this?*

She'd already figured it might be someone from the environmental club at school, but who? Sean, the president, seemed the most likely person. But could it have been someone else, like Katie's cousin? Maybe during the weekend Katie had convinced her uncle not to sign the boycott petition, so Lexi had found another way to teach Dahlia a lesson.

Then it occurred to her that Aiden may have written the note. He'd been furious at his mother for humiliating him. Maybe threatening to embarrass her with a made-up story was a form of revenge. A power play.

Out of the blue, a more troubling possibility occurred to Lily. Maybe Aiden wasn't making up the story about his mother; maybe it was true. What if yesterday when he'd been shouting at her for humiliating him—and herself—he hadn't been referring to the fire? What if he'd been referring to her relationship with Kyle?

No way, that can't be it. Dahlia swore that she and Kyle were just talking and nothing happened between them. I'd take her word over Aiden's any day, Lily rationalized. *Besides, Aiden wasn't even home the afternoon of the fire. And Dahlia would never ever do that to Martin.*

Next, her mind leaped to what Natasha had said to Kyle about being relieved that Lily wasn't as attractive as her aunt. Had Natasha suspected something was going on between Dahlia and Kyle? *Could she have been following Kyle the day of the fire? Maybe she'd seen him and Dahlia together at the shack, but she didn't want to break up with Kyle, so she only retaliated against Dahlia.*

It was a preposterous scenario but she struggled to rein in her imagination. She focused on how much Dahlia loved her uncle. Lily had witnessed her aunt's devotion to Martin for two years and it was even stronger now than when they first married. She'd seen it plain and clear in her actions on a daily basis, and especially while he was recovering from back surgery.

Although she didn't know Kyle nearly as well as she knew her aunt, Lily doubted he'd get involved with a married woman. Judging from the utter disgust in his voice when he'd told Natasha that what she'd said was inappropriate, he was too principled. He also cared too much about his reputation as an artist to do something so unseemly during his residency on Dune Island.

I can't believe I'm even considering the possibility that the note was true, Lily thought. *That's as ridiculous as any of the rumors I've heard kids repeating at school.*

Yet ridiculous or not, she still wished she knew who had taped the note to the shack wall. At least when her classmates gossiped, they did it openly, which meant that Lily could try to set the records straight, for whatever good it did. But because the author of the note was anonymous, Lily had no opportunity to respond.

And since the message could have come from *any*one, she felt mistrustful of almost *every*one. She hated hat she suspected people she'd considered to be friends, but she couldn't seem to stop turning over all the possibilities in her mind.

Her frustration about not knowing who'd written it continued into the evening and kept her awake throughout the night. By first light she knew she couldn't function until she'd slept for a couple of hours. She jotted a note and set it on the kitchen table, knowing that Dahlia would understand. It read:

I didn't sleep at all last night. I might go into school later, but first I need a really long nap. When Steve comes to pick me up, can someone please let him know?

Thanks,

L.

Then she crawled back into bed, relieved that she wasn't going to have to listen to the buzz about Aiden or Dahlia from her peers for a few more hours. Because contrary to what she'd told her aunt, Lily really didn't feel like she could handle it.

"Lily. Lily, wake up!" Dahlia's voice dragged Lily from a long, deep slumber.

Bleary-eyed and confused, she glanced at the clock: it was 3:30. She couldn't figure out what day it was, or what she was doing in bed at that time in the afternoon. "What's wrong?"

"You have a call—it's the photography association." Dahlia handed her the phone.

"Hello?" she croaked.

"Is this Lily Lindgren?" A male's deep voice questioned.

She cleared her throat. "Yes, it is."

"This is Alonzo Trapper. I'm the president of MPPA and I'm calling to congratulate you on winning this year's amateur photography competition."

Still dopey from sleep, Lily lowered the phone from her ear and earnestly asked Dahlia, "Am I dreaming or is this for real?"

"It's for real—keep talking to him or he'll think you hung up!"

Lily listened as Alonzo told her the association judges were impressed by her ability to capture the "extraordinary within the ordinary" in her photos. He also expressed how much they admired her composition and use of shadow and light. After thanking him and disconnecting the call, she stared at the phone in her hand, dazed.

"Well?" Dahlia prompted her. "What did he say?"

"He said I won." It started to sink in. She looked at Dahlia's beautiful, beaming face and repeated, "I *won!*"

"Who-hoo!" Dahlia cheered and tackled her in a bear hug. "Congratulations!"

When her aunt released her, Lily jumped out of bed to go tell her grandfather and uncle. She raced out of the farmhouse in her pajamas, shouting from halfway across the bog, "Granddad! My photos won the competition! They won, they won!"

"Well, how about that," he said when she reached him. She noticed a tear slip from his eye. He swiped it away with his heavy work glove. "If your grandma was here, she'd be even prouder than I am. She always said you were gifted."

Too choked up to speak, Lily stretched her arms as far as she could reach around her granddad's stomach. With her ear pressed against his chest, she could hear his heart beating. From the rapid pace of it, she could tell he was every bit as ecstatic as she was.

When Lily repeated the news to Martin back at the cottage, he embraced her, just as her aunt and granddad had done. Lily had noticed ever since he married Dahlia, her uncle was slowly turning into a big softie. He gave hugs more often now, but this one was especially meaningful since she knew his back was still sore.

"I'll take everyone out to Captain Clark's restaurant to celebrate," he offered. "You can bring Katie and Steve. We can invite Mrs. Henderson, if you want, too."

Aware of how tight money was, Lily was moved by her uncle's offer. But she was also concerned that she might see one of her classmates in the restaurant and they'd say something about Aiden or Dahlia that would ruin the Lindgrens' festive mood.

"Thanks, but can we order takeout and eat it at home? I'd like to celebrate here. It's kind of symbolic, since our family and the cranberry farm are the subjects of my collection."

"Sure." Dahlia answered for Martin; she was probably as

eager as Lily was to avoid going out in public. "But don't you want to invite your friends?"

"No. I'm going to wait until tomorrow to tell anyone else. Tonight, I just want it to be the four of us. Or the five of us—if Aiden comes home."

Lily was only trying to be inclusive, but when Dahlia's face clouded over, she wished she hadn't mentioned Aiden. However, her aunt recovered quickly, saying, "You never know, he just might do that."

Even though she'd slept for most of the day, that evening Lily went to her room before nine o'clock. The big meal had made her drowsy, so she stretched out in bed and reread her short but sweet text exchange with Kyle for the fifth or sixth time:

Guess what? she'd typed.

He replied: *u won!*

Yes. Can u believe it?!

Never any doubt. V well deserved

Thx.

Lily set her phone on her nightstand, ashamed that she'd ever been worried Kyle was involved in an affair with her aunt. *Maybe on some level I was looking for evidence that he wasn't as sincere as I thought he was because I felt insecure about my photos,* she thought, analyzing herself.

She rolled onto her side and closed her eyes, eager for sleep. *I can't wait until tomorrow, when the kids at school find out I won the contest,* she thought. Finally, the Lindgren family was going to give them something worth talking about.

. . .

It seemed as if hardly a minute had passed when Lily was woken by a bright light. Once again, Dahlia was telling her to wake up. Even in her drowsy state, Lily recognized that this time the urgency in her aunt's voice wasn't because Dahlia had good news to share.

Lily bolted upright. "What's wrong?"

"Your granddad was having chest pain. Martin's driving him to the hospital. They just left."

Before Dahlia could ask if she wanted to go to the ER, too, Lily was stripping off her pajamas and pulling on jeans and a T-shirt. "I'm ready, let's go," she said.

On the way there, Dahlia filled her in on what had happened. "Martin and I didn't know it, but Lars never went to bed last night because he was experiencing chest pain. He thought it was indigestion from eating such a heavy meal, so he didn't want to worry anyone. He said he considered driving himself to the hospital, but he knew he isn't supposed to drive until his new glasses come in and he didn't want me to lecture him about his safety."

Dahlia chuckled and so did Lily. She was consoled by the thought, *if Granddad was talking and making jokes, whatever's wrong with him can't be too serious.*

"Anyway, he kept taking antacids and trying to manage the pain until around four-thirty, when Martin got up and saw the light on in the house. Lars asked him for a ride to the hospital. I was worried about Martin driving—because of his back—but Lars refused to let me take him. He said this was a father and son trip."

This time when she chuckled, it sounded as if Dahlia had something caught in her throat. "He told me not to wake you—but I didn't agree to that. Lars said that after such an exciting day, you needed your sleep and that he'd be back home before you left for school anyway."

"I kind of doubt it. They'll probably make him go through

all three of the heart tests at once, now. It's going to take a while. Poor Granddad—he's not going to be happy about this."

"What heart tests?"

"You know, the tests his cardiologist told him he needed. The first one was a stress test. I don't know what the other two were. I thought you would have pried the info about them out of him by now."

"This is the first I've heard of any cardio tests. That's really odd. I wonder why he didn't mention them to me, since he would have needed a ride to the doctor's office." It took Dahlia a couple moments to figure out the answer. She clapped her hand to her forehead and expressed what Lily was already thinking. "He went to the cardiologist on the day of the fire—*that's* why he didn't tell me. Things were so chaotic afterward, he probably didn't want to make a fuss. Just like last night, when he was having chest pain and he didn't want to wake us up. I should have made a point of asking him what the doctor had said."

Lily touched her arm. "It's not your fault, Dahlia. I knew he had a stress test, so *I* probably should have mentioned it. Or Granddad should have told you after things settled down on the farm. But it doesn't matter, because he'll get them in the ER— maybe it's even better this way, because he'll get them done right away, instead of waiting for an appointment."

"I hope you're right."

So do I, Lily thought, feeling less certain than she'd felt a minute ago that her granddad's condition wasn't serious.

Hope Haven's only hospital was located in Port Newcomb, which was fewer than ten minutes from the farm. But right when Lily and Dahlia arrived in town, a long line of supply trucks disembarked the early morning ferry, blocking the inter-section they needed to cross.

By the time traffic cleared again, Lily was so anxious to find out how her granddad was that she almost asked to be dropped off at the ER entrance. But her aunt seemed every bit as nervous as she was, so Lily stayed with her while she parked the car. As they were rushing up the walkway, the automatic doors parted and Martin limped out, his features gnarled into an ashen grimace.

He must be in pain from driving here. That's why he looks like that. He probably came out here to stretch and get some air while Granddad is having the heart tests done, Lily tried to convince herself.

But when her uncle stumbled forward, buried his face against Dahlia's shoulder and wept into her hair, Lily knew what it meant: like Selma and Aiden and Kyle, her granddad was gone.

CHAPTER EIGHTEEN

THEN

After her grandfather's funeral, Lily stayed home from school for a week. By the time she returned, no one mentioned a word about Aiden leaving the island. They didn't show any sign they knew about the note posted to the wall of the shack, either. Maybe they'd forgotten about it by then or maybe they were consumed with finishing their classes and preparing for their final exams.

Many of them expressed condolences to Lily about her granddad. They also congratulated her on winning the photography competition—someone must have found out and spread the word. But Lily was so detached she could hardly acknowledge their sympathy and compliments. She felt as if she were sleep-walking through the school day until she could get home and go back to sleep for real.

She had forgotten all about the senior dance until Katie invited Lily to go to her house to see the dress she'd bought. Katie didn't have a date, but Hope Haven High's senior dance was a casual, inclusive occasion. Every graduating student was welcome, with or without a partner.

"I can't. I've got something I have to do at the farm," Lily answered. It was true—she was going to take a nap.

"Oh. Well, do you want to catch a ferry to Hyannis on Saturday?"

"Hyannis?"

"Yeah. We can go to the mall. I'll help you pick out a dress."

Lily poked at her pasta with a plastic fork. "I don't need a dress. I'm not going to the dance."

"Aww, really? Maybe you should get a dress just in case."

"I'm not going to change my mind."

Katie was quiet for a few minutes, before saying, "I can understand why you don't feel like going, but it's not going to be nearly as much fun without you there."

"Sorry if I'm spoiling your good time, but the senior dance is the last thing I care about right now."

Lily's remark came across as sarcastic, even though she genuinely regretted disappointing her friend. But she was too weary to explain herself. She stood up and went to throw her lunch in the trash, since she'd lost her taste for food, just like she'd lost her interest in everything else.

Without her granddad there, the farmhouse seemed too big and empty for Lily to live in it by herself, so Dahlia and Martin moved into one of the spare bedrooms. Regardless, Lily rarely saw them for more than a few minutes because she kept to herself, claiming she had to study. More often than not, she was napping. Dahlia and Martin were so busy on the farm and in the workshop they didn't seem to notice how withdrawn she'd become.

However, one Sunday afternoon shortly before Lily's final week of classes, Dahlia insisted she get some fresh air. "I know you're sad, but your granddad would want you to carry on with your life," she said. "C'mon, let's go for a walk on the beach."

They strolled out to the cliff, but when they peered over the edge, they saw the waves were splashing high on shore. Climbing over the slippery rocks would have been too treacherous. Lily went inside the shack and pulled the chairs from the loft so they could relax in the sun, instead.

As she was carrying them to the door, she spotted something from the corner of her eye. Dark and lumpy, it was partially obscured by the stack of boards that Lily had removed from the door and windows. She froze, imagining it might be a raccoon hiding. When it didn't move, she set down the chairs. Creeping forward, she realized it was a duffle bag.

"Look what I found under the pile of boards," she announced when she brought it outside. Without waiting for Dahlia to reply, she unzipped the tote and examined the contents. Inside was a camera, two lenses, and a leather jacket. Lily recognized them immediately and she felt like her stomach dropped to her feet. "These are *Kyle's*. How did they get inside our shack? You said he didn't step a foot over the threshold."

Dahlia gaped like a fish, the color draining from her face. Clearly, she had been caught in a lie. Lily enunciated each word as she repeated, "How did Kyle's stuff get inside our shack?"

"Like I told you, my mind was kind of addled after the fire." Dahlia swallowed. "But-but now I remember that he... he was hot, so he took off his jacket and put it in his bag and set it on the deck. And-and then we were talking and he wanted to get a closer look at that juniper tree." Dahlia gestured toward it but Lily kept her stare focused on her aunt.

"After we, uh, looked at the juniper tree, we circled around to the cliff and chatted for a while. Then Kyle left and I sat on the stairs to watch the waves. By the time I noticed he'd forgotten his things, he was already halfway down the beach. Then I-I-I heard the sirens, so I hid his bag inside under the boards for safekeeping and I ran back to the farmhouse to see what was going on."

Dahlia's story sounded so contrived it was insulting. Did she really think Lily would fall for it? "Kyle must have been awfully distracted to forget his very expensive photography equipment on the deck," she replied in a mocking tone. "I guess whatever happened inside the 'love shack' gave him temporary amnesia."

"Lily, don't talk like that. I've told you before that nothing happened between us. I love your uncle and I'd never deliberately do anything to hurt him. I swear, Kyle and I were just talking."

Lily hardly heard her because she was struck by a sickening thought. "Did Kyle... did he *photograph* you or something?"

"Pfbt." Dahlia had the good nerve make a scoffing sound at the suggestion, even though the things *she'd* been saying were a lot more outrageous. "You know how much I hate having my picture taken."

"Yeah, but you'd make an exception for him." Lily was seething. "Were you even wearing clothes or were you—"

Dahlia's nostrils flared as she pointed a finger an inch from her niece's nose. "Don't you dare finish that question, young lady."

Livid that Dahlia was acting as if *Lily* was the one who'd behaved inappropriately, she threatened, "Okay, if you're so innocent, you won't care if I look at the photos on Kyle's camera."

"Lily, no! Give that to me." Dahlia wrested the camera from her hands with a surprising amount of force. Lily was so stunned she tottered backward. Reaching to steady her, Dahlia apologized repeatedly. "Sorry. I didn't mean to do that. Sorry."

Lily yanked her arm away. "Sorry for what? For practically knocking me over or for cheating on my uncle?"

"How many times do I have to tell you, nothing physical happened between Kyle and me!" Dahlia exclaimed. She paused and rubbed her brow—Lily suspected she was stalling while she concocted a more credible story. "All right, listen. I'll tell you the whole truth, okay?"

"Why start now?" Lily began to walk away but Dahlia grabbed her wrist.

"You were right. I sort of developed a... a friendship with Kyle, if you could even call it that. We were more like friendly acquaintances." She released her grip. Lily didn't leave, but she refused to turn to face her aunt. "I felt like I knew him because you talked about him so much, and I'd met him last fall at his photo exhibition. So, whenever I'd see him in town, it was easy for us to strike up a conversation, especially since we're both relatively new to the island. Anyway, on the day of the fire, I guess I was stressed out because of Martin's botched surgery and Aiden's behavior and all the bills..."

She paused, as if she was waiting for Lily to say something empathetic. Or to acknowledge how much work Dahlia had done and how difficult her circumstances had been. *That's no excuse for getting involved with another man*, Lily thought, keeping mum.

Her aunt continued, "When Kyle stopped by, he asked if he could photograph me by the juniper tree. He said something about the angles of my cheekbones capturing the light. I was flattered, so I let him take a photo of my *face*. That's all there was to it. The rest happened just like I told you—he accidentally left his things behind, so I stashed them in the shack and I completely forgot they were there."

She sounded so sincere and Lily desperately wanted this account of Dahlia's story to be true. Turning to face her, she asked, "How am I supposed to believe you when your story keeps changing?"

Dahlia's eyes pleaded with her as she explained, "The only reason I didn't tell you everything from the beginning was because I thought it would hurt your feelings that I let Kyle take my photo, since I hardly ever let *you* take it. And because I knew how bad the situation looked after someone left that preposterous note on the door. I was afraid it might... it might make you doubt me."

Lily's gaze bore into Dahlia's eyes as she frantically tried to determine whether to believe her or not. Her aunt wouldn't lie right to her face again, would she? Lily couldn't trust her own feelings and she certainly couldn't trust Dahlia's words. There was only way to confirm whether she was telling the truth. Lily held out her hand for the camera. "Let me see the photos Kyle took."

Dahlia's hopeful expression melted into a frown. She closed her eyes and shook her head. "I'm sorry, but no. I can't do that."

A million thoughts stampeded through Lily's mind. The one she expressed was, "Now I know how exactly how Aiden felt—you've completely humiliated me and you've made a total fool of yourself, too!"

Then she turned and flew across the deck and down the stairs, racing away from her aunt and the shack as quickly as she could.

For the next week, as soon as Lily returned home from school, she went directly to her room and she stayed there until the next morning. She told Martin she had term papers to write, and she wouldn't speak to her aunt at all.

Once or twice Lily experienced a fleeting moment of guilt because she had promised her granddad she'd support Dahlia no matter what. But that promise was based on the assumption that the fire was an accident. Lily felt certain that he wouldn't have held her to her word if he'd known Dahlia had left the brush pile to go meet with Kyle.

Lily was almost as angry at Kyle as she was at her aunt, and she blocked him from her cell phone and her email. Not that she expected him to communicate, but just in case, she wanted to be absolutely sure he couldn't reach her.

When Alonzo Trapper sent her a link to the online announcement about the competition results, Lily refused to open it at first. But after a while, curiosity got the better of her and she clicked on the link. The announcement described her photos and it listed the dates when the collection would be published in print and online.

Lily was surprised to see that several of her classmates had posted remarks in the comments section, such as, "3H is proud of you." Or, "Congrats to the most creative student in our class!" And, "You're a rock star, Lily."

Everybody seems really happy for me, she thought as she scrolled through the final comments. *Maybe I've been too focused on the other kinds of stuff some of the kids have been saying lately.*

But the very next message she saw was from an anonymous commenter and it read, "It's fortunate that Lily took photos of her family's cranberry farm before her aunt started it on fire. Too bad she didn't capture pictures of the conservation land for posterity before her aunt burned that down, too."

Lily's stomach lurched and her vision went fuzzy. Thanks to Dahlia, any lingering smidgen of pride she'd felt about her accomplishment was instantly replaced with a deep sense of disgrace. She closed the website, crying to herself, *I never want to have anything to do with Dahlia or Kyle or photography again!*

The following day, while Martin was working in the bogs, Dahlia rapped on Lily's locked door, calling, "Can we please talk? I have something important I want to say to you."

I have nothing *I* want to say *to* you. But on second thought, Lily opened the door. She had *plenty* to say. "How could you do that to Uncle Martin? How could you do that to *me*? Kyle was *my* photography teacher. Are you really that needy? It's so pathetic."

Dahlia held a hand over her heart and looked Lily straight in the eyes, as if to emphasize her sincerity. "I've told you before and I'll tell you again. Nothing happened between Kyle and me —*nothing*. The headshots that he took were sappy, but they weren't indecent. While he was photographing me—"

Lily interrupted her by making a gagging sound. "Yuck. Spare me the details."

"No, please, just listen," Dahlia implored. "While Kyle was photographing me, I tried to look, I don't know, artistic or like a model or something. I've always felt self-conscious about seeing photos of myself, but I knew the ones Kyle had taken would turn out especially awful because of how I was posing—I mean, because of my facial expressions. I was embarrassed by my behavior, but I realize now I should have just shown the photos to you the other day anyway."

The more often she changed her account of what had happened on the day of the fire and the more excuses Dahlia gave for not showing Lily the photos from the start, the more implausible her story sounded. Yet as doubtful as Lily was, deep down she was still hoping that maybe, just maybe, her aunt was truly coming clean about the photos.

She challenged, "Show them to me now."

"I can't—I already shipped Kyle's camera back to him."

"How convenient." Lily snorted, furious that she'd given her aunt another chance and she'd still been burned. She taunted, "Since you've got nothing to hide, does this mean you've told Uncle Martin about your little photo session with Kyle? Have you told him about the note?"

Dahlia shook her head. "I don't want to discuss this with him while he's recovering."

"His back is a lot better now. He's out working in the bogs."

"I meant while he's recovering from losing his father, Lily.

Surely you can understand why this isn't a good time to tell him about a spiteful—and *untrue*—note someone left us." When Dahlia's comment went unacknowledged, she prompted, "I hope you're not going to tell him, either?"

As vindictive as Lily may have felt at that moment, she could never hurt her uncle by telling him what Dahlia had done.

"Of course, I'm not going to tell him your dirty little secret. That's *your* responsibility. *You're* the one who should tell him what kind of woman he married—not that you ever will." Lily's hurt and anger had reached boiling point and she couldn't seem to stop herself from adding, "You know what, Dahlia? When all the other kids at school were talking about how they couldn't believe Uncle Martin had landed a babe like you, or when they said that you were just using him, I defended you. And when Grandma died, I believed what you said about her being ready to go because she knew we'd all look after one another."

"I truly meant that," Dahlia softly replied, her lower lip trembling. "And I've tried my best to take good care of everyone, including you."

"Seriously?" Lily shrieked. "What part of the past few weeks show that you were you taking *good care* of everyone? You started the farm and the park on fire!"

Dahlia mumbled, "That was an accident."

"Was it? Because I've been thinking about that day and I remember very clearly that you couldn't wait to get rid of me. That's because you were *planning* to meet Kyle at the shack, weren't you?"

Dahlia denied it, but her voice carried no conviction. "No. He just dropped by."

"I remember the look on your face that day, too—you were really upset about something." Lily could have shown her the photo to prove it. But then she would have had to confess that she'd taken the picture without permission, and this was about

Dahlia's wrongdoing, not Lily's. "I think you felt guilty about sneaking out to meet Kyle. Or maybe you were worried that he wasn't going to show up. But the fact is, *he* was the reason you were so distracted that you walked away from the brush fire before it was completely extinguished."

Dahlia's expression crumbled and her nose and eyes were pink-rimmed, but Lily continued her tirade.

"While you and Kyle were doing *whatever* at the shack, the grass caught fire. And because of that fire, Aiden and I had to put up with all kinds of embarrassing comments at school. That's probably why he left. It's why Granddad died, too. Because if you hadn't been such a headcase after the fire, he would have told you about his cardiology tests. You would have taken him to his appointments and the doctors would have seen something was wrong with his heart and they would have saved his life."

"Li-Lily, no," Dahlia sobbed. Tears were bounding down Lily's cheeks, too, but she couldn't stop. She *wouldn't* stop.

"It's bad enough that you were fooling around with someone behind Uncle Martin's back, but did you have to do it with *my* mentor? With *my* friend? At least, I thought of him as a friend. As somebody who believed in me and thought I had talent. But I guess Kyle was just using me to get close to you, and vice versa."

"No. You're wrong," Dahlia insisted through her tears. "None of this has anything to do with your photography or your relationship with Kyle, I promise."

Lily stepped back and slammed the door to show what she thought of her aunt's promises. From the other side, she loudly informed her, "I'm going away right after I take my finals and I'm not coming back. Don't try to stop me or I'll tell Uncle Martin why I'm leaving. Then I'll tell Kyle's girlfriend and I'll tell the fire department and the conservation committee, too!"

. . .

True to her word, Lily left Dune Island the Saturday after her last exam. She told Martin, Katie, Steve and Mrs. Henderson that she was using her prize money to go on a photo-expedition in Sweden, her ancestors' country of origin.

Leaving her uncle was agonizing, especially because he was naively happy about Lily's opportunity to travel. But it would have been even more agonizing for her to live in the same house with him and Dahlia. Knowing what she knew about her aunt made Lily feel complicit in Dahlia's deception. She couldn't break her uncle's heart by telling him the truth—but not telling him the truth meant she couldn't look him in the eye, either.

Fortunately, on the day of Lily's departure, Dahlia claimed she felt sick and she couldn't accompany her and Martin to the airport. Lily had tried to tell her uncle it wasn't necessary for him to take her all the way to Boston—she could have caught a bus at the ferry terminal in Hyannis. But he insisted on seeing her off in person.

Carrying her luggage, he escorted her all the way to the security checkpoint. Then, in the middle of a throng of travelers, he embraced her and kissed the top of her head, something Lily couldn't have imagined him doing three years ago.

She suddenly felt so overwhelmed with loneliness that she almost announced she'd changed her mind. But Martin grasped her shoulders and gently pushed her away from him. Peering into her eyes, he said, "Your grandma would be so pleased that you're going on this trip. She told me she wanted you to enjoy your youth while you're still young. She made me promise I wouldn't let you become overburdened with whatever was happening on the farm."

Struck by the unintended irony of her uncle's statement, Lily could barely suppress a sob. She leaned forward and again wrapped her arms around his back, being careful not to squeeze too tight. "I'm going to miss you, Uncle Martin," she murmured. "Please take good care of yourself."

"Don't worry, I'll be fine. Dahlia's looking after me."

Lily managed not to cry until after she had boarded the plan and settled into her assigned seat by the window. Then, twisting sideways and pretending to peer at the water below, she wept all the way across the Atlantic.

Although she really did spend the summer touring Scandinavia, she never went on a photo-expedition. In fact, before she left the farm, Lily deliberately abandoned her photography equipment, along with her dreams. As a symbolic gesture, she hung her camera by its strap on the homemade wedding ring holder by the door, where Dahlia would be sure to see it.

PART THREE

CHAPTER NINETEEN

NOW

SATURDAY

Overnight, a thundershower erupted. Its reverberations jolted the tiny shack and raindrops battered the rooftop like artillery fire. Lily hardly noticed. Her mind was churning with emotion as she reflected on what had happened before she'd left Dune Island at eighteen. The memories were vivid and relentless; even her most encouraging self-talk couldn't console her and she wept a deluge of tears.

She didn't think they'd ever stop, but Lily must have exhausted herself because the next thing she knew, a seagull was screeching at her to wake up. Or so it seemed. She quickly got to her feet and stretched. There was a rain puddle beneath the front window, but a thick sunbeam from the eastern window illuminated the shack. For getting such a small amount of sleep, Lily felt surprisingly refreshed. She felt effervescent.

Maybe instead of trying to block out my saddest memories, I should have been acknowledging them head-on, she thought. *Maybe a cleansing cry was just what I needed.*

More likely, it was the anticipation of reuniting with Ryan

today that made Lily feel like dancing. There were few sorrows in her life that couldn't be assuaged—at least, a little—by her child's smile.

Hours later, Lily couldn't stop stealing glances at her son in the rearview mirror as he regaled her with tales about his adventures camping with his cousins. It had only been five days but he looked as if he'd lost a couple of pounds.

Maybe it just seems that way because of his tan, Lily reasoned. Because sudden weight loss had been Tyler's first noticeable sign of leukemia, she was constantly on guard about Ryan's weight. However, her concern now was unwarranted, because Ryan had always been on the skinny side.

Tyler had apparently been the same way as a child, and Ryan definitely looked like his side of the family. They both had straight brown hair, although Ryan had a cowlick that swirled near the front of his head, causing a thick lock of hair to stand on end. He also had his dad's brown eyes, which were so large they seemed to take up the top half of his face.

The smattering of freckles across the bridge of his nose and cheeks were the only resemblance he bore to Lily, but the tiny brown dots were already beginning to fade. *It won't be much longer before he loses them entirely*, she speculated. The thought made her sigh.

"Mom, the light's green. You can go." Ryan's urgent tone broke through her daydreaming. She accelerated onto the highway entrance ramp and merged into traffic. "You said you'd tell me more about where we're going after I told you everything that happened at the cabin while you were away. I'm done now. So, what's it like where we're going?"

"Well, it's a very small town..." Lily took a deep breath before forging ahead with the topic. "It's actually the town I grew up in. Rockfield."

"How come you had a meeting there?"

"Because the woman who married my uncle lived there, too, and—"

"You mean your aunt?"

"Well, yes, she was technically my aunt. But I didn't know her since I was little, the way you knew Aunt Leanne." Lily hoped her explanation would soften the blow of what she was about to say next. "Her name was Dahlia and she recently died, so—"

"That's sad, Mom," Ryan interjected, leaning forward to pat her shoulder.

"Yes, it is sad." Touched by his tenderness, she reached back and squeezed his hand. "Dahlia owned the house I grew up in. She stored some of my grandmother's things for me, so I had to go through them to see if there was anything I wanted to keep. I also had an important meeting with her attorney about finding a new buyer for the farm."

"You grew up on a *farm*? With cows and horses and chickens?"

"No, it wasn't that kind of farm. It was a cranberry farm. We grew cranberries."

"In one of those shallow ponds?"

"You mean a bog. And yes, that's where cranberries grow but they don't grow under water. Most farmers flood their bogs during harvest season because that's how they gather the berries. But we didn't flood the bogs on our farm." Lily had always been proud of the fact that her family was among a minority of cranberry growers who didn't sell their produce for processing. "We sold fresh fruit to the markets and we had to be careful not to bruise it. So we did something called dry harvesting. That means we picked the berries by pushing mechanical pickers—kind of like oversized lawn mowers—through the bogs."

"That's awesome. Can I help pick some?"

"It's not harvest season until the fall, but I can show you the equipment we used." Lily appreciated his enthusiasm. Maybe it was because he'd grown up in a rowhouse in the city, but Ryan was especially inquisitive about the natural world. He bounced on the seat to catch her eye in the mirror.

"How much longer till we get there?"

"Depending on traffic, it'll take another forty-five minutes to drive to Hyannis. Then we need to board a ferry, because Rockfield is in Hope Haven, which is on Dune Island."

"An *island*! How far away is it? Does it have palm trees and coconuts and coral reefs?"

Lily couldn't help smiling. "No, this island's only a few miles off the coast of Massachusetts, so there are juniper trees and scrub oaks and pitch pine. There aren't any coconuts, just cranberries. There's some coral called northern star coral—it grows in colonies pretty deep down in the water, so it's kind of hard to find. But there are beautiful shells, stones and beach glass washing ashore all the time."

"Cool," he said with the same inflection her brother-in-law Tim would have used. Ryan looked up to him and he frequently imitated his expressions and behaviors. Lily was glad that he bonded with his uncle, but she wished they didn't live so far apart. It would have been nice if Ryan could hang out with Tim and with his cousins, Bart and Zeke, more often. "I've never been on a ferry. How come we never went to where you grew up before now?"

Lily felt a small stab of guilt and she avoided answering the question. "We never visited your dad's hometown, either, honey."

"Yeah, but he lived in a city like the one we live in, not on a farm or an island like you did." Ryan added, "I didn't even know you had an aunt. I thought you grew up in an orphanage."

An orphanage? Where did he get that idea? "I've told you

several times that my grandparents raised me and that we lived in a little town in Massachusetts."

"Yeah, but you never told me anything about a farm or an island," he repeated. "And whenever you talk about your grandma and granddad, your voice sounds droopy. I thought you were making them up because you didn't want me to know your parents abandoned you at an orphanage or at a fire station or something."

The stab of guilt she'd experienced a second ago now felt like a blade twisting in Lily's chest. She should have known that Ryan was perceptive enough to sense her uneasiness on the rare occasions when she'd mentioned her youth. She'd avoided the subject as much as possible because she wanted to protect her son from her own pain. But now she realized, *He's been imagining sadder situations than I ever experienced—but he hasn't wanted to upset me by asking about them.*

"My parents didn't abandon me, but they did die," she said softly. She was aware that for a child, there was sometimes a fine line between abandonment and death. In case Ryan believed Tyler had abandoned him, Lily emphasized, "My mom and dad loved me a lot, just like your dad loved you and would have done anything to stay with you."

"I know, Mom. You told me that lots of times."

"Yeah, I guess I did." Relieved that the message seemed to have sunk in, she reminded him, "The other thing I've told you several times is that I lived with my grandma and granddad and my uncle Martin. They loved me to pieces and I loved them, too. But you're right. I haven't told you about what it was like to grow up on a farm. But you can ask me anything about it—or about my side of the family—and I'll tell you."

Ryan peppered her with questions all the way to the ferry dock. Lily answered as honestly as she could, including telling him that Dahlia and Aiden had come to live with their family so Dahlia could take care of Lily's grandmother when she was ill.

Fortunately, he didn't ask her any detailed questions about Selma's passing; he was more interested in hearing about the beach and farm.

His ears really perked up when she told him, "There's a man named Jake who has helped Dahlia manage the farm for a long time—ten years. He's made a lot of changes to it, so now it has a gift store and an education center where visitors can come and learn about growing cranberries."

"Is Jake, like, our cousin or something?"

"No. He's not related to us at all."

"Does he live on the farm?"

"No. Jake lives in his own home, by himself." She considered mentioning that Ryan might be able to meet Jake's nephew, but she didn't want to get his hopes up, in case the boys weren't able to hang out together.

"Are we going to stay in the farmhouse?"

"No. It's been converted into the gift shop and education center and offices, so we'll stay in a motel." When Ryan made a disappointed sound, Lily added brightly, "It probably has a swimming pool."

"You already said we could go swimming in the ocean. That's way better than a pool."

"Well, we can swim in the ocean during the afternoon and the pool in the evening—if the motel has one."

"How come you don't know if it has one or not?" Ryan grilled her. Lily couldn't get anything past him. "Didn't you see one when you were there?"

"I didn't actually stay at this motel," she confessed.

"Then where have you been staying?"

"Well, one night I stayed in a different motel and the rest of the time I've been staying on the farm, but not in the farmhouse. Your great-great-granddad built a little shack on a cliff overlooking the water. But it doesn't have plumbing or electricity."

"Cool! Let's stay there instead of at a motel."

"We can't. There aren't any beds in it. I've been sleeping in a lounge chair."

"I don't need a bed. I've got my sleeping bag with me."

"There isn't even an outhouse."

"I don't care, Mom. I've been peeing in the woods all week. I'm used to it."

"Hold on. Uncle Tim and Aunt Leanne's cabin has two bathrooms. Why were you going in the woods?" She eyed her son in the rearview mirror.

He shrugged. "Uncle Tim said we should mark our territory because it keeps the wild animals away."

Maybe Tim's not such a great influence after all, Lily thought facetiously. "I'm not sure if that's actually true."

"Oh, it's true, all right. We didn't see a single bear or wolf the whole week."

Lily chuckled. "You won't see any on Dune Island, either— but that's because there aren't any."

She paused to consider Ryan's request. Even though the final portion of her salary had been deposited into her account, she was going to have to make the money last until she sold some of her grandmother's possessions or secured the consulting position. Staying in the shack certainly would save them a lot of money. Even more importantly, staying in the shack was an easy way to make her son happy.

"I suppose we could try it out tonight and see how it goes."

"Thanks, Mom!" Ryan nearly strangled her with a hug from behind.

"You're welcome. But we'll use the bathroom at the house before we head out to the shack for the night. Unless it's urgent, you're not permitted to relieve yourself near the shack, on the farm or anywhere else outside on the island, understand? You'll upset some of the people on the town's environmental committee and if a park ranger sees you, I might get fined."

"Why? It's perfectly natural and it saves a lot of water

because I don't have to flush the toilet. Uncle Tim said it can help get rid of fungus, too. People should get upset if I *don't* go outside."

"Even so, there's no peeing outdoors unless it's an emergency. Got it?" Lily was beginning to regret her decision. She could almost hear the petty remarks certain residents would make if they caught her son *marking his territory*.

"I promise, I won't go outside. Not even in the ocean, 'kay?" Ryan told her. "You don't have to scrunch up your shoulders."

Chuckling, she relaxed her posture. "Okay, but if it turns out we're awake half the night, we're going to a motel tomorrow."

"How many nights are we staying on the island?"

"I'm not sure when we'll leave. Probably Wednesday. It depends on how soon the mechanic can install a new starter on our car."

"I hope it takes them a really long time."

It already feels as if it has *taken a really long time*, Lily thought, but she didn't burst her son's bubble by saying it.

There were so many vehicles ahead of them in line to board the ferry to Dune Island that Lily and Ryan couldn't make the 4:00 crossing. So they'd parked in the overflow lot and then walked to Sparky's Clam Shack on the waterfront, where Lily splurged on two early-bird specials.

It was a decision she regretted forty minutes later when the ferry sailed out of the harbor and into the rough waves, and the vessel started swaying. As they stood on the foredeck, her son looked green around the gills and Lily fretted, *The poor child. I'm used to riding the ferry, but this is his first time. I should have packed us a light snack, instead.*

She suggested that Ryan wouldn't notice the rolling motion as much if they returned to their car, which was parked in the middle of the ferry. But he insisted the fresh air was helping him feel a lot better.

Indeed, by the time they returned to their vehicle to disembark the ferry, the boy looked a lot better too. The same couldn't be said for Lily's hair, which the wind had whipped into a mat of knots. She tried to untangle it but her brush got stuck in the coils and several bristles broke off as she pulled it free. Both of them clutched their stomachs, cracking up over the mishap.

I've really missed the sound of his laughter, Lily thought, relishing the moment of shared levity.

Her boy could hardly contain his excitement as they rolled along in the heavy seasonal traffic. He lowered his window and if Lily had let him, he would have stuck his head and torso out, like a happy, panting dog. For the final mile of their trip, he was so eager to get to the farm it seemed he might jump all the way out the door altogether.

"Cool!" he exclaimed as they turned into the driveway and he spied the bogs. "I thought you said it's not cranberry season."

"It isn't. The cranberry vines are in bloom, and their flowers are a pinkish-maroon color, kind of like the color of cranberries." Turning into the parking area, Lily noticed that Jake was about to get into his truck. She absently remarked, "Looks like he's leaving for the day."

She'd barely put the car into park before Ryan leaped out. He dashed over to greet Jake and she followed him.

"Hi, Farmer Jake," Ryan exclaimed.

Farmer Jake? Lily started to tell her son that he should call him Mr. Jake or Mr. Benson, not *Farmer* Jake. But Jake caught her eye and winked, indicating he didn't mind.

"Hi. You're Ryan, right?" He extended his arm.

"Yep." He gave Jake's hand a solid shake. "My last name's Perkins, but my great-grandparents owned this farm a long time ago. Their last name was Lindgren. Did you know them?"

Jake looked amused but Lily felt a pinch of regret. Ryan had never met his relatives, yet the pride in his voice was unmistakable when he'd emphasized that they were *his* great-grandparents.

"Yes, I did know them. They gave me my first job, right here in the bogs," Jake answered. "I knew your great-aunt Dahlia and your great-uncle Martin, too. And you know what? I think you look a little like he did."

"Really?" Ryan turned to his mother. "Do you have any pictures of him you could show me?"

Again, Lily felt guilty—as well as embarrassed in front of Jake—that she hadn't told her son more about his relatives. "I've shown you photos of Uncle Martin, but you must have forgotten," she claimed, in her defense. "But there are four walls full of photos of the entire Lindgren family in the cottage, so I'll show you tomorrow. For now, we should get settled in for the night."

"We're staying in the shack," Ryan explained to Jake. "Mom said it's on a cliff and it doesn't have any plumbing or electricity. I brought my sleeping bag and she's going to sleep in a lounge chair."

Lily clarified, "Ryan convinced me he wanted to camp out there, so we're going to see how it goes for one night."

"Sounds like an adventure. Are you sleeping in the loft, Ryan?"

"There's a *loft*?" His eyes were enormous.

Lily shot Jake a look that said, *thanks a lot*. "Yes, there's a loft, but it's very dusty and that's where the chairs are stored. There's not enough room for you to sleep up there.

"We could move them and dust the place out. Please, Mom?"

Over the past few years, Lily had been forced to refuse the majority of her son's requests because she was either short on time or short on money. This was such a minor appeal and it would make him so happy, so she allowed it. "Okay, but I'll need to reinforce the ladder. It's not very sturdy."

"I can do that for you, since it, uh, was my idea for Ryan to sleep up there." Jake was clearly trying to make amends for his suggestion. "I can take down the chairs and make sure the loft is clean, too. You and Ryan must be tired from your trip, so you can relax at the house, or whatever. I'll let you know when I'm done."

"That's a great idea," Ryan piped up before Lily could say it wasn't necessary. "Can I go with Farmer Jake to help him, Mom? You could stay at the house and wash your hair, since you have so many knots in it."

Lily noticed Jake's jaw was set, but his shoulders were quaking, and she had to laugh, too. "Well, since you flattered me like that, sure. You can go with Jake. But be careful not to bang your thumb with a hammer."

"I won't, Mom. Don't worry."

That's easier said than done, my sweet boy, she thought. *Especially when it comes to protecting you.*

Two and a half hours later, Lily and Ryan were settled into their respective sleeping places.

"This is so awesome. Too bad Bart and Zeke couldn't come here, too—there's plenty of room for three people. But Aunt Leanne probably wouldn't let them sleep up here. She's afraid of heights. She didn't let us climb any trees, not even the short ones with easy branches."

I guess Leanne isn't as carefree as she thinks she is after all, Lily mused to herself. "I'm glad you're comfortable, but if you need to come down from there in the middle of the night, just say my name and I'll wake up. I can turn on my phone's flashlight for you."

"Mm-hmm." He made a drowsy noise and then was quiet.

She lay awake for a long time, listening to the rhythmic rush and retreat of waves against the rocks at the bottom of the cliff and thinking about her son. As thrilled as Ryan was to be visiting their family's farm, in a way his joy emphasized what was missing in his life.

Lily had grown up without her parents and without siblings, but she'd had her grandparents' and uncle's constant presence in her life. The only relative Ryan had on the Lindgren side of the family was Lily. Granted, Tyler's parents saw him twice a year when they visited from California. And she and Ryan got together every other month with Leanne and her family, who lived a hundred and thirty miles north of them. But Lily wished her son had more family members in his life on a daily basis—especially a man, who could be a role model for him in ways Lily wasn't.

I can't change the fact that Tyler and Uncle Martin and Granddad have died, and thinking about it is just going to make me sadder, she reminded herself as she carefully rolled onto her side in the lounge chair. *So I might as well stop wishing things were different and enjoy the fact that Ryan's so happy to be here.*

CHAPTER TWENTY

NOW

"Good morning, Mom!"

Lily partially opened one eye. Still dopey from sleep, she couldn't make sense of why Ryan's hair was standing on end. She opened the other eye and realized he was hanging his torso over the edge of the loft.

Sitting upright, she warned, "Ryan Lars Perkins, move back right now before you fall!"

"Okay."

He was so agreeable that Lily regretted starting the day by scolding him, but his safety warranted it. *Maybe Leanne and I both feel the same way about heights after all.*

"That's better. I don't mind if you peek over the edge, but please keep your shoulders in the loft," she said as he climbed down the ladder, already dressed. When he reached the third step, he twisted forward, jumped to the floor and landed with a hop, nearly knocking into the wall. Lily held her tongue about the stunt; she had to choose her battles.

"What are we going to do today? Can I see those cranberry

picking machines you told me about? Are we going to go to the beach? What time will Farmer Jake be here?" Without pausing for a full beat, he added, "I'm hungry and I sort of have to go to the bathroom."

"Okay. Just give me a second to change out of my pajamas, and then we can plan our day while we're walking to the cottage."

"I'll wait outside," Ryan told her, the door slamming behind him.

After she finished getting dressed, Lily stepped outside to find Ryan near the edge of the cliff, pitching small stones into the water.

"Too bad the top part of this cliff is so steep. Otherwise, we could sort of slide down the part near the top that's sandy and then climb down the rocks the rest of the way," he reckoned, pointing. "How far do you think it is to the bottom?"

Far enough that what you just said stopped my heart. "It's about fifty feet. And you absolutely may *not* slide or climb down it. As I told you last night, there's a staircase over there on the revetment." She emphasized again that the tides were difficult to gauge, and that he wasn't allowed to go down to the beach without her.

"I know that, Mom. You told me it isn't a good beach for swimming anyway. Can we go to the other one you told me about, the one with the sandbars where you can see seals sometimes?"

"Maybe tomorrow. Today I have a lot I want to show you around here, and I think the weather's going to be better tomorrow anyway," Lily said, fudging her answer.

The truth was, she'd prefer not to go to the beach today because on Sundays she'd be more likely to bump into her former acquaintances than on weekdays. Even though she'd begun to feel guilty for being unsociable, she couldn't let her guard down. Ryan was thrilled to be here and he was proud of his extended family. She didn't want anyone to ruin that for him by making upsetting remarks about the past.

By two o'clock, they'd explored the farm, hiked through the conservation land to see the grinding stones on the other side, assembled and disassembled the puzzle in the cranberry center twice, and eaten their lunch. Ryan was a ball of boundless energy and he had questions about everything. Watching him discover the very things she'd always loved about the farm made Lily feel like she was seeing them for the first time, too.

But because she hadn't a good night's rest since she'd arrived on the island, she could barely keep up with her eight-year-old son. So when Jake dropped by with Conner and invited them to go bodyboarding, Lily was glad that she finally had her swimsuit back from Maine again. "We'd don't have bodyboards, but we'd love to go with you and take a dip."

"That's okay. We brought extra." Conner generously offered to Ryan, "You can pick whichever one you want."

"And *you* can choose the beach," Jake told Lily, gently poking her bare arm.

"Driftwood Hollow is the best for bodyboarding. The surf isn't that high, but the sandbars make for a nice, long ride," she said. *And hardly anyone goes to that beach because the parking lot is so small.*

"I've never been bodyboarding," Ryan admitted. "Is it hard?"

"Nah. I'll show you my tricks." Conner added knowingly, "It's all about the timing."

"Isn't everything?" Jake asked Lily under his breath. She wasn't sure what he meant but his tone was unmistakably playful.

I can't believe he isn't dating anyone. The women on the island are missing out, she thought. *But I'm glad I get to see this side of him.*

. . .

When they arrived at Driftwood Hollow twenty minutes later, Lily was relieved to see that the sandy parking area, which only had room for five or six cars, was vacant. Ryan and Conner tramped over the dune ahead of Lily and Jake, holding their boards atop of their heads and jabbering as if they'd known each other for years.

"That's the long and the short of it," Jake quipped with wry affection, gesturing toward the boys.

Lily knew he was referring to the fact that Ryan was tall and skinny, and Conner was short and stout. She agreed, "Yeah, I wish I had a camera so I could snap their picture."

She'd only used the figure of speech to emphasize how cute she thought the boys looked, but Jake replied, "I remember how proud Martin was of you for going on that photo expedition to Sweden. Do you still enjoy photography?"

"Not really. I don't have time for it any more." Lily was disheartened by how quickly her mood teetered at the mention of photography. Because she didn't want anything or anyone—herself included—to ruin their pleasant afternoon, she quickly changed the subject and asked Jake if he knew what the water temperature was.

"It's a balmy sixty-one degrees."

"That's all? My poor son is going to turn into an icicle."

But somehow, he managed to keep up with Conner as he charged into the water and ducked under an oncoming wave. When Ryan surfaced, Lily could see all the way from shore that he was shivering. She turned to make a comment about it to Jake, who'd just pulled his shirt over his head.

Jake may have a farmer's tan, but he's got a bodybuilder's chest, Lily noticed, and a shiver overtook her, too.

By the time she'd fastened an elastic band around her hair and was wading into the water with Jake, her son had already caught half a dozen waves.

"He's dauntless," Jake remarked as the boy flew past them on the white edge of a wave.

That's what I'm worried about. Lily held her breath and dove into a breaking swell. She could feel her hair flattening against her skull and shoulders, and the bodyboard strap pulling at her wrist as the cold water rushed over the length of her body.

Viewing the ocean was inspiring, but being *in* the ocean was exhilarating. Even while she was still submerged, Lily wondered, *How have I survived for eighteen years without doing this every summer?*

For the next few hours, the foursome whooped and hollered and applauded each other as they rode the frothy waves so far onto the shore that they scraped their knees against the damp sand. The entire time, Ryan never stopped grinning.

His smile's so big he must have swallowed half a gallon of saltwater by now, Lily fretted. When his lips took on a bluish hue, she told him it was time to go on shore to warm up for a while. He didn't want to get out of the water, but Jake backed up her suggestion.

"C'mon, Conner. You should come out for a while, too. We'll build a sand fort."

"Okay. Let's build it by the water so we can dig a moat, too."

While the three of them were planning how to structure their fort, Lily ambled to the spot where she'd left her beach bag. She toweled off, donned her sun hat and cover-up, and sat down in the sand, where she could watch them from a distance. Once again, she felt a tug of attraction toward Jake. But this time it wasn't only his muscular biceps and pecs that captured her attention; it was the way he was interacting with the boys.

Maybe once I don't have to work such long hours and I'm not stressed about my debt, I'll start dating seriously again. It would even be good for Ryan if I remarried, she reflected thoughtfully.

In her mind, she could practically hear Leanne snickering. "Good for Ryan? It would be good for *you*—especially if you could meet a guy like Jake in Philadelphia."

Or maybe that was her own subconscious talking. Lily chuckled at the thought. Hugging her knees, she absent-mindedly buried her feet under the warm sand and then wiggled her toes, making miniature landslides. *This is the way Sunday afternoons should be,* she thought, closing her eyes and lifting her face to the sky.

Eventually, Jake and the boys returned to the water; Conner and Ryan brought their boards with them, but Jake chose to bodysurf, instead. His timing was impeccable; he didn't miss a single wave he tried to catch, and he often rode farther onto shore than either of the boys. She was just about to join the three of them again, when someone nearby shouted.

It was a woman's voice and she called, "Remember, don't go in any deeper than your waists!"

Two girls around Ryan's age and a younger boy dropped their towels in the sand some ten yards away from where Lily was sitting. They sprinted toward the water with their bodyboards, while a woman carrying a red beach chair traipsed behind them.

Lily stole a look at her from beneath the brim of her hat. *Is that Katie?* she asked herself.

The woman unfolded her chair and set it in the sand, but then she walked down to the water's edge. She was wearing a T-shirt and shorts, so Lily assumed she wasn't going swimming. Conner and Jake seemed to know the children—they momentarily clustered around Ryan. No doubt, they were introducing themselves to each other. Now that she was almost positive the woman standing in ankle-deep water *was* her childhood friend, Lily approached her. Katie might have given her the brush-off the other day, but that was no reason not to be polite and say hello. And even tell Katie how much she'd been thinking about her.

"Hi, Katie. I thought that was you," she said.

"Lily? Hi!" Her tone didn't seem as aloof as it had been on Friday. "Is that your son?"

"Yes, that's Ryan. It's his first time bodyboarding. Are those your children?"

"The boy is mine—his name's Jayce. And the girl with the brown hair is my daughter, Kaylee. The blonde girl is her friend, Mila."

"Seems like they love the water as much as you used to."

"Yeah, any day now I expect them to grow fins."

The women were quiet for a moment until Lily worked up the nerve to say, "I was really happy to see you the other day, Katie. I've thought about you a lot over the years. I have such good memories of our time together when we were young. I've never found another friend like you."

Katie stared straight ahead at the children in the water. At first, Lily didn't think she was going to acknowledge her remark but she replied, "Really? Because you had a funny way of showing it."

Lily was stunned. "What do you mean?"

"I mean it was crushing when my best friend moved across the Atlantic and hardly even kept in touch." Katie turned and stared at her.

"I *did* keep in touch. I texted. I sent letters."

"You sent *post cards*." Katie sounded like her teenage self and Lily responded a bit like a teenager, too.

"At least I wrote—*you're* the one who stopped communicating altogether."

"That's because I was sick of getting messages from you that said absolutely *nothing*," Katie retorted. "I didn't want to hear about your eight-hour flight or the weather in Stockholm. I wanted to hear about how *you* were doing. I knew you were probably having a hard time, because of your granddad dying, but whenever I tried to ask you about it, you shut me out. Before that, we used to tell each other almost everything. I missed that part of our friendship. That closeness."

Lily's whisper was barely audible. "I missed it, too."

"I mean, when I got older and I lost my grandma, I could understand why you might not have wanted to talk about your granddad. But it didn't make sense that you stopped sharing your *good* news with me, too. I didn't even find out about the photography competition results until Gretchen Turner blabbed about it at school. And after you won, it was as if you thought you were better than the rest of us."

Lily shook her head. "Trust me, I didn't."

"It *seemed* like you did. Especially when you skipped senior week. I would have understood if you didn't participate because you were grieving. But you couldn't have been that sad—you took off on a vacation in Sweden!"

Katie pushed the hair out of her watery eyes and continued, as if all the resentment she'd kept bottled up over the years was spilling out at once. "I felt like all the history we shared meant nothing to you. I didn't blame you for snubbing some of the other kids, but I was your best friend. I couldn't wait to celebrate finishing twelve years of school with you. But it seemed like all you cared about was becoming famous or finding your ancestors or whatever else it was you wanted to do in Sweden."

Lily was appalled to realize how her actions had given Katie the wrong impression. She cried, "I didn't go to Sweden to become famous. I went to become *anonymous*. The reason I chose Sweden for my destination wasn't really because of my family heritage. It was because I figured there would be other Lily Lindgrens living there. I'd thought I'd blend right in. I needed to be someplace where no one knew anything about me or my family or the farm."

Lily stopped talking when a large wave crashed into Ryan's torso from behind, knocking him to his hands and knees. Before he could rise, a successive wave crested and broke over his head, entirely submerging him. Even though Jake was only a few feet away from him, he appeared to be oblivious that Ryan was struggling to stand. Lily was about to dash into the water to help him, but he managed to get to his feet on his own. Once he was steady again, he flashed Lily the okay sign. She returned the gesture, and Ryan raced back into deeper surf to catch another wave.

Calmer now, Lily clarified, "I didn't skip senior week or go to Sweden because I thought I was better than anyone else. I went because... a lot of reasons. Mostly, I was grieving, angry and depressed. I thought getting away from what was upsetting me would make me feel better, but I never felt lower or lonelier in my life than I did that summer. I'm sorry I hurt you, Katie. I'm sorry I shut you out. I was so immature...I was so *lost*."

"*I'm* sorry you were so lonely. I didn't know." Katie wiped her eyes against the inside of her bare elbow. "I was immature, too. I should have kept writing until you were ready to open up. I guess I always felt a little bit guilty—I was worried you were still angry at me because of my uncle and that stupid petition to boycott your family's cranberries."

"No, no, no," Lily uttered. "I knew that wasn't your fault."

"For what it's worth, he never did sign it."

"Well, that's good, I guess. Why did he change his mind?"

"I threatened to boycott working at the shop, just like you suggested."

"You did? But I was only kidding!" Lily could imagine what an uproar that must have caused in Katie's close-knit family. It would have been as drastic as if *she'd* threatened to quit working on the cranberry farm. "I bet your uncle wasn't happy about that."

"Lexi wasn't either. She realized that if I quit, she'd have to take my place scooping ice cream instead of doing the cushy job of ringing up sales at the register. Suddenly, she dropped the subject of the petition—and Sean Miller dropped *her*."

Lily giggled, figuring both Lexi and Sean got what they deserved. "But you still help your cousin at the shop?"

"Yeah, on occasion, although with five children I don't have much spare time."

"*Five* children?"

"I have three more boys—they're out sailing with my husband."

"Wow, you've been busy! Who's the lucky man?"

One corner of Katie's mouth lifted in a crooked smirk that Lily remembered from when they were young. "Will."

"Will? As in, the Will Jackman you've known since you were in diapers?"

"Yep. It turns out, he's a lot more interesting than I thought." The pair laughed before Katie added softly. "I only saw Dahlia on occasion, but sometimes I'd ask about you. She told me you're widowed. I was very sorry to hear that."

"Thank you... Tyler was my first true love. I went through a pretty dark period when I lost him." *Another dark period*, Lily silently corrected herself. "But our son has been a constant bright spot in my life."

Katie nodded, and glanced toward the water at Ryan. "He seems to be having a great time. How long are you staying in Hope Haven?"

"Until Wednesday."

"That's all? I thought since you were putting the farm up for sale, you might be here for a while to work things out with a realtor and that kind of thing."

"You heard I'm selling the farm?"

"Yes. But I also heard that you were keeping it and moving back here. And there's a rumor going around that you're interested in working with a developer to build a hotel on the property." Katie rolled her eyes. "You remember how it is on Dune Island—there's never any shortage of rumors to choose from. I figured the one about you selling the farm was probably closest to the truth."

"You figured right," she confirmed. "Financially, it's just not feasible for me to keep the farm, so I have to sell it."

"Oh, that's too bad." There was a note of genuine disappointment in Katie's voice and in that moment, Lily wished she didn't have to give up the estate. The two women silently watched their children frolicking in the surf a while longer. Then, still facing the water, Katie drolly observed, "So, Jake Benson. Shirtless."

Lily giggled, "Yeah, that's a sight you and I would have waited by my window for hours to see when we were in middle school."

"Remember that time we thought he saw us spying on him, so we dropped to the floor, and you bumped your chin against my head and bit your tongue really hard?"

"How could I forget? My tongue bled so much I thought I was going to have to go to the ER," Lily exclaimed and they both doubled over with laughter.

The two women spent the next half hour filling each other in on what had been going on in their lives, until Jake and the kids came clambering up the embankment, their teeth chattering.

Before they parted ways, Katie said to Lily, "I hope you'll have another chance to drop by the shop before you leave. If you end up staying until the Fourth of July, don't forget to get your free cone." She stretched out her arms. "But in case I don't see you again, let me give you a hug."

On the way back to the farm, Lily overheard Ryan asking Conner in the back seat, "What did Ms. Katie mean about getting a free cone?"

"Every Fourth of July, Bleecker's Ice Cream Shop parks a truck at Beach Plum Cove, 'cause that's where the best fireworks are, and they give away free ice cream. You can only get a single-scoop, but it's still pretty big and it's delicious. You can choose either choco-cran or van-cran."

"I never heard of that kind of ice cream," Ryan said. "What's cran?"

"Are you serious?" Conner marveled. "Cran is short for *cranberries*. They come from the farm."

Now it was Ryan's turn to sound incredulous. "Cranberries taste good in ice cream?"

"The dried kind do. Especially if they're in chocolate ice cream," Conner raved. "I can't believe you never heard of choco-cran. It's what Dune Island is famous for."

Jake nudged Lily's elbow and gave her a sidelong grin. He whispered, "And you probably thought people flocked to Dune Island for its stunning beaches and quaint charm, didn't you?"

Although Lily chuckled, beneath her laughter, she felt a twinge of self-doubt. The reason Ryan had never heard of choco-cran ice cream was because she'd deliberately refrained from telling him about it. On the surface, it seemed like a harmless topic, but Lily had been worried that Ryan would want to know where she'd tasted the unusual flavor and she'd have to admit it was only sold on Dune Island, as far as she knew. He was so inquisitive that one question would lead to another and she'd wind up telling him more about her hometown than she'd wanted to tell him. So, it seemed best not to mention the flavors in the first place.

But once again, Lily found herself questioning whether she'd made a mistake. Essentially, she'd been pretending a big part of her life had never existed. Granted, she'd been acting that way because she'd thought it was what was best for both her and her son. And it wasn't as if he was deprived simply because he'd never tasted choco-cran ice cream.

However, as she considered the boys' conversation, Lily found herself wondering *What other good things have I withheld from my son by avoiding everything associated with Dune Island?*

CHAPTER TWENTY-ONE

NOW

MONDAY

"These are the best scrambled eggs in the world. Can I have more?" Ryan declared over breakfast. He'd made the same remark about everything he'd eaten since arriving on Dune Island—and he'd eaten a *lot*, to Lily's delight.

A healthy appetite is a sign of a healthy child, she thought, as she passed the serving bowl to him. While he was getting his fill, she reminded him of their schedule for the day. Conner's mother, Brianna, was going to drop off her son at eleven o'clock and he'd stay until his uncle brought him home at suppertime. Jake had kindly offered to help her keep an eye on both the boys around the farm.

The boys were thrilled they'd get to hang out together again today and the arrangement would be mutually beneficial to both women. Brianna had a dentist appointment and Lily had half a dozen tasks to do, including preparing for her upcoming job interview and gathering information that Steve had requested for the sales listing of the farm. Although she wished she could devote her entire day to vacationing with Ryan, Lily was pleased to know that he'd be having fun with Conner while she was occupied with business matters.

"Could you please repeat the rules I want you to follow today?" she quizzed him.

"No bothering Farmer Jake, unless he needs our help and if he does, no complaining. Conner and I can go anywhere on the farm as long as a grown-up can see and hear us. And if we need something it's okay to interrupt you at any time." Ryan was paraphrasing, but he'd gotten the gist of it.

"Very good, but one last thing. This morning I noticed the bodyboard Conner loaned you was lying in the sand by the shack. I'd like you to take better care of the things you use, especially if they belong to someone else."

"But I *was* taking good care of Conner's bodyboard—that's why I brought it to the shack. I didn't want anybody to steal it from the farmhouse when we weren't there."

Lily smiled. Dune Island had a very low crime rate, but she was glad to hear that Ryan's intention was to guard the bodyboard. "I see. The thing is, it's very breezy near the cliff. One big gust of wind and the bodyboard would go sailing over the edge like a kite. From now on, let's loop the strap around the deck railing so that doesn't happen, okay?" After Ryan nodded, Lily told him, "We have plenty of time before Conner comes, so this morning I want to show you something."

"What is it?"

"It's something my grandma showed me when I was your age. You'll see."

Long after Ryan had fallen asleep the previous evening, Lily had stood on the deck, further contemplating whether she'd been mistaken not to tell him more about her family and her youth on Dune Island. Eventually, she concluded that even if it had been unwise for her to be so secretive, she couldn't change the past—but she could change her actions going forward.

So, this morning, she led Ryan to the bogs and they each plucked a single, perfect flower from the vines. Then they hiked through the conservation land all the way to the marsh near the grinding stones on the other side.

"We have to be very quiet," she instructed him as they crouched along the edge of the mucky water.

"What are we looking for?" he whispered.

"That." Lily pointed to the sandhill crane in the distance. Then she held up her flower from the bog and showed him what Selma had shown her when she was a child. "See how the flower is shaped like the crane's head? That's how cranberries got their name—*crane-berry* became *cranberry*."

Ryan held his flower up in front of one eye and squinted as he compared it to the large, wading bird's profile. "Cool. What else did your grandma teach you?"

For the next two hours, Lily filled her son's head with dozens of facts, stories about her grandparents and uncle—several about Dahlia, too—and memories about living on the farm. Because they were hiking over strenuous terrain and Ryan kept interrupting to ask questions, Lily was too distracted to become choked up the way she'd always worried might happen if she reminisced aloud to him.

Finally, they circled back to the farm to meet Conner in the parking lot. The two boys raced toward the bogs in a blur while their mothers chatted. Brianna asked Lily if Ryan could join her and Conner for a hike and a picnic lunch at the wildlife sanctuary the following afternoon.

"You've been keeping my son entertained for almost a week now and I really appreciate it. Please, let me return the favor?"

Lily wavered. Although she trusted Brianna to take good care of her son, she wasn't comfortable allowing him to go to a public place without her. If one of the locals found out that Ryan was Lily's son, who knows what kind of remark they might make to upset him?

Ack. I'm being ridiculous, she lectured herself. *It's unlikely that anyone but Claire would make a disparaging remark directly to him. And what are the odds she'd be hiking today? She's too busy with the inn. Besides, I've got my interview tomorrow afternoon, so it would be helpful to know that Ryan's having fun while I'm tied up with business matters.*

"That would be wonderful, thanks," she finally said. "I'm sure he'll have a great time."

Lily sat beside Jake on a blanket she had spread beneath the maple tree. There was plenty of room for Conner and Ryan to sit with them, but the boys chose to eat their sandwiches while balancing on the split-rail fence, cowboy-style.

"Oh, excuse me," she said, tapping her mouth. "I can't seem to stop yawning."

"Did your sunburn keep you awake last night?" Jake asked.

"My sunburn?" Lily didn't know what Jake was talking about.

There was silence and then he'd said, "Yeah, I, uh, noticed your shoulders and the backs of your legs had gotten a little pink."

He was checking out my legs and shoulders? Or was it just a passing glance? "I don't feel sunburned. Maybe what you saw was my freckles."

"No, your freckles are tanner and they're scattered. This was an all-over pink."

Right then, Lily was pretty sure her cheeks were pink, too, because Jake clearly had taken more than a passing glance at her.

At her sister-in-law's urging, Lily had dated a few guys since Tyler had died, but she'd just been going through the motions. Jake was the first man she felt naturally attracted to in a long time, and it was intoxicating to entertain the idea he felt that way about her, too.

Not that it matters—I'm leaving in two days, she thought, with a sigh that marked a change in her attitude. She couldn't put a finger on when, exactly, she started wishing that she and Ryan could linger in Hope Haven for another week or two. But she knew there were several reasons *why* she felt that way—and one of those reasons was sitting right next to her.

"Guess what's happening tonight?" he asked. For a split-second she thought—she *hoped?*—this might be his awkward way of asking her out. But he said, "The pollinators are coming."

"Kind of late this year, aren't they?"

"Yes, but that's because the flowers were late to bloom."

Ryan piped up, "What are pollinators?"

"They're bees." Conner informed him, "They're called pollinators because they spread the pollen from the boy flowers to the girl flowers and that's how cranberries are made.

"Close enough," Jake mumbled, winking at Lily, who barely managed to keep a straight face. He explained to Ryan, "The beekeepers deliver the hives at night, because that's when the temperature is cooler, and the bees are less active. We don't want to agitate them."

"Cool."

"I told Conner he could come to see the pollinators arrive when his age was in the double digits. But since Ryan might not get another chance to see them, I'm happy to allow both boys be here when they arrive," Jake told Lily.

"Yesss!" Conner exclaimed and so did Ryan.

"Hold on," Lily cautioned. "*I* didn't agree to this yet. I'll have to think about it."

"But, Mom—"

"No *buts*. I said I'd think about it." She caught Ryan and

Conner rolling their eyes at each other, but she pretended not to notice.

"Yeah, your mom probably wants to think it over, too, Conner," Jake added.

Nice backtracking, Lily thought, because obviously, Jake hadn't received his sister's permission yet, either. Conner and Ryan gobbled down their sandwiches and then ran off in search of frogs and toads.

As soon as they were out of earshot, she said, "I wish you would have checked with me before you mentioned the bees in front of Ryan. I don't want him going near the hives. Now he's going to be upset when I tell him no. It would have been better if he hadn't known anything about them in the first place."

"You're right. I overstepped and I'm sorry." Jake leaned back on both hands, stretching his legs in front of him. "If you don't mind my asking, why don't want him to be around the hives? I mean, is he allergic to bee venom?"

"No. But I still don't want him to get stung."

"I don't want him to get stung, either. Heck, *I* don't want to get stung! You know that it's unlikely, but it might happen. No matter how careful we are, there aren't any guarantees—which I've noticed is what you seem to want."

Lily's chest rose and fell as she inhaled and let the air out in a huff. "I care about my child's safety—it's part of my job as his parent."

"I respect that. But I'm surprised that for being so intrepid when you were young, you've sure become so... *cautious*."

"How do you know what I was like when I was young?"

"I was here." Jake plucked a blade of grass from the lawn and twirled it between his fingers. "I remember how hard you worked picking berries during harvest season. Some of the guys on the crew were twice your size and age, but they didn't have half your endurance." He chuckled. "You were such a scrappy kid. I can still picture how the sky would be getting dark and everyone else would have quit for the day, but we could still see little Lily Lindgren's hair bouncing up and down as she maneuvered a picker through the vines, putting most of us to shame."

Lily absent-mindedly tucked a curl behind her ear, but it sprang forward again. "You know what I remember about you? I remember that when my grandma died, you took over with the harvest so my granddad and uncle could make the burial arrangements. You worked nonstop to pick the berries before that big rainstorm came."

"I had a lot of help from the other guys." Jake was being modest; he was the only one who worked the entire time, except when he was attending the funeral. "I'm surprised you remember that."

"What you did meant a lot to my family. It made a big impression on me."

"That's what I'm saying about *you*, Lily. Even when you were in high school, I was impressed by your strength. Not just your physical strength, either. It took a lot of courage to get through the kind of losses you've endured. Your son is strong, too. He just needs a little breathing room. A little space."

"Away from me, you mean?"

Jake didn't answer her directly. "Please let him have this experience. I'll take good care of him, I promise."

"You'd better," she warned. *He's my child and he's all I have left of my family.*

CHAPTER TWENTY-TWO

NOW

After her conversation with Steve had ended, Lily set down her phone and rubbed her temples. It should have made her happy to hear him say how eager his colleague was to view the farm over the July Fourth weekend. Instead, it had given her a headache.

It had given her a bit of a heartache, too, which didn't make sense, considering how adamantly Lily had initially insisted that selling the farm was in her and Ryan's best interests. But as reality set in, the prospect of a stranger buying her family's farm and occupying their house made her feel the same way she'd felt about a stranger wearing Dahlia's old clothes.

I left the farm and island without so much as a backward glance when I was eighteen, so I have no right to feel resentful about giving up the estate now, she told herself.

Sure, her son was overjoyed to be vacationing on the farm and his presence helped Lily not to feel so lonely for her family members who had passed away. But she couldn't bear the thought of Ryan being subject to the kinds of taunts she'd heard when she was growing up on Dune Island. And yes, she was enjoying the flirtation—if she could even call it that—between her and Jake. However, there wasn't any guarantee it would grow into a full-blown romance, even if she moved back to Rockfield. Which she couldn't afford to do in the first place. Ryan's future had to be her first priority.

Since there was no sense in thinking about it any longer, she made a snack and lemonade for the boys and then went outside to find them.

As she came down the walkway, Lily noticed the same silver sedan parked in the far corner that she'd seen the other day. *This is ridiculous*, she thought. *I know that's Olivia.*

Lily crossed the lot and tapped on the window. Olivia was searching through her purse and she genuinely seemed startled when she glanced up. *Maybe I imagined that she snubbed me the other day*, Lily thought, as Olivia lowered the glass.

"Hi, Olivia—I thought that was you!"

"Hi, Lily. How've you been?" she casually asked, as if she hadn't seen Lily for a few weeks instead of eighteen years.

"Fine, thanks. Sophie's going to be in the shop for a few more minutes. It's awfully hot out here. Do you want to come in and have a cool drink while you're waiting?"

"No, thanks. I don't mind the heat."

"Okay, but if you change your mind, come on in." She was halfway back to the house when Olivia called her name. Lily turned to see she'd gotten out of the car, so she went back to chat with her.

"I-I wanted to say I'm sorry about your aunt."

"Thank you." Lily had the sense Dahlia wasn't the only thing on her mind. Was Olivia going to inquire about Aiden?

"She was really kind to give Sophie this job."

"Your daughter's a terrific employee. The farm is fortunate to have her."

"Thanks. That's nice to hear... But I meant, it was kind to give her the job considering what I was like as a kid. I'm surprised Dahlia wasn't afraid Sophie would act the same way

I did when I was going out with Aiden. I feel terrible about that."

Lily shrugged. "We've all grown up since high school."

"Maybe, but I still regret that awful message."

"It wasn't your fault. Aiden was the one who painted the apology on the grinding stones."

Olivia knitted her brow. "I don't mean *that*—although that actually was partly my fault. I dared him to do it, to show how sorry he was. My therapist said I did things like that because my mom and dad left me to live with my aunt when I was a kid. He said I was always testing people, to see if they *really* loved me or not."

Lily wasn't quite sure what to say. "Mmm, I can see how something like that could affect a child."

"Sorry, too much information. Over-sharing is another problem I have."

She seemed so downcast and self-critical, that Lily said, "At least you're not over-sharing about other people, right? That's a lot worse than oversharing about yourself."

Her remark elicited a small smile from Olivia, but then she frowned again as she continued, "Anyway, I wasn't referring to what Aiden wrote on the grinding stones. I was referring to the message I left on the door of the shack."

Olivia had left that note? *Why?* Lily felt woozy. She reached to steady herself against the car, but the steel was so hot she pulled her hand away again. "You mean the one about..."

"Yeah. It was so nasty you can't even say it, can you?" She averted her eyes. "I felt horrible about it afterward, especially when your grandfather died. For months, I was sure he'd read the note and it gave him a heart attack."

"No. He never saw it," Lily said vacantly, trying to make sense of what she'd just heard.

"Yeah, I know that now. But at the time, I was so sick from worrying about it I couldn't eat for almost two months. So my aunt sent me to a therapist. He suggested I take ownership of what I did and apologize to Dahlia. I thought she'd be livid, but she thanked me for telling her. She said you were the only person who'd seen the note and she promised not to tell you I had written it because, you know, because we were peers and I guess she didn't want you to be mad at me. Then she gave me a hug. Can you believe it?"

I can hardly believe any of this, Lily thought ruefully. She clarified, "How did you happen to see Dahlia and Kyle together at the shack?"

"Well, originally I was waiting for Aiden in the conservation land parking lot. He was supposed to get money from Dahlia. He was going to say it was so he could buy new sneakers at the mall in Hyannis. But really we needed money because it was our turn to buy alcohol for the booze cruise."

When Lily tipped her head in confusion, Olivia explained, "We didn't go on real booze cruises—we used to meet up with some off-island kids, take a rowboat out in the pond and drink ourselves stupid. Anyway, Dahlia had been getting on Aiden's case because he never helped on the farm, so he didn't want her to know I was there, waiting for him. It was taking him forever to come back, so I walked through the conservation land, figuring I'd meet him halfway. But I got all the way to the end of the trail near the shack without bumping into him. That's when I saw Dahlia and Kyle on the deck."

Lily's mouth felt cottony and she licked her lips as she tried to think of a delicate way to phrase her next question. "Do you remember if you saw Kyle taking photos of the scenery or Dahlia or anything?"

"Nah. They were just talking."

"You're sure?"

"Positive. Anyway, Aiden broke up with me and he left the island a couple of days later and I figured it was Dahlia's fault. I thought she convinced him I was a bad influence or something.

I wanted to get her back, so I left that note, threatening to tell your uncle they were having an affair." Olivia covered her eyes and shook her head. "Even if I *had* seen something going on between them, I never would have told Martin—I thought he was kind of intimidating. But I wanted Dahlia to think I would. It was horrible that I messed with her mind like that."

My mind is pretty messed up right now, too. "Well, as you said, she was very forgiving."

"Yes, she was. I figured now that she's... at rest, it would be okay to tell you I was the one who wrote the note. I wanted to apologize to you, too. You must have been pretty upset to read a false accusation like that about your aunt."

But was it false? Lily wondered. *Or had Olivia accidentally stumbled upon the truth? If nothing was going on between Dahlia and Kyle, why was his stuff in the shack and why wouldn't she let me see it? For that matter, why didn't she ever tell me that Olivia had written the note?*

Recognizing that Olivia was waiting for her to answer, Lily said, "It was upsetting, yes. But that's in the past. You were a teenager and you were angry. I regret a lot of the stuff I said and did when I was in high school, too." She hesitated before admitting. "I guess I can understand why you wrote a note like that to Dahlia, but why did you post that comment online when my photographs won the competition? That hurt *me*, not her."

"I never posted any note online, I swear," Olivia insisted. "I'll take ownership for everything else I did, but I didn't do that."

"Oh, I'm sorry—my mistake." Lily felt her face heat up, but Olivia waved away the error, just as Sophie strolled up to them.

"Hi, Mom. Hi, Lily. Whatcha talking about?"

"Oh, we were just reminiscing about when were teenagers," her mother replied. "Right, Lily?"

It was clear that Olivia didn't want her daughter to know what they'd been discussing and Lily didn't want her to know, either. So she fibbed, "Yeah, we were just talking about the good ol' days."

Discovering that Olivia been the one who'd written the note was a relief in the sense that it finally settled the matter of who its author was. However, their discussion raised additional questions. Lily wondered who posted the online comment, since it wasn't Olivia. Was it someone from the environmental club after all? Could it have been Kyle's girlfriend Natasha?

She kept coming back to the same unanswerable question: were Kyle and Dahlia actually somehow involved with each other or weren't they? Olivia said she hadn't seen them doing anything that indicated they were having an affair. Nor had she seen Kyle photographing Dahlia. Either way, that didn't prove anything. *Maybe Olivia didn't arrive there at the right time,* Lily thought. *There had to be something going on—otherwise Dahlia would have let me see what was on Kyle's camera. No matter what she said about feeling embarrassed by her sappy poses, I don't believe that was the reason she didn't let me see the photos. Dahlia just wasn't that self-conscious.*

By the end of the day, she'd nearly driven herself to distraction trying to figure it out—something she'd vowed to stop doing years ago. *I need to forget about it. It doesn't matter any more,* she admonished herself. As she leaned on the deck railing, staring at the moon-kissed water, the lulling applause of the mild waves against the rocks began to have a calming effect on her mood. So did refocusing her thoughts on her sleeping son.

He had so much fun with Conner this evening waiting for the hives to be delivered. I'm really glad Jake talked me into letting him have that experience. Reflecting on how excited Ryan had been to tell her about the pollinators when he'd returned to the shack, Lily mused, *He himself was buzzing around here like a bee—I'm surprised he ever fell asleep. He's probably going to be up at first light, so I suppose I should go to bed now, too.*

She was turning to leave when she heard shuffling on the other side of the deck. "Jake? What are you still doing on the farm?"

"Can I come up?" he asked quietly. "I brought you something."

"Is it pizza?" whispered Lily.

"Not this time." He padded up the stairs and handed her something she couldn't quite see in the dark, but it was made of fabric. "It's two Lindgren Cranberry Farm T-shirts and caps. Ryan was admiring mine and Conner's, but I didn't want to give these to him without your permission."

Lily was touched by the gift, and by Jake's consideration. "That's really sweet. How much do I owe you?"

"Nothing. They're free for family members and staff."

"That's great, but he doesn't need two of each."

"They're not both for him—one set's for you."

"Oh, er, thanks." If she was going to try to fly under the radar for the rest of the time she was on Dune Island, Lily couldn't be seen wearing a T-shirt with her family's name emblazoned on it. She set the clothing on the deck chair near the door.

"What's the matter, don't you like this as much as your 3H class shirt?"

Lily couldn't help but laugh. "You mean the one I was *bopping around* in?"

She was only teasing, but Jake apologized. "I shouldn't have said that. I shouldn't have said anything about you and Steve, either."

"No worries, really... By the way, I spoke to him today." Resting her forearms on the railing again, she peered at the moonlit waves. "He said his colleague definitely wants to tour the farm on the Fourth of July weekend. He'll call you to arrange an exact time and date. He thinks the guy wants to get a head start before we list it."

"An impatient prospect, that's a good sign. Isn't it?"

"I suppose."

Jake rested his forearms on the deck, too; hers were luminescent compared to his. "Having second thoughts?"

"Maybe. But how I feel doesn't matter. I can't afford to keep the farm." She turned her face toward him. "At least I know I'm leaving it in good hands."

"I promise to take good care of it." He twisted his neck to look into her eyes. "Is something else bothering you?"

Yes, but I can't tell you about it. She stood up straight, tilted her head toward the moon and rubbed her neck. It was so tight. "I'm just tense—and sleeping in a lounge chair is wreaking havoc on my back."

"I can help with that, if you'll let me."

Jake moved to stand behind her. He slid his hands beneath under her curls and began kneading her shoulders. His touch was warm and firm and Lily closed her eyes, leaning into it. As he massaged her knotted muscles, it felt as if he were also caressing away the gnarled mess of emotions she'd been carrying ever since her conversation with Olivia.

Neither of them spoke a word for at least five minutes, until they heard Ryan coughing from inside the shack. Lily reflexively stiffened, and Jake's fingers froze on her scapula.

Ryan didn't cough a second time, but Jake whispered, "It's getting late. I better go before I rub the freckles right off your skin."

"All right," Lily agreed, even though every fiber of her being was crying, *stay.*

CHAPTER TWENTY-THREE

NOW

TUESDAY

Ryan was up at the crack of dawn. Lily tried to persuade him to go back to sleep for another hour, but he said he was too excited about going to the wildlife sanctuary. Since it was low tide, she took him to the bay. He was amazed at the difference between the bay and the oceanside of the island.

"Look how far the water goes out!" he exclaimed as they slogged through the tidal pools and marched over the flats. Suddenly he stopped, twisted at his waist and looked at the damp sand behind him. "It happened again."

"What happened?"

"Something squirted up the back of my ankle."

"That was a probably a razor clam, expelling water through its siphon." Lily squatted and pointed to several small holes in the wet sand. "These mean we're walking over a clam bed."

She quickly and carefully used her hands to dig through the muck and pulled out a long, narrow razor clam. It withdrew its foot and siphon into its shell before Lily could show them to Ryan. But he got a chance to see them at work when she set the shellfish down and it burrowed below the surface of the sand.

"That's so cool!" he exclaimed.

"Yeah, there are other kinds of clams here, too. In fact, one of the only things I can remember about my mom and dad was that one time we went clamming on this beach. It was kind of a foggy day and my mother dressed me in a bright yellow shirt and shorts—my grandma told me later that was because I was always running off and my mom and dad wanted to be able to see me in the fog."

"Ha—that that sounds like something you'd do to me," Ryan said. "Did you catch a lot of clams?"

"I only dug up one, but it was huge. My dad said it was big enough to feed our whole family for a week and he pretended he could hardly lift the bucket when I put it in. He was only joking, but I believed him." Lily stopped walking and squinted, almost as if she could see the scene playing out in front of her. "I got tired on the way back so my mother gave me a piggyback ride."

Her hair smelled like mint and... rosemary, I think. Lily didn't realize she could recall more about that day than she thought.

"You have a lot of good memories from living here when you were a kid, huh, Mom?"

"Yes, I do." *Even though I lost sight of them for a while.*

"Now I'll have good memories of being on Dune Island, too." Ryan said it matter-of-factly, but his remark made her misty-eyed. But before she could get too maudlin, he shouted, "Hey, look at that dog!"

A golden retriever was charging through a tidal pool, toward a sandbar where a flock of seagulls were standing in formation, against the wind. As the dog neared, they lifted and scattered. The retriever kept charging, as if it were under the illusion it could fly, too.

"Can I run out there?"

"Sure." Lily was about to warn him that there were some-times broken shells and stones in the shallow pools, but he took off before she could. Which was just as well, since she realized she was being overly protective.

She meandered slowly along the edge of a tidal pool, her head down as she thought about the massage Jake had given her last night. *I wonder if it'll be strange seeing each other in the bright light of day*, she thought.

A shrill whistle pierced her ears and she looked up. The dog's owner had come to a standstill about ten yards from Lily and he was attempting to get his pet's attention. But the golden retriever was bounding toward Ryan, who was balancing on one knee, his arms thrown open.

"Don't worry, he's friendly," the man called to Lily just as the dog nearly knocked Ryan over. She could hear her son's laughter all the way across the flats.

"It's okay, he loves dogs. Obviously." Nearing the man, Lily smiled and when he smiled back at her, she did a doubletake. His hair was shorter and grayer and he wore glasses now, but there was no mistaking his bright green eyes. Before she could decide whether to acknowledge that she knew him, he recognized her.

"Lily Lindgren!" he exclaimed.

She didn't bother to tell him her last name had changed. "Hello, Kyle."

I knew that was him I saw the other day on my way to the convenience store, she thought, even though at the time she had doubted herself. The awkwardness of seeing him face-to-face was so intense she felt as if she might be ill. But Kyle seemed delighted that their paths had crossed.

"Of all the people to bump into the first time I return to Dune Island, I can't believe it's you! I've often thought of you over the years."

I've thought about you, too—more times than I wanted to. When she was younger, Lily had often imagined the things she'd say to Kyle Wright if she ever ran into him in person again. Now that she had the opportunity, she didn't want to say anything. She just wanted to disappear beneath the sand like a razor clam.

"Do you still live in Hope Haven?" he asked, oblivious to her reluctance to engage with him.

"No. I'm only here for a few days with my son." She gestured toward Ryan, who was galloping alongside Kyle's dog. "I live in Philadelphia now."

He nodded in recognition. "Philly's a great city—and it's got an incredible art scene."

"Yes, it does. We spend a lot of time at the museums and galleries." At least, they used to, when Tyler was alive.

"How about your photography? You must have lots of requests for exhibits."

"No. I gave photography up a long time ago," Lily said, with a certain smugness that reminded her of the day Aiden announced he couldn't stand the taste of cranberries.

Kyle's eyes widened and he put his hand over his heart, which Lily thought was a bit of an overreaction, but he'd always been a little melodramatic. "Really? Why?"

Because my photography instructor shattered my confidence by having a dalliance with my aunt.

"Life got in the way." As much as Lily wanted to be indifferent about him, her curiosity got the best of her. "What are you doing back in Hope Haven? Another residency?"

"I wish. My wife and I are only here for a week. The house we rented cost a fortune and it doesn't hold a candle to the view I had when I was a fellow here." He sighed. "I guess I came back to recapture that feeling. That inspiration. That was one of the best years of my life."

Lily couldn't stand it. She blurted out, "You know something, Kyle? It was one of the *worst* years of my life. I was devastated when I found out about you and my aunt—" She stopped herself from phrasing it rudely. "About the two of you *meeting* at the shack."

Kyle removed his glasses and rubbed his face. To his credit, he didn't deny it. "I'm sorry. I felt terrible about that whole predicament. It had nothing to do with you, and I didn't want it to affect how you felt about being my photography student. I tried to be very careful so you wouldn't find out. I'm surprised Dahlia ended up telling you about it."

"Dahlia *didn't* tell me about it," Lily snidely replied. "At least, not until I found out from someone else, first."

"Aiden?"

"Aiden knew?" *So I was right—that's why he was so furious at Dahlia. He felt utterly humiliated by her relationship with Kyle.*

"Of course he knew about our meeting. After I saw him taking my things from the community center, I gave him a chance to return them, but he denied he'd stolen them. So I warned him that I was going to tell Dahlia. She confronted him, but he still denied it. Fortunately, she believed me, not Aiden." Kyle squinted at Lily, who was stupefied. "I feel like we're not on the same page here?"

"Yes, we are," she managed to say as the information sank in. She realized now for sure that she'd been wrong: Dahlia and Kyle never had an affair. He'd never even photographed her. Their meeting was all about Aiden. She said it out loud to be absolutely certain she had the facts straight. "Aiden stole your camera and lenses, and he took your leather jacket. That's why you and Dahlia were meeting at the shack on the day of the fire."

"Yeah, she wanted to meet someplace where your uncle wouldn't hear us. Afterward, when I found out about how the grass had caught fire that afternoon, I felt terrible. I kept thinking that if she wasn't so preoccupied with meeting me and paying me for my stolen equipment, she wouldn't have walked away from the burn pile before it was extinguished."

"It wasn't your fault, Kyle."

"No, it wasn't, but I still wish I hadn't asked her to reimburse me right away. Unfortunately, I was broke and I needed to buy replacement equipment to shoot a friend's wedding."

As Kyle paused to put his glasses back on, Lily was struck by an epiphany. *Aiden must have hidden the bag in the shack some time after I'd taken the boards down and before he'd left the island for good. That's why Dahlia was so aghast when I found it! Since he'd denied that he'd taken Kyle's things in the first place, she wouldn't have known what he'd done with them, and she must not have had any idea they were there. No wonder she wouldn't let me look at the camera. She must have been afraid that Aiden had taken incriminating photos with it. And she knew for a fact that there weren't any headshots of her on it. If I had seen what was—or wasn't—on the camera, her lie about what she was doing at the shack with Kyle would have been exposed.*

"If only I could have waited a while longer, she wouldn't have had to pay me. I would have gotten the camera and lenses back when Aiden confessed and gave them to her to return to me," Kyle concluded. Lily didn't correct his error since her aunt had clearly intended for him to believe that Aiden had taken responsibility for his wrongdoing. She realized she wasn't the only person Dahlia had misled about her son's behavior. "How's Aiden doing now, by the way? How are Dahlia and Martin?"

"I haven't seen Aiden in years," Lily replied. It only now occurred to her that the real reason he'd been so angry at his mother must have been because she'd sided with Kyle about the theft. *That's* what must have been so humiliating for him. She added, "My aunt and uncle have both passed away."

"Oh, hey, I'm sorry to hear that, Lily."

I'm sorry, too, Kyle—for thinking the worst of you. She

thanked him and forced herself to smile. "You mentioned you're here your wife... Did you marry Natasha?"

"Good grief, no!" he uttered. "I broke up with her after—"

"After..." Lily prompted him to finish his sentence.

"After I found out she left a disparaging comment online when you won the competition."

"The one about my aunt starting the farm and conservation land on fire? *Natasha* wrote that?"

"Yes. I'd seen evidence of her jealous streak before, but that was the last straw. I felt terrible that she tried to publicly diminish your accomplishment by posting that comment."

"Well, she's not the first person to be jealous of my aunt."

"She wasn't jealous of Dahlia—she was jealous of *you*. Natasha was an aspiring photographer, and she knew how talented you were. I'm sure you still are, because you have such a unique perspective. With a little practice, you'd be right back at it."

Her fondness for her former teacher was renewed and Lily replied, "Thanks for saying that, Kyle. You were always such an encouraging instructor."

"It's easy to encourage you, Lily—you're gifted. Don't let it go to waste."

I already *let my gift go to waste. I gave up photography eighteen years ago*, she silently lamented a few minutes later as she and Ryan trekked back to the car. *I gave up my home and my friends, too. I ran away to Sweden and left my uncle behind. All because of Dahlia's lie!* Even as she fumed, Lily recognized that she alone was responsible for her choices, especially those she made in adulthood. However, it was equally true that her aunt's deception had dramatically influenced the course of Lily's life when she was at her most vulnerable. Discovering that Dahlia had intentionally fabricated a misleading story made Lily feel as hurt, angry and betrayed now as she'd felt eighteen years ago.

Even though she told me there was nothing going on between her and Kyle, she knew *I had good reason not to believe her,* seethed Lily. *She could have eliminated my doubts by telling me the truth. Instead, she allowed me to believe something that made me utterly dejected. She* knew *that's why I was leaving and she* knew *that was why I stayed away. Yet in all those years, she never came clean. How could she let that lie come between us? Didn't she care about our relationship? Didn't she care about me? Was Aiden's reputation the only thing that mattered to her?*

She simply couldn't fathom why Dahlia had gone to such lengths to prevent her from finding out about what Aiden had done. It wasn't as if Lily hadn't already known how awful his behavior was. And she certainly never would have told anyone else that he'd stolen Kyle's things. Lily had always been able to keep a secret. Besides, she wouldn't have wanted to upset her granddad or uncle by telling them and she would have been completely mortified if her peers had ever discovered that Kyle was a thief.

Even if Dahlia didn't trust me back then, it seems like eventually she would have owned up to her lie, wouldn't she? Lily brooded.

"What's wrong, Mom?" Ryan asked. "You're making your shoulders do that funny thing again."

"Oh, I was just thinking."

"About what?"

About the fact that I used to be furious at my aunt for having an affair, and now I'm furious at her for not *having one,* she thought bitterly.

"I was thinking that if—and *only* if—I don't need to get back to Philly right away for a new job, we should stay on the farm until July fifth."

Ryan stopped in his tracks. "Seriously?"

"Seriously." It was a snap decision, but suddenly Lily felt like digging in her heels. This time, she wasn't leaving Dune Island until she was good and ready. "I know how much you want to get a free choco-cran ice cream cone and see the fireworks. And I'm sure Jake would appreciate our help with the grand opening."

Ryan nearly knocked her over when he leaped forward to wrap his arms around her. "Thanks, Mom. This is going to be awesome."

"I'm glad you're happy, but remember, we can only stay *if* I don't land this job. So don't get your hopes up too high." But as her son tightened his embrace—in public, no less—Lily realized her warning was probably too late.

CHAPTER TWENTY-FOUR

NOW

After Brianna and Conner picked up Ryan to take him to the wildlife sanctuary, Lily used Jake's office for her video interview. Although she was confident she could manage the project they'd described, she wasn't sure she wanted the assignment.

The interview had taken twice as long as Lily thought it should have taken. If upper management was that inefficient, it made her wonder how inefficient the rest of the company was, too. The departmental director said she'd call Lily in a few days to inform her of their decision.

"If you're offered the role, we'd like you to come into the office for a brief orientation and tour on Friday, so you can hit the ground running after the holiday weekend. Would you be able to do that?"

The fact that they were in such a rush to hire someone reinforced Lily's suspicion that the company was poorly managed. Experience had taught her that working for a mismanaged company would be a nightmare. The thought of locking herself into an environment like that made her feel frantic. But as Lily had told Jake, her feelings didn't matter; her finances did.

She reluctantly confirmed, "Yes. I could come in on Friday."

. . .

Because she needed to purchase a few groceries at the market, Lily had arranged to swing by the wildlife sanctuary and pick up Ryan at three o'clock. Someone must have been hosting a children's party or event because kids of all ages and numerous adults were roaming the grounds and the parking lot was full. Lily had to idle on the side of the road until she spotted Brianna and the boys coming across the lawn.

As they were driving back to the farm, Ryan was so quiet that Lily asked him if something upsetting happened at the sanctuary, but he said no, he'd had a blast.

After a few more miles of silence, she began to worry that he was coming down with something. She tried to catch a glimpse of him in her review mirror, but he must have been hanging his head, because all she could see was his hair, which looked like it needed to be washed.

"Hey, Ryan," she said. "What's blue and small and round?"

"I dunno."

"A cranberry holding its breath."

The joke failed to elicit a laugh. Lily considered telling him the one about the cranberry farmer who felt bogged down. But she doubted Ryan knew what the term "bogged down" meant, so the joke would have been lost on him. Rather than pushing him to talk, she decided to wait until he initiated a conversation.

They were nearly back to the farm when he asked, "Remember how you said I could ask you anything about our family?"

Ryan's question, coupled with the quaver in his voice, made her heart skip a beat, but Lily answered calmly, "Sure, I remember. What would you like to know?"

"Am I really Dad's son?"

"What?! Of *course*, you're really Dad's son." Lily felt as if her heart was going to burst right through her chest and she didn't trust herself to drive another mile. She pulled into the scenic viewing area near the grinding stones, turned off the ignition and unbuckled her seatbelt so she could turn to face him. "Why would you ask me that?"

Ryan shrugged and looked out the window instead of into her eyes. Lily instinctively knew that someone must have planted the idea in his mind at the sanctuary and she saw red. Why would anyone suggest that Tyler wasn't Ryan's father? They didn't even know Tyler. Was it meant to be an insult to Lily? Were they implying that she'd been unfaithful? Or that she'd had too many partners to know who Ryan's father was? The notion was preposterous, but so were most of the rumors on Dune Island and that didn't stop them from spreading.

Struggling to keep her voice even so her son wouldn't think she was upset at *him*, she repeated, "Of course you were Dad's son. I promise I'm telling you the absolute, one hundred per cent factual truth." She paused, reached over the seat and cupped his chin, forcing him to meet her eyes. "Ryan Lars Perkins, your dad and I made you. I carried you inside of me for nine months and—"

He cut her off. "All right, Mom. I believe you." He squirmed free of her grasp.

"Good, I'm glad you believe me and I'm glad you asked me about it. But I'm curious about where you got the idea that Dad wasn't your father."

"It doesn't matter."

"It matters to me. I'd really like to understand why you thought that. It's okay—it won't hurt my feelings if someone said something bad about me."

"They didn't say anything bad about *you*."

"Did they say something about Dad?" When he nodded, Lily repeated, "It's okay to tell me. Dad would want you to."

"I heard Hannah's stepmom tell another mom that maybe dad kidnapped me and that's why he died."

The words came out in such a rush and his statement was so nonsensical that Lily wondered if her anger was interfering with her language comprehension abilities. She repeated, "Hannah's stepmom said Dad *kidnapped* you?"

"Yeah." Ryan tapped the back of the seat with his foot, still not meeting his mother's eyes. "The other mom was trying to guess how dad died and Hannah's stepmom—I think her name was Ms. Claire—said maybe he robbed a cradle like Uncle Martin did and that would explain why he died so soon."

Ordinarily, Lily might have struggled to keep a straight face after hearing Ryan's literal interpretation of an idiom. But today, it took all of her willpower to keep from throwing up. She got out of the car and breathed in and out several times until the feeling passed.

Then she opened Ryan's door and crouched down beside him so her face was level with his. Choosing her words carefully, she explained what a cradle robber was, emphasizing, "It's not a very kind way to describe people and it doesn't even apply to your dad because he was the same age I was."

"Oh." He was quiet, apparently mulling over this information before asking, "Was Uncle Martin a lot older than Aunt Dahlia?"

Lily realized she had to be honest with him if she wanted him to trust the other things she told him, so she confirmed, "He was fourteen years older than she was and some people consider that to be a lot older, but it's really none of their business. What's important was that Aunt Dahlia and Uncle Martin were both grown-ups and they both loved each other very much and that's why they got married."

Ryan's cheeks were flushed; it always embarrassed him to hear about people being in love. "Can we go now? I want to look for moon snails before the tide comes in."

"Sure." She kissed the top of his head. "Afterward you need

to take a shower. It's been a few days and your hair smells like seaweed."

When they returned to the farm, he galloped ahead of her toward the shack. At his age, Lily had always been eager to get down to the beach after she'd been away for a few hours in the summer, too.

It was obvious how much Ryan loved the farm and the ocean, but as they waded among the rocks, Lily pondered whether she'd made a mistake by bringing him to the island. She definitely regretted allowing him to go to the sanctuary without her. *What he heard today is exactly the kind of remark I was worried about him hearing. It made him question his very identity*, she thought. He seemed okay now, but from her own experience, Lily realized comments like Claire's weren't so easily brushed off.

An hour and a half later, as Ryan was upstairs in the cottage showering and Lily was preparing supper in the farmhouse, Jake popped into the kitchen for a cool drink.

"There you are. I haven't seen you all day," he remarked. "I wanted to find out how your interview went."

"It was okay." Lily lopped the frond off a carrot. "They seem desperate to hire someone right away, so I think they'll offer me the job."

"Are you going to accept it?"

"Probably. I need the income." She cut along the length of the orange vegetable with a rapid succession of loud taps.

"Oh." Jake took a large swallow of iced tea before bantering, "Are you annoyed at me for some reason or are you just a very aggressive vegetable chopper?"

"Annoyed at you? Why would I be annoyed at you?" The words were barely out of her mouth when she remembered their conversation on the deck last evening. *Is he concerned that*

I regret letting him give me a massage? She hadn't intended to share what Claire had said, but she didn't want Jake to worry that he'd offended her, so she told him what had happened at the sanctuary.

"Ouch," Jake said when she'd finished the story. "No wonder you're upset. How's Ryan doing?"

"He seemed okay once I explained to him what a cradle robber was, but he's a pretty sensitive kid, so I never know for certain how something affects him," Lily said. "I had actually told him this morning that if I don't get the job, we can stay on the island through the Fourth of July weekend. But now I'm having second thoughts."

"You'd go back to Philly just because one person made an inane remark?"

"Stop insinuating I'm being overly protective," Lily snapped, chopping faster. "I wouldn't expect you to understand, but comments like the ones Claire made can have a lasting effect on a person."

"You wouldn't expect me to understand?" Jake echoed derisively. He splashed the rest of his iced tea into the sink and set the glass onto the counter with a *clunk*. "In case you've forgotten what happened when we were teenagers, my mother was arrested for a DUI after she crashed her car into a utility pole and caused a blackout for the entire neighborhood— including the high school. It was reported in all the island papers and it was covered on the local news station. My mother became known as "Louise-alcoholic-liver-disease-Benson." So believe me, Lily, I understand a thing or two about how deeply certain remarks can cut a person."

Lily set down her knife. Jake's eyes were a blustery blue and he'd crossed his arms against his chest. She reached to touch his elbow. "I'm so sorry, Jake. I *had* forgotten about that. I can only imagine how painful it must have been for you."

"Yeah, well, it was worse for my sister. She was only a kid

and her peers were ruthless. My dad had left us by then, so it wasn't as if Brianna had an adult she could turn to for support. But believe it or not, good things came from everyone finding out that my mother was an alcoholic."

"Good things? Like what?"

"For one thing, we finally got the help we needed. Until then, we'd been keeping her drinking problem a secret and trying to deal with it on our own. But once it was fodder for the rumor mill, people invited us to support groups and they brought us meals while my mother was in recovery. They also told us about their own private struggles, which helped us not to feel so alone."

While he reached to refill his class with water and then took a long drink, Lily said, "I'm really glad you had people in your life who helped you through that period."

"You know what helped me most of all?" Jake asked and she shook her head. "Working on the farm with your granddad and uncle. Funny thing was, they never talked to me about what my mother had done, but being in their presence made me calmer. They were both so patient and instructive—about a lot of things, not just farming. Working side-by-side with them gave me a sense of stability when everything else in my life was chaotic. Some of the guys on the crew complained about how boring picking berries was, but I needed that kind of routine—it was a lifesaver."

So that's why he was so dedicated to my family. And it's why he's been so dedicated to preserving the farm into the future, Lily realized and her respect for him deepened—and so did her attraction.

"Anyway, looking back on what happened, my sister and I both feel like it made us more compassionate toward other people. It also made us stronger. Sometimes hard knocks can help you develop the thicker skin, which is what you need to get through other tough things in life."

Lily took his hand and turned it upward to trace the calluses on his palm. "Thick skin like this?" she murmured.

"Nah," Jake's voice was throaty. "That's from hard work, not hard knocks."

Just then, Ryan came in, sniffing the air. Lily and Jake quickly dropped hands. "Something smells good," the boy said. "What's for supper?"

"Roasted vegetables and chicken with cranberry sauce." She turned to Jake. "You're welcome to join us."

To Lily's disappointment, he said he couldn't. "My brother-in-law is back from his business trip, so we're going out for seafood. But I'll see you bright and early tomorrow."

It won't be early enough, Lily thought as she watched him go.

"Hey, Mom?" Ryan asked from the loft that evening, a few minutes after Lily had switched off the flashlight. He sounded unusually close to her.

"What did I tell you about hanging your shoulders over the edge?" she scolded him. "Scoot back, please."

"How do you know where my shoulders are? You can't see me in the dark."

"I'm a mom. I don't need light to know when you're doing something you shouldn't be doing. Back it up." She could hear Ryan shifting in the loft. "That's better. What did you want to ask me?"

"Do you know if magnifying glasses are expensive?"

"It depends on the quality, but I think they're less than ten dollars. Why?" She wondered if he'd accidentally lost or broken a magnifying lens that he'd found in the education center.

"'Cause I wish I had one to look at bugs and plants and stuff. Did you know that if it's really sunny out, you can use a magnifying glass to burn a leaf? One of the boys at the sanctuary showed me and Conner how to do it."

Lily's stomach flip-flopped and she reflexively clenched her fingers into fists. "What was the boy's name?"

"I don't know. He was one of the older kids. He wasn't there with any of the moms."

"Well, that was a very dangerous thing for him to do and I never want you to try it." *And I'll have to warn Brianna, so Conner doesn't try it, either.*

"But, Mom, you think *every*thing is dangerous. Besides, he didn't actually start the leaf on fire. He just burned a hole through it. It was cool."

"Ryan Lars Perkins, you listen to me. There's nothing *cool* about burning leaves in the woods. All it would take is a single spark or ember to start the sanctuary on fire," Lily admonished in her strictest voice. Then she launched into the story of what had happened when Dahlia didn't completely extinguish the burn pile, including the fact that she'd had to pay restitution to the fire department. She ended by asking, "You wouldn't want to cause something like that to happen, would you?"

"No way," replied Ryan emphatically. He was quiet for a moment and Lily knew he was mulling over what she'd just told him. Then he asked, "How come Aunt Dahlia got a fine if it was an accident?"

"Because sometimes we have to pay for the consequences of our actions, even if we didn't mean for something bad to happen."

"Oh." He yawned loudly. "If I promise never ever to burn anything, can I get a magnifying glass to look at stuff?"

"I'll think about it."

"Okay. Night, Mom."

Lily lay awake in her lounger for a long time, contemplating their conversation. *I always knew there was a good possibility that someone would tell Ryan about the fire while we were in Hope Haven—but I never imagined that someone would be* me.

Yet, after sharing that part of their family's history with her son, she felt surprisingly relieved. *Now I don't have to worry about how upset he'll be if someone else tells him what Dahlia did, because he already knows.* Recalling her earlier conversation with Jake, she thought, *If a story about Dahlia prevents Ryan from getting hurt, then at least one positive thing has come from what happened that day.*

CHAPTER TWENTY-FIVE

NOW

WEDNESDAY

The cell phone signal was so weak at the shack that Lily didn't realize she'd missed two calls until she happened to check her voice mail after breakfast.

The first message was good news: the mechanic would install her starter by 10:30 this morning. The second message was also good news, but it made Lily feel awful: she'd been offered the project management job. Of course, she had to accept it—and that meant that she and Ryan would need to leave the island by the following afternoon so she could attend the orientation on Friday.

I don't want to tell him about it yet because Conner's coming here again today and it would ruin their time together, she fretted. *And I don't want to tell Jake, either, because that will ruin my time with him, too.*

Not that she and Jake had planned to do anything special together, but Lily couldn't deny how much she enjoyed his company. So she came up with a compromise: she'd return the recruiter's call and accept the position, but she'd wait until the end of the day to tell her son and Jake about it.

This way, Ryan will have time to process his feelings and he can pack his suitcase tonight. Then tomorrow, he'll be free until noon to play with Conner or go to the beach before it's time for us to catch the ferry.

Her brainstorm to soften Ryan's disappointment seemed reasonable in theory, but as Lily knew, the reality of leaving Dune Island wasn't going to be nearly so simple.

At 10:30, Jake dropped Lily off at the garage on his way to the recycling center with Ryan and Conner. All three of the boys were dressed in their Lindgren T-shirts and caps. *To steal a phrase from Dahlia, they look like three cranberries in a bog.* Lily thought wistfully, *I wish I didn't have to take Ryan back to Philly tomorrow.*

Once she'd paid the mechanic, she drove to Mrs. Henderson's house, because she figured it would be the last chance she'd have to visit her before leaving the island.

Her elderly friend was a little thinner, but she looked more or less the same as Lily remembered. If Mrs. Henderson was surprised to see her after all these years, she didn't show it. She embraced her, exclaiming, "Ah, here she is, Selma's girl."

Agnes was delighted to receive the chocolate-covered cranberries Lily had brought her and she immediately poured them into a candy dish. As Mrs. Henderson was making coffee, Lily inquired about her health and her family, and then Lily told her about Ryan and their life in Pennsylvania.

When the two women had settled into the living room overlooking the water, Agnes brought up the topic Lily had been hesitant to discuss. "I was so sorry to hear about Dahlia's passing. I didn't find out until we arrived on the island. What a shock—she was so vibrant. Such a lovely woman."

They reminisced fondly about preparing for Dahlia and Aiden's arrival at the farmhouse, and about Dahlia and

Martin's cliffside wedding. "That was a wonderful day and I appreciated it that Dahlia always took such good care of my grandma," Lily acknowledged. "But as you can probably guess, Dahlia and I had a... a falling out when I was eighteen. We sort of smoothed things over after my uncle died but we were never as close as we were when she first came to the island."

Mrs. Henderson thoughtfully patted a tuft of fluffy white hair into place near her temple. Then she said something that shocked Lily. "Dahlia and I drifted apart, too, shortly after you left. Mind you, there wasn't ever an ill word spoken between us, but I noticed she began avoiding me. At first, I felt a little slighted, but then I realized that it probably had more to do with her than with me—I think she felt a little guilty."

"Guilty? Why?"

"I believe it may have had something to do with the fire."

From the way Mrs. Henderson was hedging around the topic, Lily got the sense that she knew Aiden had stolen Kyle's photography equipment and jacket. But it was possible she just meant she thought Dahlia was ashamed of burning the conservation land. "What do you mean?"

"Oh, dear. I probably shouldn't have said anything, but hearing about Dahlia's death has stirred up old memories and doubts that I thought I'd put out of my mind a long time ago." Agnes set down her cup with a sigh and Lily nodded, to indicate she understood how the elderly woman felt. "I suppose now that she's gone, it won't hurt to tell you. The day of the fire, I stopped by the farm to drop off a treat and I heard Dahlia and Aiden arguing out back, near the burn pile."

"What were they saying?"

"I couldn't hear their words, just their voices. But it always struck me as odd that Dahlia had walked away from the burn pile before it was extinguished. She was so conscientious about everything else—Selma's medications. Her wedding ring. Lars's driving. It seems strange she wouldn't have double-checked the fire."

"Maybe she was distracted." *She had good reason to be*, Lily thought.

"Yes, maybe she was."

"You don't sound convinced."

"Oh, it's just a suspicion because that rebellious, self-centered son of hers was so irresponsible. Sometimes I wondered if..." She turned her palms upward, indicating Lily should read between the lines. What was she saying?

"You don't think Aiden set the farm and conservation land on fire, do you?"

"Goodness, no! Aiden may have been careless and maybe even destructive. But I doubt he'd ever deliberately do something that could potentially cause physical harm to another person. However, I've often wondered whether *he* was the one who was supposed to be minding the burn pile and *he* walked away before it was extinguished."

Lily was astonished. "But why would Dahlia lie about that? Why would she take responsibility for it?"

"Aiden was eighteen and he'd already been in trouble for painting the grinding stones... as well as for other things. As his mother, maybe she was trying to protect him from the authorities."

"But why wouldn't she have told me or Uncle Martin that she was covering for him?"

"Maybe she was trying to protect both of you—and Lars, too."

"From what?"

"Perhaps she was afraid that since she'd lied to the police, if someone found out, they'd question your statements, too. Maybe she didn't want to put you in that position." Mrs. Henderson suddenly looked flustered. "Then again, I'm an old lady. My memory isn't what it used to be, so please don't take anything I say to heart, dear."

But everything she'd said made perfect sense and it all fit with Lily's recollection of that day. It also matched what Olivia had said about Aiden taking so long to meet her at the conservation land parking lot.

I'd bet almost anything that Mrs. Henderson is right, Lily silently reasoned. *Dahlia must have told Aiden to watch the burn pile so she could go meet Kyle at the shack to reimburse him for his camera and lenses. Aiden was probably angry about being accused of stealing—even though he was guilty—and he ditched the responsibility of extinguishing the fire, just like he got out of being responsible for anything else on the farm.*

At least, Lily was 90 per cent certain that's what had happened. But as someone who'd been the subject of plenty of inaccurate speculation and false rumors, she knew she had to allow for the possibility that she was mistaken. She had to give Aiden the benefit of the doubt about the fire. Besides, even *if* the fire wasn't Dahlia's fault, and even *if* she'd lied about it to protect Aiden, she had still lied. And her lies had had very damaging consequences for Lily's life.

Then again, maybe she wasn't lying—not about abandoning the fire, anyway. I'm probably never going to know the truth about what happened that day, so there's no sense upsetting either Mrs. Henderson or me by dwelling on it now, she concluded. So she changed the subject and told Agnes about inheriting the estate and why she had to sell the farm.

Mrs. Henderson clucked her tongue in sympathy. "What a shame."

"Yes, it is," agreed Lily wholeheartedly.

Ryan stood on the railing of the fence, waving as Brianna and Conner drove away. *If this is how he feels when his friend leaves for the afternoon, how will he feel when we leave the island permanently?* she wondered. But Lily knew she couldn't delay telling him about her job offer any longer.

"After you put away the wheelbarrow you left on the front lawn, I'd like to speak to you about something important," she told him. "I'll be in the kitchen, starting supper. We're having cod and those sweet potato fries you like so much."

She'd barely had time to remove the glass pan from the cupboard and set it on one of the portable islands, when she heard the door open in the gift shop. Sophie must have forgotten to lock it when she left. Lily crossed the hall and stuck her head into the room. "Ryan?"

"No, it's not Ryan, Lily," a dark-haired woman replied. "It's me, Gretchen Turner."

She needed no introduction; when they were in high school, Gretchen Turner was the second biggest blabbermouth in Lily's class after Claire Griffin. She may have changed since then, but Lily had made it this long without being quizzed by Gretchen, and she didn't want to start now.

"Hi, Gretchen. It's nice to see you but I'm afraid the gift shop is closed for the day."

"Oh, I'm not here to buy anything, although I'd love to poke around. The place looks fantastic," she gushed, eyeing the displays. "My daughter, Savannah, is going to be working in the gift shop starting this weekend. Sophie set aside a name tag and T-shirt for her because she's self-conscious about her size and she wants to try the shirt on in private to make sure it fits. I'm sorry if it's a bad time, but I was on my way home from the hospital—I'm a pediatric social worker—so I thought I'd swing by and pick it up."

Before Lily could reply, Ryan called from the kitchen, "Mom? Where are you?"

"I'm coming!" she answered. Although Gretchen's request was very thoughtful on behalf of her daughter, Lily was still a little relieved to get away. "I don't know where Sophie stashed your daughter's uniform, but Jake should be able to find it. Do you mind checking with him? I think he's in the barn."

"Okay, sure," Gretchen good-naturedly agreed before making her way out.

In the kitchen, Lily served Ryan a glass of lemonade and told him to pull up a stool so they could talk while she was preparing their supper.

Spreading olive oil in the bottom of the baking dish, she said, "There's something I have to tell you that's sort of good news, but sort of bad." She set down the dish and rested her hands on the island, looking into his eyes. "I got the job I told you about, which means we have to head home tomorrow."

"Tomorrow? But you said we could stay until the Fourth of July!"

"No, Ryan. I specifically told you we could only stay *if* I didn't take the job."

"But I'll miss the fireworks at Beach Plum Cove. I'll miss the free ice cream," he wailed.

"We can go to the fireworks in Philadelphia. And after supper tonight, I'll take you to Bleecker's Ice Cream Shop—which will be even better than on the Fourth of July because you can get a double scoop. Or you can get a sundae, if you want." Even as she was speaking, Lily recognized what a pathetic consolation prize she'd just offered her son.

"Why do we have to go back tomorrow? How come your job starts on a Friday? Don't most jobs start on a Monday?"

"I need to attend an orientation."

"Can't you ask them to let you do it online?"

"No. It has to be done in person."

"Can't you do it on Monday—or on Tuesday, since Monday is Fourth of July?"

"Ryan, this is non-negotiable. I'm glad you love it here so much but now it's time to go home. If we pack tonight, you'll have all morning to hang out with Conner or to go to the beach. We'll do whatever you want to do until we have to leave. For now, I'd like you to go wash your hands, please."

Ryan didn't budge from his stool. He muttered something that she couldn't hear so she asked him to repeat it. "I said Hannah's stepmom is right."

Against her better judgment, Lily questioned, "Right about what?"

"She said you act like you're better than everyone in Hope Haven and it's true. That's why you didn't tell me I had a great-aunt and a great-uncle and great-grandparents who lived on a farm. And that's why won't let me stay here and have fun with my friends."

Peeved at both her son and Claire, Lily pointed toward the bathroom in the hallway. "Go wash your hands."

"You are the meanest, most stuck-up-est person in the world!" Ryan yelled as he used the portable island for leverage to push his stool back. His stool didn't budge, but the island tilted, causing his empty glass and the baking dish to smash onto the floor. Ryan's mouth fell open and he glared accusingly at Lily, as if to say, *Look at what you made me do.* He burst into tears, hopped down from the stool and ran outside.

As Lily was retrieving the broom and dustpan, Gretchen tentatively tiptoed into the kitchen. *This is just what I need,* Lily thought. *A nosy pediatric social worker reporting my son's meltdown to a family services agency.*

"Oh, no. That looks dangerous," Gretchen uttered, surveying the floor.

"Yeah. Clumsy me. I keep forgetting that this portable islands isn't stable and I accidentally knocked into it. Everything came crashing down." The lie sprang to Lily's lips so quickly she barely thought about it. Only after she said it did she realize that her statement might make Gretchen think Lily was downplaying her own outburst, instead of Ryan's. *What if she reports me to family services?*

"I can give you a hand if you'd like."

"No," barked Lily, before softening her tone. "I wouldn't want you to cut yourself. Thanks, but I've got this covered."

"Okay, well, take care."

After Gretchen left, Lily stood at the sink and looked out the window, practicing deep breathing. Ryan's reaction to her had been so upsetting that Lily's legs were trembling. It was one thing for Claire to say Lily thought she was better than everyone else, but it troubled her that Ryan saw her that way, too. Granted, he'd been lashing out because he was disappointed, so his opinion had to be taken with a grain of salt. But he didn't usually speak to Lily like that and she was concerned he meant it.

The only reason I've been keeping my distance from people on Dune Island is because I've wanted to protect Ryan from their gossip, she silently defended herself. Still, her son didn't know that and she didn't want to be a poor role model for him. She certainly didn't want him to become as angry and defiant as he'd been just now. *Maybe it's a good thing that we're leaving the island tomorrow after all,* she thought.

CHAPTER TWENTY-SIX

NOW

After depositing the shards and slivers of glass into the bin, Lily decided to switch their supper menu to chicken salad wraps. She had lost her appetite and she doubted Ryan would be able to eat a full meal of fish and sweet potato fries after being so upset, either.

Surprisingly, he still wasn't back by the time she'd finished rolling the wraps and setting the table. On the rare occasions when he became upset enough to cry, he usually only needed five or ten minutes to himself, but half an hour must have passed since he'd stormed out of the house. *My poor boy*, Lily thought. Any annoyance she'd felt toward him had quickly been replaced with compassion and concern. *This really hit him hard.*

As she moved toward the door to call him, an orange and white helicopter buzzed overhead. It was so close it rattled the dishes on the shelves, along with Lily's nerves. *There must have been a whale or shark sighting. Or maybe a boat capsized*, she thought. *I hope everyone's okay.*

Lily stepped outside, calling Ryan's name. Once, twice, three times, but still no answer. *Did he go to the shack? He knows he's supposed to stay within sight and shouting distance of an adult at all times.* She'd only hiked halfway across the backyard when she had the undeniable sense her son was in trouble.

This wasn't one of her usual overly protective qualms—Lily knew Ryan needed her just as surely as she'd known that her grandmother had died when she was a teenager. She charged toward the woods so fast she lost one of her sandals, but she didn't stop to pick it up.

Ryan wouldn't have gone swimming alone, no matter how angry he was at me, she tried to assure herself. But when she emerged from the other side of the trees, she spotted the helicopter hovering over the water close to shore. She sprinted so hard her momentum might have propelled her clear over the precipice, if she hadn't tripped and fallen five yards before she reached the lip of the cliff.

Although her palms felt raw and her knees were throbbing, Lily crawled the rest of the way to the edge and peered over it. The high tide was getting deeper and tall swells smashed against the base of the cliff. At first, all Lily noticed was a nearby blue and white fishing boat, bobbing violently in the surf. Then, a yellow flash caught her eye: directly below her, the waves were bouncing a fractured bodyboard against the rocks. It might as well have been Lily's heart that was being dashed to pieces.

No, no, no, not Ryan, too. Not my child, she silently implored.

If she hadn't already been lying prone against the rocky sand, Lily would have collapsed. Panting and dizzy, she was on the brink of passing out when she spotted a flicker of movement in her peripheral vision. Lily blinked and licked her lips. She inched her shoulders as far as she dared over the ledge, craning her neck. About seventy-five yards to her right, halfway between her and the conservation land staircase, Ryan was perched on the revetment wall.

Her elation that he wasn't in the ocean quickly faded when she realized one of his legs was bent at the knee and it appeared his foot was wedged in a crevice between two rocks. Although she couldn't see his face, Lily could tell he was in pain by the way he was writhing.

She craned her neck upward, wondering if the pilot had spotted him. But the helicopter seemed to be struggling to steady itself in the gusty wind. *Pretty soon the waves are going to reach Ryan!* Lily panicked. *They're going to wash right over him.*

"Don't move, Ryan! I'm coming to help you! I'm coming!" she shouted even as the aircraft drowned out her voice. Scoping out the terrain, she mentally plotted the safest path before she sat up and swung her legs over the edge and began her descent.

She had barely lowered herself down backward when her right foot slipped. Dirt and pebbles rained into the water below, but Lily managed to grab onto an exposed root and shift her weight to her other foot. Her heart thundering in her ears, she leaned spread-eagled against the cliffside and calculated her next move.

There's a rock a couple of yards to my left. It'll support me better, she thought and began worming toward it sideways.

"Stay still, Lily!" Jake's voice commanded from above her. "That ground's too fragile. You're going to start a landslide—and you'll slide with it!"

"Ryan's hurt. He needs me." She redistributed her weight and a few more pebbles bounced down the cliffside.

"He'll be all right. The Coast Guard's here. They know what they're doing."

"Ryan needs me," she repeated.

"Listen, Lily! Ryan might have hurt his leg, but he's not in danger of falling. *You* will be though if you try to go get him. So here's what you need to do. Raise your hands straight up over your head. I'm going to grab your wrists and you're going to grab mine. On the count of three, I'll hoist you up."

Lily did what he instructed. Jake didn't exactly hoist her up; it was more like he *dragged* her over the ledge, scraping her chest and stomach against the coarse earth. As soon as her feet were on solid ground again, she peered toward the revetment wall. A man was lowered down from the helicopter, like a spider on a thread, until he reached the rock where her son was stranded. The man bent over Ryan, obscuring her view for what felt like ages. Finally, he straightened up.

"What's he doing now?" Lily begged.

"Looks like he's putting a harness on Ryan. I'm not sure but I think he's going to strap him to his chest..."

A minute later, the hovering aircraft reeled Ryan and his rescuer from the rock. As she watched her son dangling in the air, Lily's knees went weak. She buried her face in her hands. "I can't look. Will you watch for me to make sure he's okay?"

"Sure." Jake must have noticed her legs were quaking, because he wrapped his arm around her side, propping her up. A moment later he commented, "They're reeling them in nice and smooth. It should only be another minute or two."

"I don't know if I can hold my breath for that long," Lily muttered. Jake chuckled, but she wasn't kidding. When he finally announced Ryan and the man were inside the helicopter, she let the air out of her lungs in a whoosh and dropped her hands and opened her eyes.

The helicopter was farther away than she expected it to be, which made her wonder if it had been flying instead of hovering as it was lifting her son and the rescuer. "What's wrong? Where are they going? There's plenty of open space to land on the farm. Why doesn't Ryan tell them to land here? I want to see him!"

Jake tipped his head and wrinkled his forehead, as if he wasn't sure what to make of her question.

"They're taking him to Hope Haven Hospital to get Ryan checked out. It's routine procedure," Gretchen answered. Lily didn't know when she'd arrived at the edge of the cliff, but Gretchen handed Lily her missing sandal. "Come on, I'll give you two a ride there."

Lily would have preferred to go alone with Jake to the hospital. But when she noticed how grim and ashen his face appeared, she realized he wasn't in any condition to get behind the wheel, either. "It's a good thing you showed up on the farm when you did, Gretchen," she acknowledged. "A ride to the hospital would be very helpful."

Before they hurried away from the cliffside, Jake waved both his arms and shouted, "Thank you!" to the little fishing boat's captain and crew, who had undoubtedly called the Coast Guard. But Lily blew them kisses.

CHAPTER TWENTY-SEVEN

NOW

Ryan had a broken ankle and a contusion near his elbow, but he was otherwise unharmed and he hardly cried at all. Lily, on the other hand, used half a box of tissues drying her tears.

"What were you doing out on the revetment wall?" she asked as they waited for the doctor to return with a pair of crutches.

Ryan explained that Conner's bodyboard had blown over the edge of the cliff and landed on the revetment. "I had to go get it because you said I should take good care of stuff I use, especially if it's borrowed. I knew I wasn't allowed to climb down the cliff, but you didn't tell me not to climb sideways. So I used the stairs to go down as far as I needed to go and then I cut straight across the revetment. I figured I could be real careful since the revetment wall isn't steep and eroded like the cliff. But I skidded and jammed my foot between two rocks and the body-board slid into the water anyway."

Lily was amazed at how much of her instruction her son had taken to heart. *He wasn't being rebellious—he just doesn't have good risk assessment skills yet*, she realized.

They were interrupted when Dr. Socorro, a handsome man

with golden ringlets, came into the room again. After reviewing her son's care plan with Lily and making sure the boy knew how to use his crutches, he told Ryan, "I'm envious that you got to ride in a Coast Guard 'copter. I keep begging them to take me for a twirl, but they never do. How was it?"

"Awesome."

"That's what I figured. But it was probably a lot more fun to fly than to watch, wasn't it, Mom?" he asked, winking at Lily.

"I don't know. I *couldn't* watch."

Dr. Socorro grinned. On his way out the door, he gave Ryan a fist bump and said, "Feel better and stay safe out there."

Jake and Gretchen were both relieved to hear that Ryan's injuries weren't more serious than a broken bone. Regardless, Gretchen offered to go get the car and bring it to the ER entrance, so Ryan wouldn't have to cross the parking lot while his foot was still sore.

Lily said she'd go with her, since she needed fresh air, but really she wanted to take the opportunity to thank Gretchen for bringing her and Jake to the hospital. "I also appreciate how level-headed you were," she said. "Thank you."

"You're welcome." Gretchen sighed. "You know, raising a child on your own isn't easy. If you want to talk about—"

Lily cut her off, firmly but kindly saying, "Thank you, but I don't need a social worker, Gretchen, and neither does Ryan."

"There wouldn't be any shame in it if you did. But I wasn't speaking to you in my professional capacity. I was speaking to you as a friend. Or at least, as a former acquaintance. And as a single mom." She paused and then added, "I realize I was a real busybody in high school, but I've changed a lot since then... Having a baby six months after I graduated from high school gave me a deeper appreciation of how destructive the local rumor mill can be."

"Mm, yes, it can be," Lily murmured, lightening her tone. She hadn't known that Gretchen was pregnant in high school and she could imagine that she'd endured her share of unkind remarks. "Thank you for the offer. We're leaving Dune Island soon, but I appreciate the thought."

"If you change your mind—about leaving or about talking to me—just look me up."

I wish I could change my mind about leaving, Lily thought.

It was after nine by the time Gretchen dropped off Jake, Lily and Ryan at the farm. Because Ryan couldn't trek out to the shack, much less climb the ladder to the loft, Lily told him they'd sleep in Dahlia's room.

"Aunt Dahlia's room has two beds?" Ryan asked.

"No, just one. But I'll sleep in the chair," Lily answered even though she doubted she'd sleep a wink that night. Because her son had mentioned he was hungry, she asked Jake, "While I run next door, would you help Ryan navigate the stairs? He's not accustomed to the crutches yet, so he could use some support. I don't want him to slip and break his other ankle."

Jake cheerfully agreed, so Lily hurried into the farmhouse kitchen. The wraps she'd prepared for supper were still on the table, but she made two slices of toast for Ryan and spread cranberry-orange jam—his new favorite flavor—on top of them.

She'd just returned to the cottage as Jake came downstairs. "Ryan's all set—I elevated his foot on a couple of pillows. His eyes are pretty heavy, so if you're going to say goodnight, you'd better do it fast."

"Thanks. I will in a sec. But I didn't get a chance to thank you for rescuing me from the edge of the cliff. I guess I shouldn't have tried to climb down it, but I was sort of out of my head..."

"*Sort of?*" Jake teased. He reached for her hair and pulled a pine needle from her curl. "No problem. I'm glad you're both safe now. Get some rest and we'll talk tomorrow, right?"

"Right." Jogging up the stairs, Lily realized she hadn't told Jake yet that she'd been offered the job, or that she'd planned on leaving.

We can't go tomorrow anyway, she decided. *Ryan isn't going to feel comfortable enough to take such a long road trip the day after breaking his ankle.* The way Lily saw it, the company who hired her was desperate; they'd wait for her to arrive next week.

In Ryan's room, she angled the armchair so she could watch him while he was eating.

"Why are you looking at me like that?" he asked, his mouth full.

"I'm just very thankful you're okay." Her eyes teared up; she couldn't help it.

He set down his toast and dipped his chin to his chest. "I didn't mean to break those dishes."

"I know you didn't. It's okay."

"I'm sorry I said all that stuff, too."

"Oh, love, I forgive you." Lily leaned over and embraced him. "I think we should work on finding new ways to express ourselves when we're upset, don't you?"

"Yeah."

"And I think I could work on being a little friendlier to people on Dune Island."

He lifted his chin. His big eyes were hopeful. "So we probably should stay here a few more days so you can practice, huh?"

Lily laughed. "Yes, we can stay, but there's something you need to know about life on a small island like this."

"What?"

"News travels very quickly, so by tomorrow, people are going to be talking about you being stranded out on the cliff."

"So, I'm going to be, like, a celebrity or something?"

"That's one way to look at it. But some people are going to have strong opinions about what happened. Some of the things they say might not be very nice."

"Like what?"

"Well, they might say I'm a bad mother for not watching you closer."

"You're the best mother in the world!"

That's quite an improvement from being the meanest, most stuck-up-est person in the world. "Or they might say you don't have respect for the environment. Or you don't care about beach erosion."

"That's not why I was on the revetment. It was because Conner's bodyboard blew down there."

"I know that and you know that, but that's not what other people might say."

"So? I'll tell them what really happened."

"They might not believe you."

"That's dumb." He was silent, mulling it over. "But I don't care. I still want to stay."

"Are you sure?"

"Yeah. Because if I stay, I get to see the fireworks at Beach Plum Cove with my new friends and eat free ice cream. That's way better than any bad things someone says about me."

Maybe his risk assessment skills are more developed than I thought they were. "Okay, then, we'll stay."

Jake was right; Ryan's eyes were drooping fast. After he'd taken the medication Dr. Socorro had provided, he nestled against the pillow and asked, "Can you tell me a cranberry joke?"

"Sure... Why did the cranberry turn red?"

"I don't know. Why?"

"Because he saw the turkey dressing."

"Hunh." Ryan made a half-laugh, half-yawning sound. She

thought he'd dozed off, but then, with his eyes still closed, he mumbled, "Mom, I really didn't like being in the helicopter that much. Or on the rope. It made me dizzy. But don't tell Conner or Bart or Zeke I said that, okay?"

"Don't worry. Your secret is safe with me. And I still think you were very brave." Lily leaned forward and kissed his head, right on his beautiful cowlick. Within a half a minute, he was sleeping. She settled into the chair beside his bed and listened to his breathing, the way she used to do when she first brought him home from the hospital after he was born.

Even though it was a balmy evening, Lily felt chilled—it was from all the emotional turmoil, no doubt. Since she didn't have an extra blanket, she rummaged through the steamer trunk to double check if there was a sweater among her high-school shirts. She removed both cardboard boxes and then all the articles of clothing, but unfortunately, the warmest top she found was a long-sleeved blouse that didn't fit her.

However, as she was replacing her wardrobe, she noticed something she hadn't seen before: two folders and a magazine were pressed flat against the side of the steamer trunk in an upright position. Lily lifted them out and examined the magazine. It was the edition of the publication featuring her winning photos—and a picture she'd taken of the farmhouse and cranberry bogs were on the cover.

I didn't know my photo made the cover! she marveled. She flipped through the pages until she came to the rest of her collection: a photo of her grandfather in his plaid flannel shirt, surveying the bog. Martin bent over a piece of machinery in the workshop. Close-ups of the vines and berries. A panoramic of the view from the cliffside. And the beloved tumble-down shack on stilts.

Viewing them now, eighteen years later, it almost seemed as if someone else had taken the photos. And Lily finally recognized that what everyone had told her was true: the girl who'd taken those photos had a gift. Was it possible she still did? Tears splattered onto the page, so Lily quickly closed the magazine and set it aside. Her aunt had taken such good care to preserve it that Lily didn't want it getting ruined now.

Next, she opened the first folder, which also contained a variety of photos she'd taken of the farm. These weren't nearly as remarkable as those she'd submitted to the contest, except for one: the portrait she'd snapped of Dahlia on the deck of the shack the day of the fire.

She must have found this folder mixed in with the other stuff I left behind. But she never let on that she knew I'd taken this without her permission, Lily thought. Slowly tracing her aunt's image with her finger, she recollected what beautiful skin she had, what high cheekbones. Dahlia's hand was pressed against her cheek and although she seemed worried, she still appeared exquisitely attractive, with her inky hair contrasting against her white shirt.

As she studied the photo, she was struck by a detail she hadn't noticed before now: Dahlia was wearing her wedding ring. Lily immediately thought of the ring holder that Martin had made. She recalled how her aunt had always been fastidious about removing her ring and leaving it on the ring holder while she was working outside, and then replacing it when she was done for the day. Hadn't Martin teased her about that, saying it was like watching someone punching in and out on a time clock?

If Dahlia had put her ring back on, that meant she considered her outside work to be done for the day! Lily realized. It was as if, after so much jiggling, a lock had finally clicked open in her mind. Instantly, she was as certain as she could ever be that Mrs. Henderson had been right—the fire was Aiden's fault.

Lily could see the scenario playing out in her mind, just as she'd imagined earlier today. *Dahlia must have told him to take care of the burn pile. Then she came back inside, put on her ring and retrieved the money to reimburse Kyle. While she was at the shack, Aiden probably got impatient waiting for the fire to die down and he left to meet Olivia in the conservation land.*

Undoubtedly, Mrs. Henderson was also right about the reason Dahlia had taken responsibility for the fire; she hadn't wanted Aiden to get into even more trouble. This morning, the possibility that her aunt had lied had seemed indefensible to Lily. But now the Thoreau quote resonated in her mind: "It's not what you look at that matters, it's what you see."

As she looked at Dahlia's photo, what she saw was a mother who had lied to protect her child—which was exactly what Lily had done today. She had told Gretchen that *she'd* broken the glass and baking dish, even though it was her son's fault. And because Lily knew if she was in the same position tomorrow, she'd accept the blame for her son's actions all over again, she realized she could forgive her aunt for lying about the fire.

It's a relief to feel like I finally know for certain what happened, she thought, reaching for the second folder.

It contained two envelopes. Dahlia's name and address was written across the first one in Lily's slanted cursive. The return label also indicated that Lily had been the sender. The date stamp was too faded to read, so she assumed it must have been a Christmas or birthday card, since that was virtually the only time she ever sent handwritten notes by mail. She removed the card from its envelope. Embossed in gold on plain, heavy stationery were the words, "In Deepest Sympathy."

A shiver fluttered across her shoulders. This was the card she had written to Dahlia shortly after Martin died. Lily and Tyler were living in Arizona at the time. She was pregnant and on bedrest for pre-eclampsia, so she hadn't been able to attend her uncle's funeral. The day after Martin died, Ryan was born.

Lily recalled how overjoyed she'd been after his birth, yet how her elation was mixed with sorrow because of her uncle's passing. She and Tyler had provided the flowers for the funeral and she'd expressed her sympathy on the phone to Dahlia, but Lily had recognized how meager those gestures were compared to the enormity of her aunt's grief. Despite the distance between her and Dahlia, she'd wanted to be a source of comfort.

She didn't know what else to do, so after a bleary, late-night feeding, she'd tucked Ryan into his bassinet and penned a heart-felt note to Dahlia. She couldn't remember exactly what she'd said, but she distinctly recalled how emotional she'd felt as she struggled to express herself in a way that was consoling, yet honest.

Lily opened the card now and read:

Dear Dahlia,

I have been thinking of you every day and wondering how you're coping. I've wanted to call, but considering my post-partum hormones and sleep deprivation, I'm afraid I'd wind up blubbering and it would make you feel worse.

I don't know if you remember when I used to say the "golden hour" was my favorite time of day, because that's when the warm, golden sunlight diminishes the harsher colors and makes everything seem softer beneath its glow...

That's how I felt about you when you came to live with us. You cast warmth and softened us all with your presence. You were my family's "golden hour"—especially Uncle Martin's. He was his brightest self beneath the glow of your smile.

I wish I could give you that kind of warmth now. I wish I could help diminish some of the harshness of your grief, the way you did for me after Grandma passed away.

Instead, I send much sympathy—

Lily

PS The enclosed photo of Ryan is from when he was one week old. I think he mostly resembles Tyler, but every now and then I see a glimpse of Granddad or Uncle Martin in him... Could it be his messy hair?!

Lily chuckled, but her smile quickly turned into tears. *I wish I had come back to Dune Island while Uncle Martin and Dahlia were still alive,* she thought.

She wished a lot of things: that she hadn't behaved so immaturely as a teenager and so stubbornly as a young adult. That Ryan could have had the opportunity to love and be loved by her side of the family. That her husband would have lived to watch their son grow up.

But mostly what Lily wished right now was that Dahlia was here. That they could trek out to the shack with a pint of choco-cran ice cream and settle into their deck chairs. As single moms and wives who'd cared for ailing husbands, they'd had so much in common and Lily imagined that they could have talked long after the "blue hour" gave way to nightfall and the stars and moon rose across the dark blanket of sky.

For the first time since she'd learned of her aunt's death, Lily allowed herself to truly mourn. Her shoulders heaving, she silently sobbed into her arms. Ten, fifteen, twenty minutes must have passed before Ryan stirred beside her. Concerned that he'd wake to find her in this distraught state, she held her breath until he was still again.

Drying her cheeks with the hem of her shirt, Lily reminded herself, *I might not have returned to Dune Island after Uncle Martin died, but Dahlia never visited me, either, and I invited her to Philly lots of times.*

It wasn't that she was blaming her aunt, because after Martin's death, Dahlia had to manage the farm single-handedly. Then she was caught up in the process of bringing Jake on board as her business manager. After that, the pair had been busy putting in a new irrigation system and converting the house and cottage into the gift shop and education center.

Lily, meanwhile, had been struggling to adjust to life as first-time mom. Shortly after Ryan turned two years old, Tyler was transferred to Philadelphia. The upheaval of relocating and purchasing a new home consumed the little bit of energy Lily had left over from working part-time while raising a toddler.

Just when it seemed as if her schedule might have allowed her the opportunity to travel, Tyler had been diagnosed with cancer and he'd later passed away. After that, it was like she'd told Steve: the women's schedules had kept them too busy for lengthy phone conversations, much less for visiting each other.

Yet even though they'd both had legitimate excuses not to see each other in person, Lily was aware that the reason they didn't make more of an effort was because their relationship had drifted too far from what it once was—and they were both to blame for that.

At least this note is a reminder of how close we used to be, she silently consoled herself. *Maybe that's why Dahlia kept it all these years. Maybe it's why she considered it a treasure.*

Sniffling, Lily picked up the second envelope addressed to Dahlia; this one had an attorney's name in the corner. She unfolded the stationery and perused the typed letter, which was dated almost a month and a half ago, shortly before Dahlia's death. It read:

Dear Ms. Lindgren:

As agreed, we have arranged to deduct the salary you earned while working for Supreme Modeling Agency from your late, ex-husband's funds prior to awarding your son the remaining assets.

The total amount (see attached) will be deposited in your account within forty-five (45) days.

It was signed by the attorney, and another attorney was cc'd on the note, as well. Reading it, Lily was absolutely stunned. *Dahlia worked for a modeling agency?* she marveled. *Was that why she* hated *being photographed?* She must have had a bad experience. Maybe she felt exploited. Or maybe it was the association with her ex-husband, a talent agent, that Dahlia resented.

Whatever the circumstances were, if she received a posthumous settlement, it must have meant he'd been withholding her salary from her during his lifetime, she thought. *No wonder she never talked about him, the snake!*

Curious, she flipped the page to view the amount on the attachment and she was even more shocked than when she'd discovered her aunt had been a model. To Lily, the figure was astounding.

Why didn't Steve tell me about this? He said the only thing in here worth real value was Dahlia's wedding ring. Then she realized maybe Dahlia hadn't had a chance to mention the settlement to him yet, since it had only been deposited recently. Her aunt had been so busy with the farm opening for the tourist season and it wasn't as if she thought she'd pass away anytime soon. She probably just hadn't gotten around to discussing it with Steve.

I'll have to confirm this with him tomorrow, Lily thought, still incredulous about her discovery. *At least now I don't feel one iota of remorse about Dahlia leaving her assets to me instead of to Aiden—he apparently received an inheritance from his father.*

It occurred to her that if the settlement rightfully belonged to her, she could easily repay her mortgage with the amount of money in Dahlia's bank account, regardless of whether or not she sold the farm. Her mind was whirring.

I wouldn't have to sell it after all, she realized. *I could sell our home in Philly instead, and Ryan and I could move here. We could live in the upstairs of the farmhouse and the students could stay here, in the cottage. I could help on the farm and with the culinary classes. Maybe I'd take up photography again. Who knows, I might even end up offering professional photography services, just like I used to dream of doing!*

Yes, she'd have to deal with people like Claire and she'd have to be vigilant about protecting her son from their gossip, too. But according to Ryan, staying on Dune Island was *way better* than anything negative they might say about him or Lily.

Was she getting carried away? Could she really make this decision here, curled up in Dahlia's old bedroom in the middle of the night, her tears still wet on her cheeks? Or was taking back the beloved home and farm she'd given up all those years ago simpler than she'd ever imagined?

CHAPTER TWENTY-EIGHT

NOW

THURSDAY

Lily hadn't slept a wink all night, but her thinking had never been clearer. At exactly eight o'clock, she tiptoed from the room, hoping Ryan wouldn't wake quite yet, and called Steve. She'd barely finished confirming that she had, indeed, inherited whatever money Dahlia had been awarded, when she heard Jake's truck pulling up the driveway.

She quickly told Steve she'd speak to him again later. She ran downstairs, burst out the door and darted across the parking area to where Jake was unloading bags of mulch from his truck bed.

"Hey, Lily, is everything all right?" he asked as soon as he saw her approaching.

"Everything is *awesome!*" she exclaimed. "Do you mind putting that down for a sec? I have something important I need to tell you."

Jake dropped the mulch back into the truck bed with a *thunk* and clapped the dirt from his hands. "What is it?"

"You're not going to believe this, but it turns out that Dahlia left me enough money to cover the loss of selling my house in Philly. I've decided I'm keeping the farm and Ryan and I are moving here." Her heart was racing and her palms were clammy but she had never felt more sure of anything in her life.

Jake scratched the back of his head but he didn't say anything for a long time. It wasn't the response Lily had expected to get from him. Finally, he asked, "Are you sure? I mean, this is a huge decision. Finances aside, a week ago it seemed like you couldn't wait to leave Hope Haven. You said you'd never uproot your son from Philly and you had qualms about him being in this environment. What changed?"

"A week ago I hadn't spent a week on Dune Island—and neither had Ryan," she quipped, but he didn't smile, so she tried to explain it a different way. "Being here reminded me of everything I love about this place, despite a few drawbacks. Not to mention, yesterday I thought I'd lost my son—and for a moment before you pulled me off the cliff, I thought *he* might lose *me*. An experience like that has a way of giving a person a lot of clarity. I've always wanted the best for Ryan, and now I see that means giving him a home in Hope Haven, which is also what's best for me."

Jake nodded thoughtfully, but his expression was still serious.

"I thought you'd be glad I'm not selling the farm," Lily said. "Is there... is there some reason you're unhappy about it?"

"No, it's not that I'm unhappy, not exactly." There was a tentative note in his voice and he scratched his head again.

"Then what is it? Don't you want to work with me?"

"I *do* want to work with you. It's just... well, remember the other night when you asked me if I was in a relationship with Dahlia?"

Unfortunately, I do—but I wish I could forget it. "Yes, I remember."

"Well, one of the reasons I think Dahlia and I worked so

well together was that we *didn't* have a personal relationship. A *romantic* relationship." He rubbed his jaw and shuffled his feet. "My business decisions weren't affected by my personal feelings for her and vice versa. But with you... it might be..."

Was he saying what she thought he was saying? Lily paused before speaking carefully. "Yes, I can see how that would be a problem for you. I'm facing the same dilemma myself."

"You mean...?" He raised an eyebrow.

"Um. Yes. I... I can't pretend I'm not attracted to you, too." Her voice was lilting, definitely not businesslike, the way it should have been. *See, this is already a problem*, she thought. But what she said was, "I'm sure we'll find a way to work it out as we go."

"Sounds good to me." He grinned. "So that's that? You're officially staying?"

"That's that."

"Well, let me be the first to congratulate you on being the newest owner of Lindgren Cranberry Farm." He stuck out his arm and they shook hands. Then his grasp softened but he didn't release her fingers. "I'm glad you came back, Lily. And I'm even gladder you're staying."

"So am I." Her tone was lilting again. "And Ryan's going to be ecstatic. Let's go tell him together, Farmer Jake."

EPILOGUE

NOW

LATE SUMMER

"I don't know about this, Jake..."

Lily scanned the road in each direction. Because she'd missed leaping off Herring Run Bridge with her graduating class on the last day of school, Jake had suggested that she should jump off it on the last day before school *started*. They couldn't risk being seen, so they couldn't jump until the second high tide, which occurred shortly after eleven-thirty in the evening. By then, the slow-moving water would be deep enough that they wouldn't hit the squishy riverbed with their feet.

Jake had arranged for Ryan to spend the night at his sister's house; the boys were camping in her back yard. Initially, Lily was nervous about allowing her son to sleep on the ground in a tent. The temperatures were supposed to drop into the 50s overnight and there was a chance of rain in the morning, so she worried he'd become chilled and overly tired. But she'd worked through her anxiety and now the only thing she was nervous about was getting in trouble for violating a safety ordinance.

"We could be fined a thousand dollars each for doing this and I don't have that kind of money to spare," she said.

"Actually, you do—or you will soon." Jake hung his towel over the railing and turned to face her. "I just reviewed our books with the accountant this afternoon and thanks to a steady stream of summer tourists, we've made good money. Who-hoo!"

"Shh." Lily playfully cupped her hand over his mouth. "We're going to get caught."

"Who's going to catch us?" he asked, his breath warm against her fingers.

She lowered her hand and joked, "At this very minute, some nosy gossiper is probably hiding in the grass and spying on us with a pair of binoculars."

"If he is, it's only because he's hoping to catch a glimpse of you in that swimsuit."

"Hey, don't make fun. It's left over from high school—my other suit is frayed from all the bodyboarding we did with the boys this summer."

"I wasn't making fun. I think it looks great." He fingered one of the straps and a million little shivers fluttered up her spine.

"Thanks." Lily stood on tiptoe, clasped her hands behind Jake's neck and pressed her lips to his for a tender, intimate kiss.

"You're welcome." When Jake leaned in to kiss her a second time, she held him back, her hands flat against his bare chest.

"We'd better jump before I lose my nerve."

"Okay."

He hopped up onto the railing in a smooth, swift motion. Since Lily was shorter, she had to climb onto it slowly, using the lower, vertical board like a ladder. As she straightened from a crouching position into an upright stance, her legs began to quake and she wobbled forward. But Jake wrapped his arm around her waist and helped her catch her balance.

Resting her head against his shoulder, Lily again recalled her aunt's advice, "There's something even better than falling head-over-heels in love, and that's being with a man who steadies you."

I learned so much about love from Dahlia, reflected Lily. *Not only because of the things she said, but because of the thoughtful, attentive way she looked after each of us— even if she made mistakes along the way...*

After a few quiet moments, Jake asked, "Are you okay."

"Yes, definitely." Lily lifted her head and kissed his shoulder. "Let's do this."

"Do you want to go first or should I?"

"We're partners, so we should leap together." She interlocked her fingers with his. "Ready, set, GO!"

As they lunged forward, they lost their grip on each other's hands. Jake hit the water first, in a large, moonlit splash of white. A split second later, Lily was submerged—and just as quickly, she surfaced, half laughing, half gasping from the chilly plunge.

"I can't believe how cold it is already. It's not even September yet," she said, treading water.

Jake paddled closer. "Here, let me warm you up." The salty kiss he gave her really did make her flush with heat. "Better?"

"Much. But my toes are still cold."

He grinned. "We can't have that."

As he was kissing her a second time, someone shouted, "Hey, you two in the river—knock it off!"

Her heart thumping, Lily spun around in the water to see who it was. Three people were clustered on the bridge and the silhouette of a very tall man towered over them from the railing. They all appeared to be wearing swimsuits.

Lily squinted. "Is that... S*teve?*"

"Watch out!" he hollered. Springing forward, he hugged his knees to his chest and landed with such force the water rocked with waves. When he surfaced, he sprayed water from his mouth, like a whale spouting.

"How's that for being a big fish in a small pond?" he asked.

Lily and Jake cracked up and so did the other three people on the bridge; Katie, Will and Gretchen. While Steve was coaxing them to jump, Lily quietly asked Jake, "Did you invite them here?"

"Yeah. It seemed like the kind of celebration that's more fun with a group than just a couple. You don't mind, do you?"

"No, I'm glad they're here," she said, treading water beside him. "Everyone here is part of my past—I want to leap into the future with them, too."

A LETTER FROM KRISTIN

Thanks so much for choosing to read *Lily's Secret Inheritance*. If you enjoyed it and want to keep up to date with all my latest releases, just sign up at the following link. Your email address will never be shared and you can unsubscribe at any time.

www.bookouture.com/kristin-harper

The setting for this book came to mind easily. I've always loved the sight of cranberry bogs in coastal Massachusetts. In autumn, I can't get enough of the fresh cranberries sold at my favorite Cape Cod roadside produce stand, owned by a local family. Likewise, in summer, I indulge in cranberry ice cream from my favorite Cape Cod ice cream shop. But perhaps the best cranberries I ever tasted were the wild ones my nephews and I discovered on a hike in the Province Lands. If you're ever on the outer Cape, I highly recommend taking this strenuous trek through the dunes. Even if you don't find any wild cranberries, you'll be rewarded with otherworldly views!

If reading *Lily's Secret Inheritance* was a wonderful experience for you, I'd really appreciate it if you'd share what you loved about it in an online review. Your perspective means a lot to me and your enthusiasm makes a big difference in helping new readers discover one of my books for the first time.

Keeping in touch means a lot to me, too, so please don't hesitate to reach out through Twitter, Goodreads or my website.

Thanks,

Kristin

Kristinharperauthor.com

 twitter.com/KHarperauthor

ACKNOWLEDGMENTS

The more books I write, the less capable I feel I am to adequately express my deep and abiding appreciation for the many, many individuals who support me on every level. So, to my editor, Ellen Gleeson, and the entire team at Bookouture, as well as to my family and friends, and to my wonderful readers, I simply say: thank you.

Made in the USA
Las Vegas, NV
15 April 2023

70636489R00173